Tangled Up in Tuesday

Jennie Marts

Copyright © 2015 Jennie Marts

All rights reserved under International and Pan-American Copyright Conventions

By payment of required fees, you have been granted the *non*-exclusive, *non*-transferable right to access and read the text of this book. No part of this text may be reproduced, transmitted, downloaded, decompiled, reverse engineered, or stored in or introduced into any information storage and retrieval system, in any form or by any means, whether electronic or mechanical, now known or hereinafter invented without the express written permission of copyright owner.

Please Note

The reverse engineering, uploading, and/or distributing of this book via the internet or via any other means without the permission of the copyright owner is illegal and punishable by law. Please purchase only authorized electronic editions, and do not participate in or encourage electronic piracy of copyrighted materials. Your support of the author's rights is appreciated

No part of this book may be reproduced or transmitted in any form or by any electronic or mechanical means, including photocopying, recording or by any information storage and retrieval system, without the written permission of the publisher, except where permitted by law.

Cover Design and Interior format by The Killion Group
http://thekilliongroupinc.com

Thank you.

DEDICATION

This book is dedicated to Carolyn V—
an honorary member of the Page Turners Book Club
Because she loved the Page Turners and they made her laugh
Rest in peace, my friend

Acknowledgements

First and foremost, I must always thank my husband, Todd. For believing in me, for supporting me, and for loving me through it all.

My family means everything to me and I thank my sons, Tyler and Nick for their support of my writing career.

A special thanks goes out to my mom, Lee Cumba, for her invaluable support of this book. Thanks Mom, for listening to hours of plot lines and working through countless ideas of how to make this story better.

I have an amazing group of proofreaders and beta-readers, who will drop everything and read my books as soon as I call. Each has their own skills and they find commas, legal issues, plot holes, and logistical impossibilities. My books benefit greatly from their keen eyes, support, advice and grammar knowledge. Thanks to Carla Albers, Lee Cumba, Terry Gregson, Linda Kay, and Mona Egger.

I am blessed to be surrounded by an awesome group of writers who continuously offer guidance, support and critique help. I would be lost without the friendship and support of Michelle Major, Lana Williams, and Annie MacFarlane.

Big thanks goes out to my editor, Alyssa Linn Palmer for coming through for me in a pinch and for her great editing skills.

I cannot say enough about The Killion Group and their amazing work with my covers and marketing material. My thanks goes out to Kim Killion and Jennifer Jakes for your fast and efficient work. I value your creativity, your advice and most of all, your friendship.

My biggest thanks goes out to my readers! Thanks for loving my stories and my characters and for asking for Mac's book. I am making each of you an honorary member of the Page Turners Book Club! And I can't wait to share the next Page Turners novel with you.

ONE

THUD!

Zoey Allen's eyes popped open.

She waited for her vision to adjust to the dim light of her bedroom. Searching the room, she noted her bedside clock read one-thirty-eight AM.

Nothing seemed out of place, but something had woken her up.

Her heart raced as she pushed herself upright in the bed.

Something was off. She could feel a disturbance in the air. Her heart jumped to her throat as she detected movement, a shift in the darkness.

Her ears strained for the slightest noise, and the hairs stood up on her arms as she detected a whisper of fabric, followed by a footstep.

"Zoey."

Her name, spoken in a man's voice, breathy and deep, sent shivers racing up her spine.

She reached for her cell phone on the bedside table. Her fingers barely touched the edge of the phone before it was knocked to the ground as a huge bulk of a man fell across her bed.

She screamed.

Pushing against him, her nostrils filled with the scent of sweat and a metallic coppery scent. And Axe body spray.

Wait. She knew that smell.

"Zoey," he said again. Just one word. Just her name.

But it was enough. She stopped struggling. She recognized the voice. The body spray. The frame of the large man that had just fallen on her. "Teddy?"

She reached for the bedside lamp, but his big hand clamped on her arm. "Don't. They're coming. I had to warn you."

"Teddy, you're scaring me. What's going on?" Teddy Grimes was her coworker at Cavelli Commerce. Both accountants, they'd had neighboring cubicles for the past several years.

Teddy was a big guy. Tall, slightly overweight, always hurrying into work and out of breath as he sunk into his office chair, a light sheen of sweat often dampening his drab brown hair against his forehead. Fast food wrappers littered his messy desk, the complete opposite of Zoey's meticulously organized cubicle.

Still, she liked him. He made her laugh, and they'd become friends. Like his name, he was gentle and kind like a big teddy bear.

She was used to Teddy offering her an extra donut or grabbing her a coffee on his way in to work. And she trusted him enough to give him a key to her apartment to water her plants and pick up her mail when she'd recently been out of town.

But she hadn't heard from him in days, and his presence in her bedroom at one in the morning told her something was very wrong.

He'd landed across her when he fell, and she reached out to push him off her lap. Her hands met his solid girth, and his shirt was wet. She jerked her hands back, her fingers tacky and damp.

Her heart leapt to her throat. Oh no.

She reached out and touched the small lamp next to her bed, bathing the room in soft light. She didn't care what he said. She needed to see what was going on.

Her fears were realized. The coppery scent, the sticky wetness. Teddy's eyes were closed, his chest heaved with effort, and his white shirt bloomed with a large wet circle of crimson blood. So much blood. The deep color looking almost black in the soft light.

Zoey looked down at her hands and almost gagged. They were covered in blood as well. A perfect red fingerprint showed on the side of the lamp where she'd touched it.

She swallowed her instinct to scream. "Teddy, you're hurt. You've got to let me call 911."

He should his head. "No, I'll be okay."

"You're not okay. You're bleeding. What happened?"

"Stabbed me. Tried to fight them." His breathing was labored. He opened his eyes and looked at her. "I barely got away. I need to tell you something, then you need to run. Get somewhere safe. Before they find you."

"Who?" She asked the question, but in her heart, she already knew.

"The Cavelli brothers. They know I have the final proof to put them away. Not just Carmine, but all of them."

"What kind of proof?"

"Numbers. Data. Figures showing the money coming in and going out and who's involved. I've been collecting the details of their money laundering scheme. I've known something was wrong for a long time but didn't want to say anything 'til I had concrete evidence. Then you called them out in the audit." He gave her a half-hearted grin. "You are one brave chick."

She didn't know if she was brave or stupid.

She hadn't known the extent of the scheme when she'd first uncovered it a few weeks ago. She'd collected as much evidence as she could before she reported it, then they'd fired her.

After receiving threatening messages, and having reporters constantly hounding her doorstep, she'd fled to the safety of her grandmother's house in Pleasant Valley, about a half an hour's drive from her apartment in Denver.

It hadn't been much of an escape. In fact, she'd found herself in more danger there, and she still had the cuts, bruises, and purplish knot on her forehead to prove it. But at least in Pleasant Valley, she'd had the protection of Officer McCarthy, a local cop.

She'd only been back in Denver for a few days and was already missing the handsome police officer. Especially now—with holding the weight of her friend as he bled onto her comforter. Yeah, she could use Mac right about now.

Gathering the corner of her sheet, she pressed a wad of fabric against Teddy's side. "Listen, you can tell me all of this later. Right now we've got to get you to a hospital."

He shook his head, fear in his brown eyes. "No. You listen. You need to get out of here. After you reported them, the bosses brought in some computer guys to figure out what all you'd dug up. All the heat's been on you, so I thought I was flying under the radar. But they must have found out I'd been downloading the figures, because a guy broke into my apartment tonight."

He grimaced in pain as she applied pressure to his wound. "He told me he knew I had the evidence and to give it to him or he'd kill me."

"So, did you give it to them?"

"No, it's hidden. On a flash drive. I didn't even have it, so I tried to fight him. But the bastard stabbed me. Then I knocked him in the head with my Xbox."

"Oh, no."

"I know. But it's okay. I was gonna upgrade to the new PlayStation anyway."

She rolled her eyes. "I meant 'oh, no' to him stabbing you, not to the loss of the gaming system."

"Oh, right. Well, that machine really came through because he went down, and I got out of there. But before we started fighting, he said something about needing to take care of the blonde bitch accountant that started this mess. I knew I had to warn you."

She was terrified for herself, but her heart raced as she thought about the people in her family that the Cavellis could also threaten. Her mom and dad lived on a hippy commune out in the country with a whole community of people, but her Grandma Edna and newly-found grandfather, John, were easy targets in the small town of Pleasant Valley.

Teddy pressed his hand on top of hers. "Zoey, you're the only person I trust, but they could be on their way here now. You've got to get out of here. Go somewhere safe. To someone you trust. These guys are so powerful, they have friends in the police department too."

As if his words had conjured them, she heard a slam against her front door.

"They're here." Teddy tried to press himself up off the bed, but seemed too weak to stand. "You've gotta get outta here. Now."

Zoey scrambled from the bed as she heard another crash against her door, this time accompanied by a sharp crack as the door frame splintered.

A pair of tennis shoes lay on the floor by the canvas backpack that she'd filled last night in preparation for going to the gym when she woke up. She stuffed her feet into the shoes and looked around for a jacket or shirt, but the room was in its normal tidy state with no stray clothes strewn about.

She wore a sexy blue pajama set of short-shorts and a spaghetti-strap tank top. The material was a satiny light blue, and she normally didn't wear pajamas like this at all. She usually wore shorts and a T-shirt. But there'd been a sale last week at Vickie's Secret, and she'd bought the pajamas on impulse.

Thoughts of Mac, the cute cop, had filled her head when she'd made the purchase, and she'd put them on earlier thinking that tonight she just might be brave enough to text or call him.

But the satin pajamas held no super powers of bravery, and she'd chickened out again.

Now the sexy little top was covered in blood.

Her wallet was in the bag, and her keys lay on the side of her dresser. Good thing she *was* so organized. It helps to be prepared in case a wounded coworker and an intruder dropped by your house to kill you at one in the morning.

All of these crazy thoughts ran through her head in a matter of panicked seconds. She bent to look under the bed. "I need my phone."

Teddy pushed her way. "Forget the phone. Get the hell out of here."

"What about you?"

"Forget about me too. I'll try to stall them. Get the drive. It's hidden in my office. But then only give it to someone you trust completely." He pushed to his feet.

She ran to the window and pushed the sill up. The window opened to a fire escape, and she dropped the backpack onto the metal grating. "Hidden where? How am I supposed to find it?"

Another loud crack, and she heard the front door give way.

Teddy held a finger to his lips, signaling her to keep quiet. He pointed at the window and mouthed the word *go*.

A male voice carried to the back bedroom. If he was speaking aloud, there must be at least two people. "You check up here, and I'll find the bedroom. Somebody needs to teach this stupid bitch a lesson."

This bitch wasn't stickin' around for any lessons.

Zoey climbed through the window, pulled it shut, then grabbed her backpack and ran down the stairs of the fire escape.

Her car was parked on the street, and the thought of being in the dark alley in the middle of the night sent shivers of fear racing down her spine. But the imagined threat of a crazed rapist waiting in the alley didn't compare to the *real* threat of the men that just broke down the door of her apartment.

She hit the pavement of the alley and took off at a sprint. The cardio she did at the gym every week paid off. Her legs were muscled and strong, although the adrenaline alone could have fueled the race through the alley.

With her running shoes on and her chest threatening to pop free of the tiny blood-stained pajama top, she felt like some kind of burlesque track star in a B-rated horror film.

She held her car keys in her hand, the keys extended between her fingers—like she'd been taught in the self-defense classes her grandma had given her as a Christmas gift last year. Some people had grandmothers who gave them crocheted sweaters or towels for their bathroom as gifts. Not Edna.

Zoey reached her car and shuffled the keys in her hand. Her breath came in ragged gasps, her heart racing due to the running and the fear of being chased.

The keys fumbled from her fingers and dropped to the ground. Swearing, she bent to retrieve them.

"Nice jammies. Pretty sexy."

She froze at the leering voice coming from behind her. Grabbing her keys, she stood and slowly turned to the man standing behind her.

Okay, more of a boy really. A kid of about eighteen or nineteen stood on the sidewalk. He wore baggy pants and a flat-billed baseball cap. Typical punk attire. His smug expression changed to one of horror as he took in her blood-smeared clothes. "Holy shit, lady. Did you just kill somebody?"

Despite the fear racing through her veins, she narrowed her eyes and tried for her best tough voice. "Not yet."

He held up his hands in surrender and backed away. "Hey, I don't want no trouble. You go on, and get in your little car there. I'm just gonna take off."

She clicked the keyfob to unlock her door and reached behind her to open it. Giving him one more hardened stare, she slid into the seat and slammed her door shut. Starting the car, she engaged the locks, but the kid was already gone.

A distant gunshot sounded, and she jumped in her seat.

Oh no.

She prayed it wasn't Teddy that had just been shot.

The sound of sirens filled the air. Someone must have called the police.

Please let Teddy be okay.

Pulling away from the curb, she floored the car and headed toward the one place she felt safe.

It took putting ten miles between her and the city for her heartbeat to finally slow down. She shivered in the cool Colorado night air and checked the rearview mirror. Again.

There didn't seem to be any one following her. So far.

She sped up the highway toward the small town of Pleasant Valley. Toward the safety of her grandmother's house. Most people wouldn't think to go to their grandparents' house for protection. But most people didn't have a grandmother like Edna.

Even in her early eighties, Edna Allen, now Edna Allen Collins, was a feisty spitfire that was known to carry a gun, pepper spray, and a Taser in her purse. Or sometimes her bra. You never knew with Edna.

The speedometer inched toward ninety and for the umpteenth time, Zoey wished she'd been able to grab her cell phone. She alternately prayed not to get caught and wished she'd get pulled over.

She hoped the sirens she'd heard were headed to her apartment. Surely her neighbors had heard the sounds of those men breaking down her door.

At last, the lights of Pleasant Valley came into view, and she breathed a sigh of relief as she finally turned down her grandmother's street.

Zoey parked her car a few houses away and cut through the yards to get to Edna's back door. She knew she'd be scaring her grandmother to death by knocking on her door at three o'clock in the morning on a Tuesday night—well, at three o'clock in the morning on any night, really. But this Tuesday night, it couldn't be helped.

She knocked on the back screen door and heard John's dog, Havoc, go into a barking frenzy. Who needed house alarms when there were small yappy dogs around?

It only took a few minutes for the light to pop on and for Edna to appear in the kitchen. "Who's there? I've got a gun, and I know how to use it."

She was indeed carrying a gun, and Zoey waved at her through the back door window. "Don't shoot, Gram. It's me."

Edna squinted at the window as she rushed forward to unlock the door. "Zoey! What in the devil are you doing here at this time of night?"

She opened the door, and Zoey stepped inside. She wanted nothing more than to fall in to the arms of her grandmother, but she didn't want to get blood on her.

Both women gasped as they took in the sight of each other.

"Oh honey, is that blood? Are you hurt?" Edna asked.

"What are you wearing?" Zoey asked, before she could even form an answer to her grandmother's question. Edna had on bright pink slippers and the same Vickie's Secret pajamas that Zoe wore. Except Edna's were in leopard print.

Edna looked down at herself and shrugged. "What? There was a sale at the mall. I thought they were cute."

John walked into the kitchen and gasped at his granddaughter. "Zoey, good God, are you hurt? What happened? Should I call 911?"

Zoey shook her head. "No, I'm okay. I'm shaken up, but I'm fine." She looked at the dark stains of blood now drying on her pajamas. "It's not my blood."

Johnny crossed the room in three long strides, his arms outstretched.

Zoey shrunk back. "I don't want to get blood on you."

Waving away her protests, he pulled her into his arms. "I don't give two hoots about this old robe. I care about you."

She let herself sink into her grandfather's embrace. He smelled like Old Spice and laundry detergent.

Edna placed her hands on her hips. "I'm glad you're not hurt, but you're here in the middle of the night, and you're covered in *somebody's* blood. So we need to either call an ambulance or the police."

"No police," Zoey said, heeding Teddy's words of caution. She pulled away from Johnny. "I don't know who we can trust with this situation."

"Well, I know we can trust Mac." Edna had the number chosen and the phone pressed to her ear before Zoey had time to object.

And she didn't really want to object. The thought of seeing Mac filled her with warmth, and her heart picked up a beat as she listened to her grandmother address the police officer.

"Mac, this is Edna Collins." She paused. "Yes, sir, I am in fact aware of what time it is. It's almost three in the morning and my granddaughter, Zoey, is standing in my kitchen covered in blood."

She paused again. "No, she's okay. It's not her blood. But she doesn't want to call the police." She sighed. "I know you *are* the police, but I'm only calling you."

Edna pulled the phone from her ear and looked at Zoey. "He said don't move, he'll be right over, then he hung up."

She shuffled to the living room. Pulling a throw off the back of the sofa, she brought it back to wrap around Zoey's shoulders, then guided her to the kitchen table. "Zoey, sit down here. Johnny, why don't you start a pot of coffee? Getting a warm cup in your hands will keep them from shaking."

Zoey sank into the chair and glanced at her hands. They *were* shaking. Her heart was hammering in her chest, and her mouth was dry.

She was going to see Mac again. That thought alone had her heart rate accelerating.

But the realities of the night were also sinking in.

Someone was after her. Had broken into her apartment with the intent to harm her. A friend had been stabbed, and his blood was streaked along her bare arm.

She scratched at the burgundy-colored stain, and it flaked off onto the table as if it were dried paint. But it wasn't paint. It was blood. Teddy's blood.

What had happened to him? Had he gotten out of her apartment? Had the men found him? The gun shot she'd heard. Who'd fired a weapon?

Oh God, had Teddy been shot?

Was her friend lying dead on the floor of her apartment?

Her body began to shake. She hugged her arms around her middle as if warding off a stomach-ache.

She looked up at the clock above the sink.

How long would it take Mac to get here?

TWO

Mac jammed his bare feet into a pair of tennis shoes and grabbed a T-shirt from the stack of clean clothes piled on his dresser. He took a minute to brush his teeth and stuff his wallet and badge into the pocket of the gym shorts he'd worn to bed.

Grabbing his shoulder holster, he strapped on his gun as he raced for the door.

What the hell was going on? Why was Zoey here, in Pleasant Valley?

And covered in blood? And who the hell's blood?

The questions flooded his mind as he sped toward Edna's house.

He knew the house. Had been there more times than he would rather count in recent months. If there was a pile of trouble anywhere near that old woman, she'd find a way to step in it.

But Zoey was different. She didn't ask for trouble. He gathered that Zoey led a life as trouble-free as possible.

It was why this thing with the Cavelli brothers had been so upsetting to her. He knew about the trouble at her firm, had been involved in trying to protect and help her the last few weeks while she'd been threatened and hounded by the press. He'd been caught up in trying to keep her safe.

If he were honest with himself, he'd admit that he was caught up in more than just her safety.

His sleep had been troubled by thoughts of the danger she'd been in, by visions of her escaping the crashed car, scenes of her being held captive by a madman. And memories of her face as she looked to him for help, thoughts of her lush body as she ran into his arms, images of her long blonde hair and her smooth skin as she walked down the aisle of the church at her grandmother's wedding. The way she'd smiled at him as she walked toward him, like he was some kind of hero.

Well, he was nobody's hero. Far from it.

The last thing he wanted was her thinking he could save her.

He absently rubbed at the scar on his shoulder—the torn tissue where a bullet had ripped through his skin the last time he had tried to save someone.

Tried and failed.

So what was he doing racing toward Zoey Allen in the middle of the night?

Turning down Edna's street, he pulled to a stop at the curb, and exited the car. Pausing, he took in the surroundings of the quaint neighborhood cul-de-sac.

Bright flowers edged every neatly mowed lawn. A small spotlight lit an American flag that hung from the porch across the street, its red and white stripes swaying in the gentle breeze. It was an idyllic picture of small town Americana. Peaceful. Innocent.

That's why he'd left Chicago and moved back to his hometown. To escape the rampant crime and brutal violence of the city.

But he'd learned lately that danger could lurk anywhere. Even in the most innocent of places.

He cocked his head, listening for any disturbance in the night air. Only the sound of crickets chirping and the hum of a window fan met his ear.

A quick movement caught his eye and he turned, reaching instinctively for his gun. The clatter of metal broke the quiet, and he started, spinning toward the sound. A raccoon scurried around the edge of a garage. The noise had only been the lid of a trashcan hitting the ground.

Other than the masked garbage raider, he didn't see anything suspicious, so he hurried up the sidewalk to Edna's.

The door opened as he hit the front stoop, and John Collins waved him in. "Hey there, Mac. Good of you to come over so quickly."

"Where is she?" He was already inside, taking in the empty living room and striding toward the kitchen.

Zoey was standing at the kitchen sink, washing her hands. Pink-tinged water swirled against the white porcelain as she rubbed her hands under the faucet.

She wore running shoes and a tiny set of blue satin pajamas. Pajamas that were caked with blood. A long streak of a rust-colored stain ran down the outside of her calf.

She turned to him as he walked in the room, her face lighting with—what?—Hope? Need? Or simply recognition?

He didn't care. She smiled, her lips curving up in a brave attempt even as he saw tears pooling in her blue eyes.

She looked scared and vulnerable. And beautiful.

Without thinking, he stepped forward and pulled her into his arms.

She pressed into him, her body fitting against his in perfect unison. Two cool spots formed on his back where her wet hands clutched the fabric of his T-shirt. Strands of her hair brushed his bare forearm, and a sensation of desire ran through him.

Everything about her was perfect. The scent of her surrounded him—shampoo, perfume, soap, and the underlying coppery scent of blood.

He could feel her trembling and he looked down at her. "Are you okay?"

She nodded against his chest. "I am now."

He tilted her chin up to him. "Are you hurt? Whose blood is this?"

"I'm not bleeding, just bruised and shaken. My coworker, Teddy Grimes, showed up in the bedroom of my apartment about an hour ago. He'd been stabbed, and this is his blood."

"That doesn't make any sense. When someone gets stabbed, they go to a hospital, not to a coworker's apartment. Do you know who stabbed him, or why he came to you?"

Her bottom lip trembled slightly as if she might cry, but she swallowed the emotion down. "He came to warn me."

"About what?"

"He said he'd been collecting evidence about the money laundering scheme at the firm, and that a guy broke into his apartment and threatened to kill him if he didn't give it to him. Teddy fought him and got stabbed in the fight. The guy had said he was coming to take care of me next so Teddy came to warn me. A couple of guys broke down the door of my apartment, and I ran. Teddy told me that he'd try to hold them off and to get out of there. I didn't want to leave him, but I was scared. I climbed out the window and drove straight here."

She looked up at him, her voice shaking as she spoke. "As I drove away, I heard a gunshot. And I heard sirens in the distance, so someone must have called the police."

"Why didn't *you* call the police?" *Why didn't you call me?*

"I didn't have my phone. It had dropped behind my bed, and I didn't have time to grab it. And Teddy told me not to call the police. He said the Cavellis have guys on the force on their payroll and to be wary of who I trusted. I didn't know what to do, so I just got in the car and drove here."

"He could be right. Cops are underpaid, and there are always a few crooked ones who'll take a payoff to look the other way." He touched her cheek. "But you can trust me."

What the hell was he doing? Could she really trust him?

The look in her eyes said she already did. And everything in him wanted to live up to the look she was giving him.

But he knew he couldn't. Knew he would only let her down.

He needed to step back. Like actually step back. Get his arms from around her and stop touching her face. But her skin was so soft, and she felt so good pressed against his chest.

He dropped his arms but couldn't seem to pull away from her just yet.

Get a grip, man. Focus on the tasks. Do the work.

He narrowed his eyes at her. "You need to take those clothes off."

Her eyes widened in surprise, then she grinned and offered him a small nervous laugh. "You're not even gonna offer to buy me a drink first."

Shit. That hadn't come out exactly right. He'd gone straight into cop mode. Easier to think of her as a victim of an assault than as the lush woman currently pressed against him.

Except now he was thinking of her with her clothes off. Damn. He was really in trouble here.

"I meant, we need to get you out of those clothes."

Her grin deepened, and he felt a warm flush spread up his neck.

Geez, what was wrong with him? He took a deep breath. "We don't know what kind of evidence you have on your clothes. Do you have something else you can wear? I've got an evidence bag in the car. I'll grab it while you get changed."

She nodded and pulled away from him. "I knew what you meant." Her expression lost its humor as she looked down at herself. "I'd really like to wash this blood off of me. But I'm worried about Teddy."

"At this point, another ten minutes isn't going to make much of a difference. You probably have time to wash off quick in the shower. Just be careful putting your clothes in the bag. We want to preserve any kind of evidence that might lead us to who was after you."

"I can help her."

Mac looked up to see Edna standing in the doorway of the kitchen. She wore a short robe that had come open in the front, and he was fairly certain she was wearing the same style of pajamas as Zoey. Except in—*Lord have mercy*—leopard print.

He frowned and averted his gaze. "Evenin' Miss Allen, er... Mrs. Collins. I'm still not used to the married name."

She walked up and patted him on the arm. "Evidently you're not used to seeing a lot of women in their night clothes either. Geez Mac, they're just pajamas."

Pajamas that he never, ever wanted to see again.

He took a step back from Zoey and cleared his throat. "Well, I'll just go get that evidence bag if you want to help her get undressed. Um…taken care of."

He turned and headed for the front door before he said another stupid word. What was wrong with him? He was usually cool, calm and collected. Totally in control.

What was it about Zoey Allen that had his stomach turning in uncomfortable knots and idiotic words tumbling out of his mouth?

The night air was cool against his flushed skin, and he pulled a plastic evidence bag from the trunk of his car. He carried it back into the house and knocked on the closed bathroom door.

The door opened just a crack, and he passed the bag through.

"Thank you," Edna said, and shut the door.

But not before Mac caught a glimpse of Zoey's reflection in the mirror. She was naked, her back turned to the mirror as she stepped into the shower. Her blonde hair fell across the creamy skin of her back. Her waist was slender above curvy hips that shaped her perfectly rounded bottom.

Mac swallowed and imagined running his hands along the curved length of her. Touching his fingertips lightly to her smooth bare skin. His fingertips, his lips, his tongue.

Okay. He needed to stop. Get back some professional perspective. She'd just been through a highly traumatic incident, and he was imagining her tangled up in the sheets of his bed.

He needed to focus on what he could do for her.

Like figure out who the hell had broken into her apartment tonight. He pulled his phone from his pocket and checked in with his dispatch. Maybe they'd heard something about the break-in.

Rosie was on duty tonight, but she claimed she hadn't heard anything. She offered to make a few calls to some of her connections in Denver and get back to him.

"That'd be great, Rosie. Thanks." He hung up the phone as John walked in from the kitchen.

He handed Mac a thermos. "I filled it with coffee. Figured you'd be headed back to Zoey's apartment and thought you could use the pick-me-up."

Mac took the container. "Thanks, John. Yeah, I figured I'd take her back down. See if we can figure out what happened and hopefully find her friend."

John lifted his own cup of coffee and eyed him over the rim. "That seemed like a lot of blood. You think the guy's still alive?"

Mac shrugged. "Any blood always seems like a lot. But, you'd be amazed at what the body can survive."

The bathroom door opened, and Edna stepped out. She handed the evidence bag to Mac. "I wasn't sure if I should seal it."

"It's fine. I've got it. Thanks."

Edna stared at Mac, her eyes narrowed and stern. "You find out who's trying to hurt my grand-baby. And don't let anything happen to her."

He nodded. "I won't. She's safe with me."

But was she? Really?

Edna turned and hurried down the hallway.

Zoey emerged seconds later. She wore black yoga pants and a snug fitting pink T-shirt. Her hair was wet, but combed, and hung down her back.

Flashes of her hair resting against the naked smooth skin of her back filled Mac's head, and his mouth went dry. He focused on pulling the tape and sealing the evidence bag.

Zoey's feet were bare, and she carried her tennis shoes in her hand. "I'm ready. Gram's just going to find me a pair of socks, and I'll put my shoes on in the car."

Edna appeared with a pair of low cut socks in her hand. She gave Zoey a quick hug. "You be careful."

"We will." She grabbed the socks and crossed to the front door. "Let's go."

Mac followed her to the car and held the door open. Her arm brushed against his as she slid into the seat, and he had to grit his teeth at the response his body gave to her slightest touch.

He walked around the car and dropped into the driver's seat.

Get a freaking hold of yourself. She's just a woman.

A woman whose scent filled the interior of his car. A heady mixture of soap and shampoo and something floral.

"I love this car. I never really pictured you as the hybrid kind of guy." Zoey gestured to the dash of his Toyota Camry Hybrid as she pulled her shoes on.

He shrugged. "I do what I can for the environment. Plus it's great on gas mileage." Wow, could he sound any cooler—talking about the fuel efficiency of his car?

They headed for the highway, Mac concentrating on the lines of the road instead of the woman in the seat next to him.

She had her legs pulled up in the seat and her arms wrapped around them. A slim band of her bare ankle showed below the cuff of the yoga pants.

Criminy. He knew he had it bad when he started admiring a woman's ankles.

His cell phone rang.

"Mac here," he said, holding the phone to his ear.

"Yeah, Mac. It's Rosie. I made a couple of calls, and Denver reported a homicide downtown about a half an hour ago. Neighbors called it in. Said they heard someone breaking down a door then later heard a gunshot. PD found a body at the scene. Door was broken in, but that's about all I know."

"Thanks, Rosie." He disconnected and pressed the accelerator, now anxious to get to her apartment. "That was dispatch. Denver PD reported a homicide in an apartment downtown."

She sucked in a breath. "Teddy?"

Mac shook his head. "Listen, we won't know anything until we get there, and it doesn't do any good to assume the worst." He flew by two cars in the right lane as the speedometer inched close to ninety-five miles an hour. The hybrid might be fuel efficient, but it had a great engine, lots of horsepower, and the car could fly.

She nodded, two quick bobs of her head, and pulled her arms tighter around her knees. "You're right."

He may have been right that they didn't really know anything, but his assumptions always went to the worst possible scenario. It would most likely be Teddy's body they found at the scene, but he wasn't about to tell her that.

Best to keep her mind occupied on other things. "Tell me again everything that happened from the minute Teddy entered your apartment. Try to concentrate and don't leave anything out, no matter how insignificant it might seem."

Zoey spent the next twenty minutes of the trip recanting the details of the evening. She stopped as they turned the corner and saw the myriad of emergency vehicles blocking the street in front of her apartment.

Mac parked the car a block back, and he and Zoey walked down the sidewalk.

He had the insane urge to hold her hand. Like they were a couple. No, not a couple. Just to offer her support, like a friend.

Yeah, who was he kidding?

He settled for placing a hand in the small of her back as he guided her through the small throng of people standing on the sidewalk in front of the building. Holding up his badge, he got a nod from the officer on duty, and he lifted the plastic caution tape for Zoey and him to duck under.

The stairs were empty, and Mac followed her to the apartment door. A couple of first responders were on the scene and a few cops. He knew they didn't have much time before the place would be crawling with emergency personnel.

Zoey gasped and reached for his hand as she saw the wide open space where the door had been kicked in and the devastation of her apartment. Signs of a struggle were obvious by the broken furniture and glass littering the floor.

Crossing the threshold, Mac glimpsed the body on the floor of the living room. Thank goodness it was covered with a sheet. He spoke to one of the officers. "You got an ID yet?"

"Who are you?" the officer asked.

Mac held up his badge. "Officer McCarthy, Pleasant Valley PD."

"You're a little out of your jurisdiction, aren't you? What are you doing down here?" The officer eyed Mac and Zoey's joined hands.

Mac dropped her hand and pulled Zoey forward. "This is Zoey Allen. She's the occupant of the residence. And a friend."

Zoey looked down at the body, her face stricken with horror. "Is it Teddy?"

The officer's face softened a little at her frightened tone. And it probably didn't hurt that she was gorgeous. "You think you know the guy? Wanna try to ID him?"

She nodded slowly, her eyes glazing over in shock.

"I'll take a look first," Mac told her. "What does Teddy look like? What color hair?"

She drew her bottom lip in. "Umm, brown. Brown hair, kind of scruffy. He's a big guy, well over six feet. Probably in his late twenties."

The officer shook his head. "You're welcome to still take a look, but that ain't your guy. This one is in his late forties and balding. And there's no way he's even close to six feet."

Zoey let out a rush of air. "Oh, thank God." An expression of confusion crossed her face. "Then who is this?"

Mac pulled back the tarp to reveal just who the officer described. Male in his late forties, balding, stocky. He wore a leather bomber jacket and looked like he'd stepped out of the cast of the Sopranos. Dried blood caked along the side of his forehead where he'd suffered a blow to the head and crimson blood pooled around a torn hole in the fabric of his shirt.

He looked toward her. "Do you recognize him?"

Zoey shook her head. "No, I've never seen that man before."

Mac noticed the way her hands had started to shake and dropped the tarp back over the body. He looked at the other cop. "Sorry. She doesn't know him."

He shrugged. "Oh well, the guys from the crime scene lab will be here any minute, and we're waiting on the Medical Examiner."

"Well, I'm no ME, but I'd hazard a guess that the cause of death was the single gunshot wound in his chest."

The other cop grinned. "That's a possibility." He nodded at Zoey who had headed down the hallway. "Hey, you better get your girlfriend. This is still a crime scene, and I don't want her messing up any evidence."

Shit. He was right. Zoey's apartment was now the scene of a murder, and he guessed the first person they were going to look at was the owner of the apartment.

He strode down the hall after her. After his girlfriend. Ha. He hadn't used the term 'girlfriend' in years.

So what was Zoey? Dating material? A friend with possible benefits? A potential love interest? Ugh. Those were all worse than girlfriend.

The hallway led to a bathroom with two bedrooms off to either side. He followed Zoey as she ducked into the room on the left.

Entering the room, the first thing he saw was the blood-covered comforter. Holy hell. It looked like someone had been murdered in here too. Zoey lay on the floor by the bed. "What happened? Are you okay?"

"Oh yeah, I just—um—tripped when I came in here."

He narrowed his eyes as he saw her draw her hand back from under the bed skirt and slip her phone into her pants pocket. "You do know that I'm a detective, right? We're trained to be observant and to know when someone's lying."

She pushed up off the floor and sighed. "All I want is my phone. I'm sure no one even knows it's in here."

Mac cocked an eyebrow at her then relented. "Fine. That guy was killed by a gunshot to the chest and had blunt force trauma to the head. I'm pretty sure your cell phone isn't the murder weapon." He looked around at the immaculately kept bedroom, trying to imagine Zoey's life here. "Besides, they don't need the actual phone to pull all of the records anyway."

"Pull the records? Why would they do that?"

Seriously? "Zoey, you're in a bit of trouble here. There's a dead guy in your apartment and your bed is soaked in blood. I'd say that makes you a strong suspect in his murder."

She gasped. "A suspect? I didn't kill that man. I don't even kill spiders. And I don't even know who that guy is."

"Regardless of your humanity to spiders, at the very least, the Denver PD is going to view you as a person of interest. We're going to need to go down to the station so you can fill out a report."

"What? I can't go now. We have to find Teddy. We don't know what happened to him. If he's still even alive. We have to at least go to his house and see if he's okay."

She took his hand and looked up at him. "Mac, please. I'll go down to the police station. I'll answer whatever questions they want. But first, I need to check on Teddy. Will you take me to his house? Please?"

Damn. A guy could get lost in those blue eyes. And he was seriously losing his way.

The increased noise in the front of the apartment signaled that more law enforcement had arrived. If they were going to get out of here, they needed to do it now, before it was too late.

He shook his head and gestured to the window. "All right. We'll go check on Teddy. I'd feel terrible if the guy died. But then we're going down to the police station."

"Thank you. Thank you." She hurried to the window and raised the sash then climbed through like she'd done earlier that night. It was still dark and so far, the alley behind her apartment was deserted.

Mac climbed out the window and slid it closed behind him. For just a moment, he questioned his decision before he followed her down the fire escape and through the alley. They hurried to where he'd left the car, and he unlocked and opened the door for her.

He could see more people had arrived, including the press, and he was glad they'd parked a few blocks away. He slid the car into gear and pulled a U-turn in the street. "Okay, so where does this Teddy Grimes live?"

Zoey pulled out her phone and read him the address from her contacts. "It's only about ten minutes from here. I gave him a ride home once when his car was in the shop."

He focused on her directions, willing his lips to stay shut. Had she only given him a ride home? How close was she to this coworker? No. He did not need to know.

It was none of his business. "So, you and this Teddy guy? Were you always just coworkers—er—I mean, friends?"

Zoey laughed. He liked the sound of her laugh. Liked it way too much.

She tilted her head at him. "Why do you ask? Are you jealous?"

"No. What? I was just asking for the purpose of the investigation. It's none of my business who you want to date. Or not date. Or whatever."

Wow. Really smooth.

"Teddy and I are just friends. When I first started working there, he may have asked me out for coffee a couple of times, but I'm sure it was only to be nice. He's a sweet guy. But there's never been any romantic interest there."

"At least on your part."

"On any part, as far as I'm concerned."

Good. As much as he hated the jealous little streak that was running through him, he really didn't want anyone else interested in any of her *parts*.

"Look, Teddy's a nice guy. He's only ever been good to me. And I trust him. Instead of going straight to a hospital, he tried to protect me. And he may have the evidence to back up my testimony against the Cavelli brothers in this money-laundering scheme."

They turned into a suburban neighborhood of small cookie cutter houses. Well-kept lawns and varying shades of taupe houses lined the street, the homes distinguished only by their trim color or front porch design.

Zoey pointed. "There, that's his. The one with the Denver Bronco flag."

At least the guy had good taste in football teams.

They pulled up in front of the house, and Zoey had her door open before he'd even stopped the car. He turned off the engine and raced to catch up with her. "Zoey, slow down. You don't know what—or who—we're going to find here."

The place looked quiet, no car in the driveway and no lights on in the house. The porch light glowed softly and everything looked tidy in the living room visible through the front windows of the house.

Part of him hoped this was all a mistake. That they'd knock on the door and a grumpy guy in boxers would answer and say that he was fine.

But the dead guy currently inhabiting Zoey's apartment made him think they weren't going to be so lucky.

Zoey rang the doorbell then knocked on the door. "Teddy? Are you okay?"

The door budged open an inch when she'd knocked on it, and she looked up at him in fright.

An unlocked open door was never a good sign.

He put out his arm and gently moved her behind him. Taking his gun from the holster, he carefully pushed open the door, his senses on alert for any indication of danger.

They stepped slowly into the living room. Everything seemed normal.

Crossing the room, Mac could see a light on above the sink in the kitchen and a family room to the right. This seemed to be the room most lived in. A big recliner and a comfortable sofa turned toward a big screen television on the wall. Shelves on either side of the TV were lined with video games, controllers, and stacks of DVDs.

In the dim light from the kitchen, he could see overturned furniture and a smashed gaming system on the floor. A red smear of blood stained the tan carpet.

Definite signs of a struggle.

He pressed Zoey against the kitchen wall. "Stay here. I'm gonna check out the rest of the house," he whispered. "Yell if you see anything."

She nodded, her eyes wide with fright.

He quickly checked out the upstairs. A bathroom, office, and bedroom were on the upper level and all were empty. The bed was a mess of sheets and blankets, but that could be the way it looked all the time.

"I don't think anyone's here," he said, coming down the stairs.

Zoey hadn't moved. She stood in the same spot and let out a breath as Mac stepped into the room.

He pointed at the door off the kitchen. "That's probably the garage. I'll check it out, but the place seems empty."

A scratching sound followed by a soft keening came from the direction of the door.

Mac raised his gun and motioned for her to be quiet.

Obviously the place wasn't completely empty.

THREE

A chill raced up Zoey's back as another frantic scratching noise sounded.

Could it be Teddy?

Could he be lying on the floor on the other side of the door, too weak to do anything but scratch at the door? Maybe he'd heard them and was trying to signal for help.

Mac approached the door, his gun held up, his body alert for any sign of danger. As nervous as this situation made her, she still couldn't help the sensations that ran through her as she watched his muscled physique tense and flex. Lord, he was good looking.

Everything about him appealed to her. She liked his neat appearance, his clean-shaven head, his quick precise movements. She liked things neat and tidy, organized, and Mac seemed to share that sense of precision.

He reached for the door then slowly turned the knob. She held her breath, praying that it was Teddy, and he was okay.

Mac yanked the door open, and a big ball of white fluff raced into the room, yapping and crying as it beelined for Zoey's legs.

"Oh no. Poor thing." She reached down and lifted a small white poodle into her arms. A pink ribbon hung limply from its forehead, and the dog was trembling as it pawed at her chest trying to get close enough to her face to lick her cheek.

Mac disappeared into the garage. She tentatively crossed the room to follow him.

Maybe this little dog was trying to signal them that Teddy was in the garage. It didn't look much like Lassie but its frantic yips could mean 'Help, Timmy fell in the well' or 'Help, Teddy's bleeding out on the garage floor."

Poking her head around the door, she peered into the garage.

No Teddy.

The garage was actually fairly empty. A deep freeze hummed in one corner, and a mountain bike leaned against the wall. A few storage boxes were stacked along one side of the room, and a small workbench filled the back wall.

She clutched the poodle to her chest. "Check the freezer."

Mac raised an eyebrow. "For what? Are you suddenly hungry for ice cream?"

"No." She lowered her voice and glanced around the empty room. "For a body. On TV, they're always hiding the body in the freezer." Why was she whispering?

Mac sighed and opened the freezer door. Stacks of pizzas and frozen dinners covered the shelves. "No body."

Zoey let out her breath. Thank goodness. "Then where the heck is Teddy? Do you think those men took him?"

"If so, it would only be man, singular. If you were right about there being two men breaking in to your apartment, one of them never left." Mac crossed the garage and led her back in to the kitchen.

"What do you think they'll do to him?" Her voice trembled, and tears threatened as she thought about Teddy risking his life to protect her.

"Hey now. None of that." Mac reached a hand up and laid it gently on her arm. "We don't know what happened. For all we know, Teddy may have escaped and gotten himself to a doctor. When we get to the station, I'll check in with the local hospitals and see if they had any stabbing victims admitted tonight."

She nodded, trying to put on a brave face. And ignore the sudden warmth that filled her at the touch of Mac's hand on the bare skin of her upper arm.

He touched the paw of the dog, and its pink tongue snuck a quick lick of his finger. "What's the story with this little guy? Did you know Teddy had a dog?"

"Yeah, but I wasn't expecting this dog. Teddy talks about his dog, Bruiser, all the time. But I always imagined it as a pit bull or a mastiff, something big and hairy like him. The kind of dog that drools and tears up your garbage. This dog looks like it gets pedicures."

Mac lifted the pink crystal-ringed tag from around the dog's neck and grinned. "This tag says Bruiser, so this must be his dog." He ducked his head to look under the dog's body. "But he's actually a *she*."

Zoey cuddled the dog under her chin. "Hey, Bruiser. You're a good girl. I wish you could tell us what happened here. And what happened to Teddy."

"I wish she could too." Mac surveyed the disheveled living room. "The destruction in this room corroborates your coworker's story about someone breaking in and him fighting them off." He toed the edge of the smashed Xbox laying near the smear of blood on the carpet. "Try not to touch anything. I'm going to have to call in this scene as well."

"I haven't touched anything." But she'd certainly thought about touching a few things. A few of his things. Funny tinglies ran through her when he said the word 'touch' and she tried to focus on the situation at hand. She needed to find her friend and figure out who the dead guy was in her apartment.

"That's good. I'm sorry we didn't find your coworker." He took another look around the room. "I don't think there's anything left to find here. We should head over to the police station. Somebody's probably going to be pretty pissed off that we left the scene earlier. The only way I'm going to save any grace if I get you over there now."

She looked around the kitchen. "Okay. I just want to find this little girl's food and her dishes."

"Good idea. We should grab some of her food so she'll have what she's used to at the shelter. We can drop her off at the Humane Society on our way to the station. They'll take care of her until Teddy's found."

She gasped. "I'm not leaving her at a shelter. Who knows when Teddy will get back?" Or *if* he'll get back.

Stop it. Don't even think like that.

"I'm bringing her with me. I'll get Gram to help me take care of her until we know what happened to Teddy." She peered into the open door that she assumed was a pantry and spied two small dog dishes on the floor. Bingo.

"You're just going to take the guy's dog?"

A bag of dog chow sat on the pantry shelf, and she grabbed both the bag of food and the dog dishes. A quick glance at the rest of the pantry told her that Teddy ate a lot of chips and Pasta Roni.

She passed the bag to Mac. "Look around. I can't leave her here."

He held his hands up in surrender before taking the bag of food and crossing to the front door. "He's your friend. I just want to go on record that I had nothing to do with this dog-napping."

"We're not dog-napping her. You make it sound like I'm concocting a note demanding a ransom for Bruiser, the fluffy French poodle. I'm just taking care of her until we find Teddy." She found a scrap of paper and a pen in a drawer and scribbled a quick note that simply read, "I have Bruiser—Z". A little cryptic but hopefully wouldn't give too much information if someone else saw the note.

She stuck it to the refrigerator with a magnet shaped like a football helmet. Then she sent up another quick prayer that Teddy was okay, pulled the front door closed behind her and followed Mac to his car.

He put the dog food into the back seat then held the door for her while she got situated in the front. She put on her seatbelt, and the dog settled in her lap while Mac walked around the car and slid into the driver's seat.

"I'll call in to dispatch and see which precinct we need to go to," he told her as he started the engine.

"I'll call Gram and let her know what's going on."

"Good idea. I'm surprised she's not already down here. I'll bet she's already heard about the murder. That woman seems to know everything. I have a feeling when she hears, she'll race right down to see if she can offer the CSI guys any tips."

Zoey laughed. "You're probably right." She dialed Edna's number and filled her in on the events of the morning.

"I'd already heard about the murder. And I'm coming down there. I just saw this new thing on CSI that helps—"

"You don't have to come down here, Gram. I'm sure the Denver PD have it all handled. Besides, we're not going back to my apartment. I have to go down to the police station to give them a statement."

"I figured that. I'm already one step ahead of you and have been arranging for a good lawyer to help you out. I've already called Maggie, and she's on her way over here to pick me up. We'll meet you down there in a half hour."

Maggie Hayes was a member of her grandmother's book club, the Pleasant Valley Page Turners. That summer the Page Turners had found themselves in quite a few messes that had required Tasers, lawyers, and the police to help clean up.

Zoey's wasn't the first dead body that they'd encountered that summer.

Ugh. Why was she thinking of it as *her* dead body?

"Thank you, Gram. But I really don't think I'm going to need a lawyer. I'm just going to give them a statement."

"Of course you're going to need a lawyer. Don't you watch television at all? Honey, a dead body was just found in your apartment. That makes you the number one suspect. The police aren't just going to ask you a few questions. They are going to try to determine if you murdered this guy and if they should arrest you for it."

"What? Arrest me? But I didn't do anything. I'm the victim here."

"That's what they all say. And I'd wager that the dead guy in your living room thinks he's the real victim."

"Well, he doesn't really think anything anymore." She hadn't even considered that she'd be regarded as a suspect. "Hold on, Gram."

She covered the phone with her hand and turned to Mac. "My grandma thinks that the police are going to consider me a suspect in the case, and she wants to bring me a lawyer. Do you think I need legal representation?"

Mac shrugged as he turned the corner and headed into downtown Denver. "I hate it when I have to admit this, but Edna might be right on this one. The victim *is* in your apartment, and there are obvious signs of a struggle. Your front door was broken down in the middle of the night. It's easy to suspect that you shot an intruder that broke into your home."

Probably best not to repeat her claim of being the victim. "So, you think I *do* need a lawyer?"

"I don't think it would hurt. It's better to be prepared."

She uncovered the phone. "All right, Gram. Mac agrees with you."

"Of course he does. We've worked together on several cases. It's like we're practically partners, and they say partners start to think alike."

Edna had offered her advice to Mac during previous investigations that summer. Advice that was often culled from the latest mystery or crime show she'd seen on television. Zoey wasn't sure that actually made Edna Mac's partner but it didn't pay to argue with her grandmother when she had her mind set.

"Okay, I guess. I'll text you the address of the police station, and please tell Maggie thanks. I'll see you in a little bit." She hung up the phone and glanced at Mac. "Your "partner" is evidently now on the case."

He groaned. "At what point did Edna Collins become my new partner?"

"She said now that you're practically partners, you tend to think alike."

"I don't think she's thinking the same thing that I am right now."

Zoey laughed. "She already called Maggie, and they're going to meet us at the police station."

"Good. Maggie's smart. She'll be able to help if you need her."

Maggie was smart. And beautiful. Not just beautiful, but knock-out gorgeous. Tall and slender, with long dark hair that turned heads whenever she walked into a room. Including Mac's.

He'd been interested in Maggie earlier that summer. How deep that attraction went, Zoey wasn't sure. And she wasn't sure if she wanted to know.

Just leave it alone. There was no reason to even ask about it. "So, did you and Maggie have like, a thing, earlier this summer?"

Nice. Subtle. She wanted to grab the question back out of the air.

"I wouldn't exactly call it a 'thing.' There was a little interest, but it never went anywhere, and now we're just friends. Would it bother you if we'd had a 'thing?'" He gave her a sideways glance, and the corner of his mouth tipped up in a grin.

Did he think she was jealous?

Was she jealous?

She got a weird feeling in the pit of her stomach when she thought of Mac being interested in anyone else. And Maggie was so gorgeous.

"I've certainly had 'things' with other men before." Not a lot of 'things,' and certainly never with men like Mac. But she'd had 'things.'

She usually dated men in the corporate world. Men who sat at desks and got their shirts dry-cleaned. Men who fit into her controlled world of structure and organization. Not men who had crazy muscled biceps or wore a gun holstered to their shoulder.

And she hadn't had a 'thing' in a while. Quite a while actually. She'd been focused on her career and trying to get a promotion. She had plans and an outline for her life. Uncovering a money-laundering scheme and getting fired hadn't fit in to those plans.

And neither did a tall policeman who worked odd hours and probably didn't care about eating at six on the dot every night. She'd wager he even had a tattoo. And he'd had the *interest* of a woman like Maggie. "I wouldn't say it bothers me. It's just that Maggie is so beautiful. It's hard to compete with her."

Mac pulled into the lot of the police station and parked the car. He turned to Zoey. "You don't have to compete with her. In my book, there is no comparison."

Hmmm. Did that mean she didn't even compare to Maggie? Or did he think Maggie didn't even compare to her?

"Besides, I've always preferred blondes." He gave her a devilish wink before stepping out of the car.

Her stomach did a funny little flip as she watched him walk around the front of the car and open her door. Even in gym shorts and a T-shirt, he still walked and moved with authority. And he opened her door for her. An officer *and* a gentleman.

And he'd said he preferred blondes. He *was* flirting with her. Even while they were talking about Maggie. That was a good sign.

"You ready for this?" Mac's eyes darkened as he looked toward the busy police station. "I don't know how rough they're going to be on you in there. It's a little different than the laid back station in Pleasant Valley."

She took a deep breath, the flirtatious flutterings in her stomach replaced with nervous jitterings. "I'm good. I didn't do anything wrong." Cuddling the dog close to her chest, she grabbed her backpack and stepped onto the sidewalk.

"That's what they all say." He set his hand on her back and guided her into the noisy station.

FOUR

Drawing strength from his warm hand pressed against her back, Zoey let Mac guide her through the door of the police station.

The stale smell of body odor and marijuana hung in the air, and a low hum of activity interspersed with bursts of noise filled her ears.

A long hallway lined with chairs led to a glass-enclosed check-in desk. The majority of the chairs were filled. It was a melting pot of races and ages, some people sitting anxiously on the edges of their seats and others slumped in their chairs, either asleep or passed out.

Mac directed her to a chair next to an elderly woman. "Have a seat. I'll let them know you're here."

Zoey eased onto the plastic chair, hesitant to touch the arm rests. Did she have time to dig her antibacterial gel out of her bag? She glanced over at Mac as he waited in line to get her checked in.

Oh yeah. It would seem she was going to have plenty of time. She could probably sanitize her hands and the whole chair before Mac would even get to the front of the line. Who knew the police station would be that busy before the rays of the sun had even lit the morning sky?

She dug through her pack and found a tube of antibacterial gel. The scent of plumeria filled the air as she rubbed the gel on her hands. She offered the tube to the woman sitting beside her.

The elderly woman held out her hand, and Zoey squeezed a dab onto her wrinkled hand. "Thank you. It smells nice. But I think you're gonna need a bigger bottle if you want to kill all the germs in this place."

She laughed softly. "Yes, you're probably right." She tucked the tube back into her pack.

The woman held out her hand for Bruiser to give it a sniff. The dog's little pink tongue darted out and licked the woman's hand. She laughed. "She's a cutie. But I'm not sure you're allowed to have dogs in here."

Zoey smiled. "She's my therapy dog." Okay that was a lie, but she certainly felt that petting this cuddly dog was offering some therapy after such a stressful night. Best to change the subject and get the attention off of Bruiser. "Are you waiting for someone?"

The woman nodded, her lips forming a disapproving purse. "My grandson. Called me at two AM to come down and bail his butt out of jail. His momma's addicted to meth and his daddy's in prison, and I swear that boy is doing his dangdest to follow in his father's footsteps. He moved in with me earlier this year, and I'm pretty sure taking care of that boy is going to kill me. I'll be surprised if my old heart lasts through Christmas."

"Sorry." What else could she say? She offered her an encouraging smile. "He's lucky to have someone that cares enough about him to come down to the police station in the middle of the night to bail him out. And I have a feeling you're tougher than you look."

The woman offered her a wry grin. "Probably. They say the Lord doesn't give you more than you can handle, but my grandson may prove that theory wrong." She gave Zoey a once-over. "What are you here for? You don't look old enough to have kids in trouble and even in workout clothes, you're dressed better than most of the hookers in here."

"Thanks. I think. I mean—er—the police found a dead guy in my apartment tonight."

"Was it your husband?"

Zoey thought of the older guy laying in her apartment, with his paunchy stomach and wrinkled pale skin. "Ew. No. I don't even know him."

"Did you kill him?"

"What? No, of course not."

The older woman shrugged. "That's what they all say."

She wished people would quit telling her that. It was not helping her confidence.

Twenty minutes later, Mac dropped onto the seat next to her. "Geez, this place is a madhouse. But, they're finding one of the detectives working the case and setting up an interrogation room. They'll call you when they're ready."

"Interrogation? What are they interrogating me for? I didn't do anything. I'm the victim."

The woman next to her gave a soft 'mmm-hmmm' sound.

Zoey turned toward her. "Not helping." She turned back to Mac. "Do you think I'm really in trouble here?"

Before he could answer, the door to the police station opened, and Edna burst in. Her arms were filled with a large box of donuts, and she had a huge tote bag thrown over her shoulder. Her eyes lit on her granddaughter, and she made a beeline to where they sat. "Zoey, there you are. Now don't you worry about a thing. I'm here, and I brought donuts."

"If I didn't think you were in trouble before, I'm pretty sure you're going to be now," Mac said, not quite under his breath. He stood up to offer Edna his chair. "Hello, Mrs. Collins. Thanks for coming down."

She wrapped an arm around Mac's waist and gave him a quick squeeze. "Of course I came down. Zoey's my granddaughter. And you know you can always count on me when you need a little help."

He shook his head. "I didn't say I *needed* your help."

She waved away his comment. "Of course not. You didn't have to." She held up the box in her hands before he could reply. "And I brought donuts. I know how you cops like your donuts."

Mac rolled his eyes. "Yes, ma'am. You do know a lot about cops."

Zoey smiled at the way Mac dealt with her grandmother. She'd seen that he had a gruff side. That he could be tough and all business when he needed to be. Even though she could tell Edna frustrated him, she liked the way his gruff demeanor softened when he was around her grandmother.

Edna bent down and gave Zoey a quick squeeze before she sank into the chair. She smelled like gardenias and maple frosting. She rubbed Bruiser's fuzzy head. "Who's this little guy?"

"It's actually a girl. Although her name is Bruiser. She's Teddy's dog. We found her at his house, and I couldn't bear to leave her there—in case—you know—he doesn't come back."

Edna nodded. "Any word from him?"

Zoey shook her head.

"While I was waiting in line, I called up to my dispatcher to have her call around to the local hospitals to see if they'd had any stabbing victims admitted last night or this morning," Mac said. "But so far she's had no luck."

Zoey smiled up at him. "Thanks for trying." She peered down the hallway and turned back to Edna. "I thought you were bringing Maggie."

"I did. She's parking the car."

The doors of the police station opened again, and Maggie Hayes entered the building. Every head in the room turned toward her.

Even the dog looked up.

Little traitor.

Maggie wore a dark gray pencil skirt with a matching jacket over a white button-up blouse. Her long legs were muscled and tan, and the expensive high heels she wore put her over six feet tall. Her long dark hair was loose and fell over her shoulders.

Ignoring the catcalls of a thug handcuffed to a chair, she walked with purpose and authority, a grim look on her face.

She nodded at Mac as she approached them. "Hey, Mac. How're you doing?"

"I'm good. Thanks for coming down. I'm not sure how much Zoey's going to need you, but it's good for you to be here, just in case." He turned his eyes back to Zoey and gave her a smile of encouragement.

Zoey liked that he talked to Maggie, then turned back to her. He wasn't acting awestruck by Maggie's beauty or unable to tear his eyes away from her.

Why was she worrying about Mac's reaction to Maggie now? She needed to be focused on her own situation and how she was going to convince the detective that she had nothing to do with the dead body they found in her living room.

She stood and gave Maggie a hug, squishing the little poodle between them. "Thanks so much for coming. I really appreciate this." She held up the dog. "She belongs to my friend Teddy. I'm keeping her until we find him."

Zoey had known Maggie for years through the book club and had always admired her. Maggie was clever and smart and had a wry sense of humor. She was tough in the courtroom and didn't put up with bullshit.

Putting aside her earlier worries over a mild 'thing' with Mac, Zoey couldn't be happier to see her grandmother's friend. Maggie was exactly what she needed.

Maggie hugged her back, then petted the poodle's head. "Of course. We would have been here sooner if Edna hadn't insisted we stop for donuts."

"Hey," Edna said. "I plan on using them for leverage. Cops love donuts. We'll use them to soften 'em up before they start their interrogation."

Maggie arched an eyebrow. "I am not using donuts to bribe the investigating detective. Most cops think that donut stereotype is insulting anyway."

"Insulting? Oh, that's just silly. Everyone loves donuts."

"I love donuts," said the elderly woman who'd been talking to Zoey earlier.

Edna stuck her tongue out at Maggie. "See." She turned and offered a donut to the woman.

"Zoey Allen." The woman at the front desk yelled her name and motioned to the door next to the counter. "They're ready for you."

Zoey and Edna both stood up.

Maggie gave Edna an exasperated look. "Edna, you can't come in with us. This isn't like the doctor's office. They don't let your grandma come in to the interrogation room with you."

Edna huffed. "Well, that's just rude." She held out the box. "Do you at least want to take the donuts?"

"No."

"Watch out for that old 'good cop/bad cop' routine. Don't let them pull that one over on you."

"I've done this before." Maggie pointed to the chair. "Now sit down and please behave. Zoey's in enough trouble. I don't want to come out of that room and find that you've been arrested for disorderly conduct."

"Fine." She plopped in to the chair. "You don't have to get all snippy about it. I'll just sit here and mind my own business. I certainly know how to *behave* and my conduct is *always* orderly."

Maggie cocked an eyebrow in her direction. "Yeah, right. I'll believe that when I see it."

Zoey passed the dog to Edna. "Can you hold Bruiser while I'm in there? It would really help me."

"Of course I can, honey." Edna set the little dog on her lap and huffed at Maggie. "At least I'm good for something around here. It seems as if I'm good enough to take care of the dog."

Maggie ignored her and followed Zoey and Mac through the door. She leaned down to speak quietly into Zoey's ear. "Listen, I only know what Edna told me on the way down here, so for now, just answer their questions. You don't need to volunteer any extra information that they could later use against you. Keep it simple until we've had a chance to talk."

Zoey nodded, her nerves ratcheting up a notch. She looked around the busy station and remembered Teddy's warning about the Cavellis having local police on their payroll and being careful about who to trust.

She knew she trusted Maggie. And Edna.

And she hoped she could trust Mac.

But that was about as far as she got in this room.

Taking a deep breath, she willed her hands to stop shaking. What she would do for a coffee right about now. Black with two sugars and just a dollop of cream. Not that she was particular.

Oh who was she kidding? She was particular about every single thing in her life. She liked things neat and orderly, a place for everything and everything in its place. And she did not have a place for a dead body in her life. She couldn't bear to think about the stain all that blood would leave on her rug.

Would plain bleach work on a blood stain, or maybe something abrasive? Maybe throwing it out would be easier than even attempting to clean it.

Just thinking about cleaning helped to calm her nerves. She could do this.

A detective in his mid-forties with drab brown hair and wearing a rumpled suit met them inside the door. He held a hand out to Mac. "Detective Schmidt—good to meet ya."

Okay, he seemed nice. Maybe he was the 'good' cop. She really wanted to offer to iron his jacket though.

Mac shook his hand. "Officer McCarthy, Pleasant Valley PD. I was with Ms. Allen earlier when we discovered someone had been shot in her apartment."

He ran his gaze over Zoey and Mac's clothes. "What, were you working out at the gym together?"

Ignoring the detective's barb, Maggie stepped forward and held out her hand. "I'm Maggie Hayes. I'm Ms. Allen's lawyer."

His eyes took a lengthy tour of Maggie's body, stopping for a drink around her slim waist and her ample bust.

Hmmm. Maybe not exactly the 'good' cop.

He tore his eyes away from Maggie's bust and turned to Zoey. "You already think you're gonna need a lawyer?"

Zoey shrugged. "I like to be prepared."

Although she felt anything but prepared as she followed the detective down the hall and into a room that smelled like stale cigarette smoke and old coffee. A single table sat in the middle of the room, and she and Maggie took the chairs opposite Detective Schmidt.

"I'll wait for you," Mac said from the doorway. "I've got a buddy that works here. I'm going to try to track him down. Call me when you're done."

Zoey nodded, wishing he could stay. Wishing he could sit beside her and hold her hand again. She clasped her fingers together in her lap, trying to control the trembling that was back. How much trouble could she really be in here?

The detective gestured to the recorder sitting on the table. "Mind if we record this?"

She shook her head.

Taking a notebook from inside his jacket, he pressed play on the recorder and narrowed his eyes at her. "So, why don't we start by you telling me why you killed this guy?"

Uh-oh. More trouble than she'd originally thought. "I didn't kill him. I didn't even know him."

"Okay. So, a stranger breaks in to your apartment in the middle of the night, and you pop him. Makes sense to me. Do you have a license for the gun?"

"No. What? I don't even own a gun. I wasn't in the apartment when he was shot. I heard him break in, and I crawled out the back window of my apartment."

"Ahh. So you're saying he must have shot himself?"

"No, of course not. I don't know who shot him." Her answers sounded breathless and confused. Why was he trying to trip her up?

"Look, you've got a dead guy in the middle of your living room, and your bed is covered in blood. Something's not adding up here, and I think you know a lot more than you're letting on."

Maggie held up a hand. "All right. Quit bullying my client. She came in of her own free will. Just ask her your questions."

"Okay. Don't need to get your panties all in a twist," the detective grumbled.

"I can assure you that my panties are nowhere near twisted. But you'll be the first to know if a rotation of my undergarments is imminent." Maggie's voice stayed cool and low. "Now ask your questions."

He grunted and rolled his eyes before focusing back on Zoey. "Fine. Let's go through the timeline of your whereabouts tonight. We know the victim was shot between the hours of midnight and three AM."

"More like between two and three because he broke into my apartment a little before two."

The detective cocked his head at her. "How are you so sure about the exact time?"

She took a breath, thinking about how to answer. She wanted to protect Teddy, but she was also worried about him. She had to weigh the threat of revealing his presence with the possibility that he could be lying in a gutter somewhere bleeding to death. Or that someone had taken him.

Her apartment was a crime scene, and they were dusting for fingerprints so Teddy's presence would be discovered anyway.

Heeding Maggie's advice, she just answered the question. "Because I looked at the clock, and it was about a quarter to two when my co-worker showed up unexpectedly in my bedroom and woke me up. He'd been stabbed, and that's his blood all over my bed. His name is Ted Grimes, and we worked together. He'd been attacked at his apartment, and his assailant had threatened me. He came to my apartment to warn me. Before he had a chance to tell me everything that happened, we heard someone breaking down my door."

"Did you know who it was?"

"No. I don't normally have visitors in the middle of the night and if I do, they don't usually break the door down. But I knew something was wrong, and I believed Teddy that I was in danger. Plus, I heard the two men who broke into my house say that they needed to teach this blonde bitch a lesson and that was enough for me. I didn't stick around to introduce myself. I just got the heck out of there."

"Why didn't you call the police?"

"I didn't have—" Oh crud. If she said she didn't have her phone with her, she'd have to explain how she had it now. And taking something from the scene of the crime wouldn't reflect well on her or Mac. "I didn't have time. And I was scared. I just wanted to get somewhere safe. And I did call Officer McCarthy as soon as I got to my grandmother's house."

"And you're sure you didn't recognize the dead guy?"

"Yes, positive." She looked at the tinted window behind the detective's head and wondered if Mac were standing on the other side of the two-way glass. She took strength in the idea that he was watching and would be waiting for her when she finished.

"I don't know. Something doesn't add up here. It doesn't make sense that some random guys would break in to your house and one of them ends up dead. I feel like there's still something you're not telling me here."

"She's answering your questions," Maggie said, before Zoey even had a chance to defend herself. "She told you what she knows, so quit badgering her. It sounds like these guys were there to hurt or even kill her. She's lucky she got out of there alive. It seems to me that she's the real victim here."

Finally. Somebody *finally* agreed with her.

The door opened and another policeman walked in and passed Detective Schmidt a note. He read it, then looked up sharply at Zoey. "You're the key witness in the money laundering scam against the Cavellis?"

She nodded.

"Why didn't you tell me that before?"

"You didn't ask."

"All right. All right. So do you think this dead guy was one of Cavellis?"

"I have no idea. I would assume so. Teddy and I were both accountants for the Cavellis." She didn't want to reveal that Teddy had uncovered more evidence against them just yet. "Look, Teddy stayed behind to give me a chance to get away, and now he's missing. I think the other guy must have taken him. He was bleeding and hurt, and you've got to find him."

"All right. I wrote down his name, and I promise we'll look for him."

"I don't have a lot of enemies. And the fact that Teddy and I were both targeted makes me think the Cavellis have to be involved." She could still point them in the direction of the finance company without disclosing that Teddy had found more incriminating evidence. "And I *have* received a few threats from them over the past few weeks."

His demeanor changed to one of concern. "What kind of threats?"

"Just phone calls, really. I turned in copies of the messages to the police in Pleasant Valley. That's where my grandmother lives and where I've been hiding out the last few weeks."

"Maybe you need to consider hiding out for a few more weeks." He made a few more notes in his pad. "Do you think you need police protection? We're pretty short around here, but I could probably get a couple of guys to drive by your apartment a few extra times."

Zoey shook her head. "No. I'm sure I'll be fine."

Maggie pointed a thumb toward the door. "I'm pretty sure Edna's planning on having you come back to her house. I don't think she's going to let you out of her sight."

"I can't go back to my apartment anyway. It's officially a crime scene." She looked to the detective for confirmation. "When do you think I'll be able to get back in my apartment? I need to get some clothes."

He shrugged. "Who knows? Could be a couple of days. Could be a couple of weeks. It sounds like you're going to be staying at your granny's house, kid." He stood and indicated they were free to go. "You can go, for now. But make sure you stay available, in case we need to reach you with other questions."

Zoey pushed back from the table, anxious to get out of the stuffy little room.

She'd had enough of police stations. Enough of being surrounded by criminals and questioned by the cops. She just wanted to get out of here. To go back to Edna's and get some real coffee.

She needed caffeine and a clear head so she could work on how to find the evidence against the Cavellis.

And to figure out what the heck happened to Teddy.

FIVE

Mac checked his watch for the third time in the last two minutes and peered down the street.

Where the hell was Pat?

He'd sent Zoey and the dog home with Edna and Maggie a half an hour before, and he now stood on the sidewalk in front of the police station waiting for his old friend to show up.

He'd known Patrick Callahan since they were in high school. They'd both gone to Pleasant Valley High and entered the police academy the same year. Pat had come back and worked on the local police force, and Mac had gone to Chicago. A few years back, Pat had been promoted to Detective with the Denver PD, and now Mac was back at their hometown station. Funny how things worked out.

They'd kept in touch. Not so far as friending each other on Facebook or anything, but they got together for a beer once or twice a year when they were both in town. Mostly they talked about the old times, who they'd seen from high school and what the old gang was doing. They shared a laugh over who'd been arrested or who they knew who had accumulated the most parking tickets.

Thinking back, Mac realized he hadn't seen Pat in close to a year. Not since he'd been back to Pleasant Valley, and not since Pat had started working in Denver.

The thrum of an engine drew his attention. He looked up to see a navy blue classic Ford Mustang pulling up to the curb with Pat at the wheel.

He rolled down the window as he stopped in front of Mac. "Hey there, you handsome piece of shit."

Mac chuckled and slid into the car. "How ya doing, Patty?"

His friend shrugged. Half a toothpick clung to the corner of his lip as he grinned. "Could be better, could be worse. What the hell's up with you? I haven't heard from you in forever. You don't call. You don't write. Then suddenly I get a text that you're in my precinct, and you need me." He placed a hand over his heart. "I feel like your "I'm in the neighborhood" booty call."

"Yeah, well I'm not interested in your sorry-ass booty."

"Ouch. That hurts. Many ladies seem to find my booty quite fine."

Mac laughed. "Well, they can have it. Right now, I need you for your connections. I need to interview a guy connected to a case your precinct is working on, and I'm hoping you can go with me to see the guy."

"Geez, I feel so used."

"Get over it." He tilted the air vent toward him. It was late summer, but already the morning was heating up. "So will you help me?"

Pat shrugged. "Sure. Who do you want to shake down?"

"Salvatore Cavelli. He and his brother Carmine run Cavelli Commerce. It's a financial advisory firm downtown. Or at least it claims to be."

"Yeah, I know those guys. They've got some pretty hefty connections themselves. Aren't they involved in some money-washing scandal right now?"

"Those are the guys. And I think one of their 'connections' ended up dead on the floor of the key witness's apartment last night."

Pat grimaced. "Sucks to be him. But what do you have to do with it?"

"I know the key witness."

"Isn't she the blonde? I think I saw her on the news. Nice ass? Great tits?" Pat wiggled his eyebrows at him and knocked an elbow against his arm. "So do you really just know this broad or do you actually *know* this broad?"

Mac shoved his elbow away. "Shut up, asshole. It's not like that." But it was kind of like that. He didn't really *know* Zoey in that sense, but he sure as hell thought a lot about getting to *know* her better.

In fact, he thought about her way too much. He was already in way over his head with this woman. He did not need to get more involved in this case or more involved with her. He should just back out now. Drop the whole thing.

He turned to Pat. "So, are you going to go with me to the Cavellis or not?"

Pat chuckled again. "Yeah man, keep your panties on. Let's go. I'll call over to dispatch and see if I can find out anything more on your stiff." He put the car in gear and pulled away from the curb.

The car was a classic but the engine revved with power. Even though the body was old, it shone with a metallic dark blue paint job and everything inside the car was new and up-to-date. Mac was familiar with a detective's salary, and Pat must have been pouring every dime he made into this car. Either that, or he recently had a rich relative kick the bucket and leave him an inheritance.

Mac ran a hand across the dashboard. "Nice ride."

"Thanks. I've been putting a lot of work into her."

"I can tell."

"Check out this sound system." The stereo was playing a song by the latest rap artist and he turned the volume up to somewhere between loud and deafening. The car shook with the reverberations of the bass.

The music, if you could call it that, was punctuated with lyrics about violence and drugs. Personally, Mac would have preferred a little classic rock. But it was Pat's car, so he let it be.

The drive into the center of Denver took about fifteen minutes, and the traffic reminded Mac of what he liked about living in a small town. Pleasant Valley only had three stop lights in the whole town.

They parked the Mustang at a meter on the street in front of Cavelli Commerce. The firm was on the top floor of a skyscraper, and the sun shone against the tinted glass windows of the building.

Pat's phone hummed as they walked into the building. He pulled it from the case at his hip and read the text message. "Just heard from dispatch. They've ID'd your stiff. His name is James Louchenza, otherwise known as Jimmy Two-Fingers. He's got a few priors, some petty burglary stuff, but no jail time. And no known connection to the Cavellis."

Mac blew out a breath and rubbed a hand over his head. "Then who the hell *is* he connected to, and what did he want with Zoey?"

Pat shrugged. "You still want to talk to Cavelli?"

"Yeah. If nothing else, I want to see his expression when we tell him this guy is dead. I've only talked to the guy on the phone. It would help to get a read on him in person."

"I gotcha. Sometimes you just gotta get a cop-sense about somebody." He pushed the button for the elevator.

"You got a mug shot of the guy?" Mac asked as they stepped into the elevator.

"Yeah, they just sent it to me with the ID."

"Can you text it to me?"

Pat pulled out his phone. "Sure."

Ten minutes later, a pretty receptionist in a tight skirt and a white blouse led them in to the office of Salvatore Cavelli. The office was plush in its furnishings, and a state of the art computer monitor sat on the expensive oak desk. Cavelli Commerce seemed to be doing pretty well for itself.

Salvatore sat at his desk and snapped a folder shut as they walked in. Mac watched his face and thought he saw a spark of recognition when Pat stepped through the door.

"Morning, officers. To what do I owe the pleasure of a visit from Denver's finest men in blue this morning?" He stood and held out a hand, his generous gut threatening to burst free of the single button holding his suit jacket closed. His suit was expensive and tailored, but something about the cut just seemed off.

Maybe it was the shape of the man. Salvatore Cavelli couldn't have been more than five foot seven, and was shaped liked a barrel. His chest may have once been muscular, but now was soft with flab. Mac put him somewhere between forty-five and fifty.

Pat shook Salvatore's hand. "I'm Detective Patrick Callahan. And this is Officer McCarthy. We're just here to ask you a few questions."

That was weird. Pat was acting as if he'd never met the guy, yet earlier in the car he'd mentioned that he'd had a few dealings with him. Maybe he hadn't made much of an impression and figured Salvatore wouldn't remember him, or more than likely, Pat was exaggerating his connection to the wealthy financier.

"Salvatore Cavelli. But you can call me Sal." He shook Pat's hand, then Mac's.

Shaking his hand, Mac was surprised at the strength of his grip. "I'm actually with the Pleasant Valley PD. We spoke a few weeks ago about some threatening calls to Zoey Allen, the CPA that used to work for your firm."

Sal brushed a hand through the air. "Oh yeah—that was all just a misunderstanding. My brother just got a little overzealous—watches too many cop shows on TV."

Hmm. Maybe he should introduce him to Edna.

"He hasn't done anything lately, though. I told him to lay off of her."

"Well, somebody broke into her apartment last night, and he ended up with a bullet in his chest."

Sal shook his head in regret. "Poor schmuck—did she shoot him?"

"No. Of course not."

"Yeah. That broad's a pain in my ass, but I can't imagine her shooting anyone." He sat back down at his desk. "I never even knew her name until this accounting fiasco. I mean, sure, I noticed her—who wouldn't notice a pretty woman working at your firm? But I never even knew her name 'til this bullshit happened with the audit. And that's what it is—all bullshit. You'll see. It's just a mix-up with the numbers."

"Yeah, I'm sure that's it." Mac tried to nonchalantly ease into the next question. "Speaking of accounting, we were hoping to talk to another one of your accountants, Teddy—er, Ted Grimes. Nothing major, just a couple of routine questions."

Sal shrugged. "Sure. Whatever. Don't want it to seem like I'm not cooperating with the boys in blue." He picked up the phone and spoke into the receiver. "Hey Megan, can you call down to accounting and see if—" he looked up at Mac, "What's the guy's name again?"

"Grimes. Ted Grimes."

"See if Ted Grimes can talk to a couple of cops." He paused. "Yeah, okay. Thanks." He hung up the phone. "I guess the guy hasn't shown up yet and hasn't called in."

Mac checked his watch. It was past ten. "Isn't that kind of unusual for an employee to be this late and not even call in?"

Sal shrugged again. "How the hell would I know? Do I look like the HR department? I deal with the clients and their money. I don't have time in my day to worry about whether some accountant shows up on time." He pointedly glanced at his watch. "And speaking of time—if's there's nothing else—I need to get back to work."

"Just one last thing." Mac drew out his phone, pulled up the picture of Jimmy Two-Fingers, and held it out for Sal. "This is the stiff we found in Ms. Allen's apartment. You ever seen this guy before? Maybe he works for you?"

Sal leaned forward to peer at the picture, then shook his head. "Nope. I don't know him."

"You sure? Maybe take another glance. You sure you didn't send this guy out to *take care* of your little problem of a nosy accountant? Maybe you just told him to threaten her a little and things got out of hand?"

"Look, I've never seen that guy in my life. Does he really look like he works here? Listen—I'm a frickin' financial advisor. The most danger I see is dodging falling interest rates. I don't know anything about any threats. I barely know those employees in accounting and whatever connections you think I have—you're wrong. The only way I know how to 'take care' of anyone is to take care of their stock portfolio. And I resent the implication. You're treating me like an inner-city mob boss or something."

"If the bad suit fits—"

"Hey, this suit costs more than you make in a month."

"Then maybe I need to invest some of my salary here, 'cause I didn't think the stock market was paying that much lately."

"Listen, how about you go do your job and find these guys that are supposedly threatening my employee and let me get back to doing my job." Sal waved a hand dismissively at them. "We're done here."

"Oh, we're far from done here."

Pat circled his hand, gesturing for him to wrap it up and Mac nodded. "But I guess we're done for today. You'll be sure to let us know if you hear from Mr. Grimes?"

"You'll be the first one I call."

"You do that." Satisfied he got the last word, Mac followed Pat out of the office. "Well, what do you think? Do you feel like he knew the guy?"

Pat shrugged as they headed for the elevator. "I don't think so. But he got awful testy after you started questioning him." Pat offered him a sideways grin. "You probably shouldn't have insulted the guy's suit."

Mac laughed as they stepped in to the elevator.

"Hold the door, please." The pretty receptionist called to them and hurried toward the elevator car. She stepped in and waited for the doors to close before she turned to Mac. "Listen, I probably shouldn't say anything, but I'm worried about Teddy. He never calls in sick, and he's rarely ever late." She looked down at her hands. "He's been bringing me coffee for the last month and we've texted—you know—a little. He's a sweet guy, and he makes me laugh."

Mac raised an eyebrow, remembering the photos he saw of the big shaggy-haired man he saw at Teddy's house. *Right on, Teddy.* "Have you heard from him today? Or last night?"

She shook her head and bit down gently on her bottom lip. "I heard you asking Sal—Mr. Cavelli—about him. Do you think he's okay?"

Mac handed her a card from his wallet. "I'm sure he's fine. But I'd really like to talk to him. He's not in trouble or anything. I just want to ask him some questions. I'd appreciate it if you'd get ahold of me if you hear from him. Or give him my number, and ask him to give me a call."

She took the card and pressed it into her palm. "Okay. I just hope he's okay. He's a good guy."

Mac nodded. He hoped Teddy was okay too. But he had a bad feeling about this whole thing.

Teddy might have been the accountant, but even he knew something about Cavelli Commerce wasn't 'adding' up.

SIX

Zoey looked around the table at the Pleasant Valley Page Turners book club. She held Teddy's poodle in her lap. It peered its head over the edge of the table, sniffing for spare crumbs.

And there *were* crumbs. Coffee cake crumbs. Cinnamon roll crumbs. Cookie crumbs. Because one thing you could count on with the Page Turners book club was that there would be food. And usually the delicious calorie-laden rich dessert kind of food.

Zoey stabbed another bite of coffee cake with her fork. The last thing she was thinking about now was calories. She felt like her heart had been racing since two o'clock that morning and that had to be similar to cardio. Right?

By the time she, Edna, and Maggie got back from Denver, the remaining members of the book club had arrived at Edna's with a full lunch spread.

Cassie Bennett, the mom of the group, had prepared sandwiches and whipped up a homemade macaroni salad. She loved to bake and had the coffee cake on hand. Her seventeen year old niece, Piper, the youngest member of the book club, had offered to call in sick to her summer job, but Cassie had assured her they could handle this one on their own.

Maggie, Cassie, and Sunny Vale had been friends since college. When they decided to form a book club, it seemed natural to invite Sunny's neighbor, Edna. They'd been doing the club for years, choosing a new book each month, but meeting every Wednesday. When Piper had moved in with Cassie earlier that year, it was easy to include her in the club as well.

They were an odd bunch. Plus-size, cardigan-wearing Cassie's cheery demeanor was the opposite of slender and stylish Maggie's sarcastic personality. Like her name, Sunny's personality was happy and positive. And Edna provided the comic relief with her often dirty mind and harebrained schemes.

They seemed different, but they loved each other and depended on the friendship of each. Especially the last summer when they'd found themselves turning from average book club readers into amateur sleuths.

That summer had been more than steamy, with hot men and murder plots invading the sleepy town of Pleasant Valley. And the Page Turners had found themselves in the middle of it all.

Eager to help, the Page Turners had rallied that morning when Edna had called to tell them Zoey was in trouble.

They now sat around Edna's large kitchen table, eating lunch and planning their next move. Cassie may have brought lunch, but Sunny, the school teacher, had brought office supplies. Notebooks and different colored pens littered the table and an easel with a large pad of paper stood in the corner.

Edna set down her fork and let out a small burp. "Well, Zoey, what's our plan?"

"How should I know? You're the amateur detective. Or at least you watch more crime television than I do. I'm just a boring accountant."

She liked numbers and charts. Things that made sense and could be calculated. All this drama and mayhem was sending her blood pressure through the roof. Although she had to admit that having a pencil and paper in her hand did seem to calm her down.

"All right. Settle down. I know this is probably hard for you since you like things neat and orderly. And there's nothing neat about murder." Edna winked at her. She did know her granddaughter well. "But there is order in solving a crime. Let's take what we do know, then figure out what we need to still find out in order to crack this caper."

Her grandmother was enjoying this way too much.

"We're not 'cracking a caper,'" Maggie said. "This isn't an episode of Murder She Wrote. A guy is dead. But I do agree that we should start with what we know."

Sunny grabbed a marker from the center of the table and wrote 'Zoey's Murder' across the top of the big pad of paper.

The color drained from Zoey's face.

Realizing her error, Sunny quickly added the word 'Case' to the end of her title. She shrugged at Zoey. "Sorry."

Cassie gave Zoey a reassuring nod. "All right, now tell us everything you remember about last night. Sunny will keep track of the most important facts. You just tell us what happened."

Zoey looked around the room at the faces of the women she had known for years. She may not have been an official member of the book club, but they'd always included her when she was visiting Edna and she knew she was loved by them.

And she knew she could trust them.

She took a deep breath and told them what happened the night before. Talking about Teddy got her choked up.

Cassie slid an arm around her shoulder and gave her a squeeze. "That must have been terrible for you." She lowered her voice for only Zoey to hear. "And the stains that blood is going to leave will be atrocious. You'll never get it out of your bedding if you didn't pretreat it."

This is why she loved Cassie. And for her hugs. Cassie was a great hugger.

Maggie rolled her eyes. "Who cares about the bedding? Buy some new stuff. Even if she could get the flippin' stain out, who wants to cuddle up in a comforter that someone bled all over. Let's focus on the facts."

Sunny studied her paper. "It seems the three most important things here are to find Teddy and make sure he's okay, to find the evidence on the flash drive that he was talking about, and to figure out why this guy wants to kill you."

"The 'why' seems obvious," Cassie said. "She's the key witness in a big case against some really powerful people. The 'why' would be to silence her to keep her from testifying."

Zoey shook her head. "That's not the why. I haven't had a chance to tell you yet, but Mac texted me a little while ago to say that the dead guy's name is James Louchenza, otherwise known as Jimmy Two-Fingers, and he has no known connection to the Cavelli brothers."

"What? How can that be?" Edna asked. "He has to be connected to the Cavellis somehow. Otherwise, what in the world could he possibly have against you?"

Zoey shrugged. "I have no idea. That's why this whole thing is such a mystery to me."

"Okay, so the best way to solve a mystery is to focus on the evidence," Maggie said. "Teddy told you the evidence is on a flash drive. We need to find that drive. Did he give you any kind of clue as to where he hid it?"

Zoey shook her head. "No, he didn't have time. All he said was that it was in his office."

"Okay, that narrows it down. Do you think he meant his home office or his work office?"

"I assume he meant at work. If the flash drive were at his house, then he would have just grabbed it before he left."

"Unless he didn't have time," Cassie said. "He had just been stabbed and was fleeing for his life."

Zoey twisted the end of her napkin, trying to think through Teddy's actions. "You might be right. But he knocked the guy out. I think if he had the evidence at home, he would have just grabbed it and had it with him. And if he had it with him, he would have just given it to me last night. I think my best guess is that it's still at his work office."

"Okay," Sunny said. "So we just run downtown and nonchalantly check out his office."

"Except for one tiny nonchalant problem," Zoey replied. "I don't work there anymore. And they won't let me in. I tried to go back to get something from my desk that I had forgotten and the receptionist wouldn't let me past her desk."

"Good point." Sunny tapped the page with her marker. "So that means we need to find another way in."

"You know what that means?" Edna asked.

Zoey did not like the gleam that'd just lit Edna's eye.

"We're going undercover."

"Gram, I don't know if that's a good idea. What if we get caught?"

Edna shrugged. "What if we do? What are they going to do—fire you?"

"No, but they could call the police. Since I was fired, I would be trespassing."

"Well, then—we need to make sure that we don't get caught."

"And how do you suggest we do that?"

Her grandmother wiggled her eyebrows. "We go in disguises."

"Oh, Lord help us," Maggie said. "What kind of disguise is going to get us all four through the door and allow Zoey to search Teddy's desk."

"Give me a minute. I'm thinking." Edna wiggled her mouth from side to side then slammed her palm on to the table. "I got it. Maggie and I will go in as a wealthy mother and daughter looking for advice on my portfolio. We can cause a distraction and you three can sneak in as cleaning ladies. Nobody really pays attention to the cleaning people."

Maggie looked doubtful. "You realize I could get in trouble for this."

Edna waved away her concerns. "You don't really have to even do anything. I'll do the talking. I just need you to be part of the distraction. So you just have to put on a short skirt, some high heels, and show a lot of cleavage."

Maggie rolled her eyes. "Oh, well, if that's all."

"I'm not much for going undercover," Cassie said. "But I can drive us down in the minivan, and I can supply the cleaning products for Sunny and Zoey's disguises."

"Good." Edna turned to Zoey. "What do the cleaning people at your firm usually wear?"

Zoey shrugged. "I don't know. I don't think I've ever noticed."

"Ha," Edna cackled. "My point exactly. No one notices the cleaning people. Especially if they are dressed in drab clothes and don't bother anyone."

Cassie snapped her fingers. "Oh, I know. I have some tan colored scrubs from years ago when I worked at the dentist's office. Those would be drab. But I don't know if they would fit. Even then, I was still quite a bit bigger than both of you are, but they have a drawstring."

"That'll be perfect," Edna said. "We can give them some padding to make them look even dumpier."

"Thanks a lot," Cassie mumbled.

"Oh stop it," Edna said. "You know what I mean."

"I don't think some extra padding and tan scrubs are going to be enough of a disguise," Zoey said. "I've worked there for years. My coworkers know me."

Edna tapped her finger against her chin and narrowed her eyes at her granddaughter. "No, we're going to need a little more. Like a wig and some makeup. Maybe create a big juicy zit on the end of your nose. When people see a pimple, they usually turn away and avoid looking at your face."

Zoey laughed. "You're terrible, Gram. Besides that being sort of disgusting, I don't have a wig or makeup. And I don't have time to grow a big juicy pimple on the end of my nose."

"You don't have to," Edna said. "We'll do it with stage makeup." She waved her arms with a flourish. "We'll use my connections with the theatre."

"What connections?" Maggie asked, skeptically.

"I'm a member of the Pleasant Valley Community Theatre. Remember last year when you all came to see me in the local production of *The Sound of Music?*"

Maggie dropped her forehead into her hand. "I have tried to forget that night. That was two hours of my life I will never get back."

"Oh, stop it," Edna told her. "That was a wonderful production. And I personally thought I did a stirring rendition of the Baroness and of Nun #7. I still know all the words to *The Morning Hymn*. And I can prove it."

Maggie held up her hands before Edna could start to sing. "I believe you. And you were fabulous as Nun #7. But how is your stint in community theatre going to help us get into Cavelli Commerce?"

"Because I know the makeup guy. He's very sweet. And I'm sure I could call him, and he could help with our disguises. We could probably even 'borrow' some of the costumes."

"You think this guy is just going to let us waltz into the community theatre and help ourselves to costumes? I think you may be overestimating your connections."

Edna winked. "You haven't met my connection. He's pretty relaxed, and he's a bit of a rule-breaker himself." Edna looked around the table. "All right. Who's in for Operation Flash Drive Retrieval?"

Zoey and the rest of the Page Turners raised their hands. Even Maggie grudgingly held up her hand.

"Okay, I'll call my guy and tell him to meet us at the Community Theatre in an hour. Everyone go home and get whatever you need for the operation, and we'll meet back here in forty-five minutes to ride over together. Cassie, you grab the cleaning supplies and the scrubs. Maggie, try to find something to wear that will attract attention. Go for classy yet still a little slutty with a lot of cleavage and bring some high heels."

"Is this an undercover operation or a date?" Maggie asked.

Sunny laughed. "What can I bring?"

"Can you ask Jake if we can borrow some of those fancy earpiece walkie-talkie thingies that he uses so we can communicate with each other?"

Sunny had met Jake earlier that summer when he had mysteriously shown up in the middle of the night and taken over the house that sat between hers and Edna's. Even though he was gorgeous and had abs you could crack an egg on, the Page Turners had questioned if he was a good match for Sunny or if he was possibly a murderer.

He turned out to not only be a good match, but an undercover FBI agent who had since retired and now worked as a private investigator.

He was also a pretty good neighbor and got along well with Edna and Johnny. He had offered to take Johnny to the doctor today when Edna had to race to Denver. They were hoping Johnny's x-rays would look good, and he'd be able to get the cast off his leg. Or at least be able to switch to a boot.

"I'll ask him," Sunny said. "But then he'll probably want to come along."

Edna nodded. "That's okay. We could use the muscle."

SEVEN

Forty minutes later, the Page Turners reconvened in Edna's living room.

Zoey's phone rang and a warm tingle ran through her when she saw Mac's name on the caller ID screen. She slipped down the hall to talk in private. "Hello."

"Hey, Zoey. It's Mac."

She loved the way her name sounded coming from his mouth. His voice was deep and filled with authority, but it seemed to hold a touch of tenderness when he spoke her name. Or at least, she imagined that it did. "Have you heard anything more? Any news on who the mystery guy is?"

"No, nothing new. But I've think I've done all I can down here for now. I'm headed back up to Pleasant Valley. I need to grab a shower, then I'll head in to the station. I want to dig around a bit and see if I can find out anything about him."

"Yeah, that sounds good."

"What are you doing? Is Edna feeding you her famous cinnamon rolls?"

She laughed. "Yes, the Page Turners brought over lunch. And dessert, of course."

"You must be tired after last night. Maybe you should try to get some rest this afternoon."

She wasn't quite ready to share their plan to sneak into Cavelli Commerce with the cop working on the case. "That's a good idea. Yep. I will probably just take a little nap. Maybe watch some TV."

"I'll call you later to let you know if I find out anything. Don't let that grandma of yours talk you into any harebrained schemes until then."

"Nope. No, sir. No harebrained schemes going on around here." She winced at the lie. "I should probably go. I'll talk to you later."

"Okay. And Zoey?"

There it was again. Her name dripping with the deep resonance of his voice. She could have melted into the phone. She swallowed, her voice soft as she replied, "Yes, Mac?"

"Be careful."

"I will."

He clicked off, leaving her standing in the empty hallway, leaning against the wall for support. How could a simple phone conversation make her weak in the knees?

She needed to pull it together.

She had a harebrained scheme to carry out.

Ten minutes later, she and the Page Turners pulled up in front of the Pleasant Valley Community Theatre. Piling out of Cassie's minivan, the sidewalk looked deserted except for a scruffy-looking guy in his early twenties. He had a full beard and wore jeans and a faded Pokémon T-shirt. He also smelled faintly of marijuana.

Maggie held up her hand as he approached them. "Sorry buddy. None of us have any spare change."

Cassie held up her purse. "I don't give out money to the homeless, but I might have a granola bar in my bag if you're hungry."

"He's not homeless," Edna said. "This is Scooter. He's my theatre connection."

Scooter waved. "Hey, dudes." He lifted his chin at Cassie's purse. "So can I still get that granola bar?"

Cassie offered him a sheepish grin. "Sure."

"I can see what you mean about him being a bit of a rule breaker," Maggie said. She narrowed her eyes at Scooter. "Do you work at The Travel Inn?"

He nodded. "Yep, cover the desk for the night shift on the weekends." Snapping his fingers, he pointed a finger at her. "Didn't I see you there a while back with Luke Skywalker?"

Maggie dipped her chin and lowered her voice. "Obi-Wan Kenobi, actually."

He pointed at her and let out a chuckle. "Lara Croft, right? Tomb Raider babe?"

Sunny laughed. "A little role-play action, Miss Maggie?"

"Cut it out. It was the night we all went undercover at Comic Con. Remember you and Jake were dressed as Batman and Catwoman?"

Sunny smiled, a sheepish grin that made her eyes twinkle. "Oh, I remember, all right."

Cassie covered her ears. "La-la-la. I do not need to hear this."

"I do," Edna said. "Jake looked hot in that Batman suit."

"Let's just focus on the task at hand, shall we?" Maggie pointed at the Community Theatre doors. "Can you get us inside, Scooter?"

He held up a set of keys. "Dude."

Evidently that meant 'yes' because they all traipsed after him into the building.

An hour and a half later they all traipsed back out and headed toward the minivan. Cassie was the only one who looked the same as when she walked in.

Maggie was dressed to the hilt in a figure-hugging dress that showed off every curve of her tall body. She wore dark panty hose with a black seam running down the back of her leg, ending in a pair of black stiletto heels. Well-endowed to begin with, the addition of a push-up bra had her breasts bursting over the front of her blouse.

Maggie would cause a distraction just by walking into the room.

Edna still looked like an old lady. There was only so much that makeup could do, but Scooter had refined her makeup and outfitted her in a cream-colored Chanel dress with matching jacket and demure tan heels. He had filled her head with notes on her character—a rich heiress that was angry with her financial advisor and looking for a new place to house her millions.

Scooter had found her a cane and advised her to stoop forward as she walked and lean on the cane. Already in character, she moved with the haughty air of a woman accustomed to wealth. She stood to the side of the van, her nose slightly lifted as she waited for someone to open the door for her.

Sunny pulled at the door and offered her a hand into the van. Both Sunny and Zoey wore the tan scrubs that Cassie had brought. Sunny had found an old pair of tennis shoes, and Scooter had found a dark colored wig to cover her blond curly hair.

The biggest transformation was in Zoey. They had told Scooter enough that he knew they were going undercover into Zoey's old firm to get something from her desk. He said he'd watched enough of the news to know that Zoey was a key witness, and he assured her that when he was through, not even her own mother would recognize her.

He'd covered her body with padding under the scrubs, making her appear heavier and her belly seem thicker. A short drab wig of mousy brown hair covered her head, and thick brown-rimmed glasses sat on her nose. Everything about her screamed boring and un-noticeable.

At Edna's insistence, he even added a fierce red pimple in the crease of her nose. He'd applied a thin layer of foundation to give her an almost grayish pallor and a pair of Edna's tan orthopedic shoes adorned her feet. She might look dowdy, but at least she had great arch support.

Scooter waved from the sidewalk. "Good luck, dudes."

Cassie fired up the engine of the van and buckled her seat belt. "Who's ready to go get their spy on?"

Edna was the only one who raised her hand.

Maggie adjusted her cleavage around the seat belt strap. "Who's ready to just get this over with?" This time, she, Sunny, and Zoey all raised their hands.

On the drive to Denver, Sunny showed them all how to use the ear pieces. She told them that Jake hadn't made it back yet from the doctor's appointment so she hadn't exactly *asked* to borrow the equipment. She said she hoped he wouldn't be mad, but if he was, she'd have a fun time making it up to him later.

Sunny passed an earpiece to Zoey. "I could only find two, so I think each team should get one so we can keep in contact. Zoey, you can wear the one for our team." She looked skeptically at Maggie and Edna who both held out their hand for the other one.

Edna grabbed it and fit it into her ear. "It makes sense that I would wear it. I'm old enough that it could just look like I'm wearing a hearing aid. Besides, everyone's going to be staring at Maggie so we don't want a suspicious-looking thingie sticking out of her ear."

Maggie rolled her eyes. "You're giving my boobs a lot of credit."

Edna pointed at her cleavage. "Have you seen your boobs? Every man in that room will be staring. No one will even notice me."

Yeah, right. Edna had never gone unnoticed in a room in her life.

Maggie shrugged. "Whatever. You can wear it. I know you just want to have it so you can pretend you're an agent with CIA."

Edna grinned. "How do you know that I'm not?"

They had concocted a basic plan of Edna and Maggie, posing as a wealthy heiress and her snobbish daughter, working the main area.

Edna had an idea of how to create a diversion, and she tapped the cane against the floor of the van. "I'll just keep raising my voice louder, and as soon as I start knocking things off of desks with this cane, you two should be able to sneak in and search Teddy's desk."

Zoey's hand flew to her mouth. "Oh, Grandma, you wouldn't."

Edna scoffed. "You bet I would. Those weasels fired my granddaughter. I'm not worried about knocking around a few of their staplers or file folders."

The pace of her heartbeat doubled, and Zoey's palms broke out in a sweat. Her mind raced with the hundreds of things that could go wrong with this plan.

This was not her. She did things by the book—kept her life in tidy order. Unlike their laid-back theatre connection, she was *not* a rule breaker.

No—she was definitely a rule follower. And everything about this plan seemed to break the rules.

Cassie drove into the parking garage of Cavelli Commerce. She pulled into a spot close to the elevator and put the van in park. She waved a hand in front of her, fanning her face. "All right girls, I'll wait here. I'm close to the elevator in case we need to do a quick getaway. And I'll leave the car—and the air conditioner—running since this dang garage is so stuffy."

Quick getaway? Zoey hoped to get in and out without even being noticed. She imagined them running from the building toward the van, wigs askew, as gunmen raced after them, weapons drawn.

Except most of the men that worked at Cavelli Commerce wore business suits and many hadn't *run* after anything in a long time. Except maybe a cab.

She took a deep breath. They were going to be fine. This was a financial corporation with a bunch of employees who were mostly bored with their jobs and watched the clock until their next break or until they could go home for the night.

Nothing was going to happen. She just needed to stay calm.

She looked around the van at the Page Turners. Cassie still wore her sunglasses and nervously scoped out the rest of the parking garage. Sunny had the front visor down and was adjusting her wig. Maggie's high-heeled foot jiggled with impatience, and Edna's shoulders bounced in time with the music playing in the van.

Born to Be Wild was on the radio, and Edna belted out the lyrics with gusto.

Her grandmother was enjoying this *way* too much.

Zoey adjusted her earpiece and reached for the door handle. "All right, let's do this thing."

The four rode up the elevator in silence. Zoey and Edna had checked the microphones, and they could easily hear each other. Sunny had assured her that she could talk normally, and the mike would pick up her voice, but Zoey kept tilting her head to talk as if she could get her mouth closer to her ear.

The elevator dinged and the doors slid open. This was it. Ready or not.

Sunny and Zoey hung back as Edna and Maggie swept through the glass doors of Cavelli Commerce.

A receptionist sat at a large front desk, but Edna strode purposely by her and into the main room where the majority of the financial advisors sat at their desks. Well, maybe not strode, but hobbled forward with her cane, her expensive handbag swinging from her arm.

From their vantage point, Zoey and Sunny could see every head in the room swivel toward Maggie, men and women alike. All she had to do was walk into the room. She didn't even have to open her mouth. Just had to stand there and look bored and aloof.

And as a lawyer used to sitting in court, Maggie was excellent at that.

Through the earpiece, Zoey could hear her grandmother's voice.

Edna's tone was bold with authority and conceit. "Who's in charge of this place? My name's Imogene Buckingham, and I've got more money in my piggy bank than most of you pencil-pushers make in a year."

Imogene Buckingham? Like the palace? Where in the world had Edna come up with that name? Maybe they should have discussed their aliases when they were concocting this plan.

Two men in business suits approached Edna, both holding out their hands in greeting, false smiles plastered on their greedy faces as they each clearly hoped for the commission on a rich old lady's investments.

But Edna was having nothing to do with them. "I don't want to talk to you wankers." Wankers??? She really was channeling Queen Elizabeth. "Neither of you look like you even have your suits tailored. I want to talk to someone who is really in charge." She banged her cane against the side of a desk, making the man sitting there jump. He'd been ogling Maggie and obviously hadn't been prepared for his desk to be assaulted.

But Zoey was more concerned with her grandmother's last statement. What did she mean by wanting to talk to someone who was in charge? Was Edna trying to get in to talk with Sal?

Suddenly this felt way more dangerous.

Sunny tugged at her sleeve and motioned to the window where they could see Edna's cane take out an unsuspecting tape dispenser that went sailing off a desk. "That's our cue. Let's go."

The receptionist had her back to the door, seemingly too engrossed in the scene Edna was making to pay any attention to two drab cleaning ladies.

Cassie had supplied them each with a bucket filled with dusters, paper towels, and Windex. They slipped down on the hall on their soft-soled shoes, the thick carpet absorbing any sound. Zoey had told Sunny earlier that the accountant's offices were down the hall and to the right.

The firm employed three accountants and their cubicles sat side-by-side, running the length of the room.

Zoey motioned for Sunny to follow her, and they slipped through the door and into Teddy's cubicle. Her heart was racing, and she grabbed the duster from her bucket and started dusting Teddy's monitor.

"What are you doing?" Sunny whispered.

"I'm cleaning. It's what I do when I get nervous." Or stressed. Or depressed. It was her fallback habit. And Teddy's desk could definitely use the cleaning. It was littered with fast-food wrappers and dozens of sticky notes. Faded brown coffee stains formed rings that were dotted across his desk calendar. Doodles of three-dimensional boxes marched down the side of the calendar and assorted pens were scattered across its surface.

The only neat thing was the perfect row of Star Wars Lego action figures that were affixed to the top of his computer monitor.

Sunny pulled out her bottle of glass cleaner and wandered down the row of cubicles. "It looks like we're the only ones in here."

"Mary must be on one of her breaks. In the afternoon, she usually takes a couple of smoke breaks and a couple of bathroom breaks followed by a couple of snack breaks. I'd guess we have about five or ten more minutes before she wanders back in."

"Which cubicle was yours?"

Zoey pointed absently at the next cubby over.

"Geez, they really tidied it up for the next person coming in. It's spotless over here."

Zoey poked her head around the wall of the cubicle and looked at her old workspace. "No. That's just the way I left it."

She didn't know why she felt like she had to clean it after they had fired her. Well, she didn't *really* clean it. Just wiped down the surfaces with an antibacterial cloth and cleaned out the drawers. She pointed at a pink stapler shaped like a high heeled shoe. "Hey, grab that stapler. I bought that with my own money."

The stapler had been a gag. Something she'd bought to show that she did have a sense of humor and wasn't just a stuffy old OCD accountant.

She snatched the stapler off the desk and handed it to Zoey who dropped it into her front pocket.

Sunny moved back in to Teddy's cubicle and pulled open the top desk drawer. "Geez, this guy is a mess."

"Yeah, but he was—is—a big lovable goofy mess." She prayed he was still okay. She pointed at the cabinet above the desk. "Check that cabinet. Look for anything that could possibly be a flash drive. They make them to look like all sorts of things now, and Teddy especially loved the ones that looked like little toys."

She searched the drawers while Sunny looked through the cabinet. Everything was jumbled together, and it took everything in her not to stop and organize at least the loose paper clips and rubber bands.

Their search netted four flash drives, two matching silver ones, a black one, and a neon green one in the shape of a frog.

Zoey dropped all four into her front pocket then caught a whiff of cigarette smoke. "Oh shizzle. Mary's on her way back in." She turned her back to her ex co-worker and focused on dusting while Sunny stepped in front of her.

Mary walked in to the office holding a diet soda and a Snickers bar.

Zoey held her breath as she heard Mary walk by Teddy's desk on the way to her own. Her breath caught as she heard her footsteps stop.

"Hey, don't you guys normally clean at night?" Mary asked.

Zoey dipped her head and mumbled, "Donde esta?"

Sunny nudged her with her elbow. "This guy's desk always takes a little longer. And we heard he called in sick today, so we thought we'd get a little head start."

This answer seemed to make sense to Mary because she nodded her head in agreement. "Yeah, Teddy's a bit of a slob. But he's a good guy. I heard he didn't show up today and didn't call. Which is totally not like him. I've worked with the guy for three years, and he's never called in sick. Even when he *was* sick. The jerk came in this winter with strep throat and shared it with half the office. Where did you hear he called in sick?"

Zoey felt Sunny's shoulders shrug. "Um, I'm not sure. Maybe I just assumed that. We just do what we're told."

Zoey scrubbed the desk with a paper towel trying to shrink into herself. "No ablo englais."

"We didn't know you'd be here. We don't want to bother you." Sunny grabbed Zoey's arm and pulled her from the office. "We'll come back later."

They hurried down the hall, their buckets knocking against their knees.

"We got what we needed." Zoey spoke toward the earpiece. "We're headed to the van." She'd been so focused on their task, she hadn't been paying much attention to Edna's voice in her ear.

It had crackled and seemed to cut in and out like it was getting bad reception when they had moved down the hall, so she had turned down the volume a little.

She hoped Edna wasn't having trouble hearing her. She could make out bits of conversation as they hurried down the hall. A man's voice mixed with Edna's shrill one.

As the voices cut in and out, she picked up bits of conversation with words like "service" and "lots of money" and "is this how you treat your customers." She clearly thought she heard the word 'penis' but knew that couldn't be right, and her brain tried to decipher what other word it could have been. Venus? Pianist?

That couldn't be right. Why would her grandmother be talking about a piano player or another planet? Then again, why would she be talking about a penis?

Sunny nudged her side. "Donde esta? Seriously?"

Zoey laughed. A nervous giggle. "I panicked. It just popped out. Then I had to go with it."

She turned up the tiny earpiece and spoke toward it again. "Abort plan. We are heading to the garage. Got what we needed. Get out of there."

They slowed their pace and calmly pushed through the door and out in to the foyer. Sunny pressed the button to the elevator.

A commotion drew her attention, and Zoey turned to see Maggie and Edna being led through the doors by two large men. The men both wore black suits but their biceps bulged, drawing the fabric tight against their muscled arms.

"This is an outrage!" Edna bellowed. "I have rights! Take your hands off of me. I'm reporting you for elderly abuse." Her face was flushed with anger. She was either really into character or her grandmother was seriously pissed off.

"I'm not abusing you, ma'am," one of the men said to Edna. "I'm simply escorting you out of the firm. And asking that you not return."

"What's wrong? Is the Buckingham money not good enough for you?" Her head only came up to the taller man's chest, and she tipped her chin up to glare at him. "I've been saving this money since Nixon was in office! Probably before you were even born."

"That very well could be, ma'am," he replied, his voice dull and monotone. It was obvious he wasn't letting one little old lady shake his nerve. "But it doesn't matter how much money you have or how long you've been saving it, you can't come into someone's business and call the CEO a penis-face."

Oh, Lord. She had used that word.

Edna huffed. "I'm eighty-two years old—I can do whatever I damn well please."

"Not here you can't."

They moved closer to where Zoey and Sunny stood. Zoey tucked her head into her chin and studied the floor. The elevator dinged, and she stepped on, head down, shoulders hunched and backed into the far corner of the elevator.

She snuck a glance at the men as they deposited Edna and Maggie into the elevator. She didn't recognize either of them. But she recognized the glint of steel under his jacket when one raised his arm to hold the elevator door for Maggie.

Why did he have a gun?

Who were these guys? They were acting like financial advisor bouncers—since when did Cavelli Commerce have security? And what in the world would they need it for?

Something felt really wrong here.

She would have to think all of this through later. In precise detail. With lists and a chart. Possible even create a spreadsheet.

But for now she just wanted to get back to the van. Wanted to get away from Cavelli Commerce to where she felt safe.

And where she could take this silly itchy wig off.

Maggie and Edna stood next to her and Sunny in the elevator. Maggie wore an expression of humiliation, and Edna's shoulders shook with indignation.

"I belong to the Red Hat Society, and I'll be telling all of my friends to *not* invest their money here," Edna called as the elevator doors slid shut.

They had discussed the possibility of cameras in the elevator, so Zoey pressed the button for the parking garage and feigned indifference at the old lady panting with exertion. Her cleaning bucket bumped against her leg as she dared a glance at the others.

They all stood perfectly still, the canned music playing softly in the background, but Zoey caught a look pass between Sunny and Maggie. The corner of Sunny's mouth twitched as she obviously tried not to laugh. She pressed her lips tightly together and looked at the ceiling. Anywhere but at Edna.

After what seemed like about an hour, the elevator doors slid open and Edna hobbled out, her back bent over her cane. Maggie followed behind. Following the plan, Sunny and Zoey stayed on and rode down one more floor then raced back up the stairs.

Zoey slowly pushed open the door to the parking garage's main level. She could see Edna and Maggie getting into Cassie's van. She spoke in a loud whisper, hoping the earpiece picked up her voice, even in the concrete stairwell.

She could certainly hear Edna complaining about the way her girdle was pinching her. "We're over by the door. Look to your right, and you'll be able to see us."

She saw Edna's head swivel to the right and point at the door. She waved. "Have Cassie drive over and get us, just in case there are cameras watching the garage. Especially now that security has seen us."

"Roger that. We're on our way." Her grandmother's voice took on a tone that crossed between a spy and a truck driver. Zoey fully expected to hear her say "ten-four, good buddy" next.

Relief poured through her as Cassie pulled the van up to the door, and she and Sunny slid into the back seat. Maggie slammed the door shut, and Cassie gunned the engine as she pulled out of the parking garage.

No one spoke for a few minutes as Cassie maneuvered the complicated streets of downtown Denver.

Merging onto the highway, Cassie turned her head. "Well, how did it go?"

Zoey looked from her grandmother, to Maggie, to Sunny, and they all dissolved into hysterical giggles.

Sunny grabbed her chest and tried to catch her breath. "Oh. My. Gosh. That was so much fun. And so scary. I was sure we were going to get caught. Especially when Zoey's coworker walked in and looked right at her." She grinned at Zoey. "Good thing you went with that awesome Spanish accent."

"Spanish accent?" Edna gave her a disapproving look. "Now, honey, with that wig's hair color and your skin tone, you'd have been better off going with a Russian accent, or Polish even. You need to think these things through."

Zoey laughed. "I wasn't thinking at all. I'm not even sure what 'donde estas' means. It just popped out. I certainly wasn't planning on affecting *any* kind of accent." She looked pointedly at her grandmother. "I can assure you that I'm *not* in the CIA."

Edna huffed. "Well, not with that attitude anyway."

Cassie switched lanes and passed a red compact car. "And by the way, I think 'donde estas' means 'where are you?' Which doesn't seem like the appropriate phrase if she was standing in front of you."

Zoey laughed. "No. It wasn't the appropriate phrase for anything. And I didn't even say it to her. I mumbled it to the desk I was dusting."

"Who cares about the accent? Or the dusting," Maggie said. "Did you accomplish the mission? Oh shit. Now *I'm* sounding like Miss CIA." She ducked sideways to avoid a swat from Edna. "Did you get the flash drive?"

Zoey checked her pockets and pulled out the drives and the comical high-heeled stapler. "We found four of them in his desk. We won't really know if they're the right ones until I can get them in a computer and see what's on them."

"You can put them in here for now." Edna held out her giant handbag, and Zoey dropped the flash drives and the stapler inside. "You can use my laptop when we get back to the house."

"Thanks. Mrs. Buckingham." Zoey dissolved into a fit of giggles, and the others joined in.

All except Cassie. "Wait. Who's Mrs. Buckingham? Like the palace?"

"That was the alias the CIA extraordinaire decided to go with," Maggie explained between hoots of laughter. "She even called a guy a *wanker*."

"That's not all she called a guy," Zoey said. "Grandma, did you really call Salvatore Cavelli a penis-face?"

Edna grinned. "Not to his face. The coward wouldn't come out of his office. I said it to his secretary after she called the goons in."

Zoey's expression sobered. "Yeah, that was weird. I don't remember seeing those guys around before. Granted, I didn't work directly with the Cavellis or in the executive offices, but why would a financial advisor firm need muscled and armed security?"

"Armed?" Sunny asked.

"Yeah, I saw a gun holstered on his hip when he held the door of the elevator."

"I saw that too," Maggie said. "And I noticed the dark-haired one had a tattoo on his wrist. It looked like an eagle or something with some numbers. Like kind of a bad-ass eagle though. Maybe military. Could be the numbers were his platoon or squadron or whatever."

Cassie pulled a small notebook with a pen attached from a basket on the floor of the van. "Here. Try to draw it while it's fresh in your memory. It could be nothing, but maybe we could have Jake look into it. See if it means anything."

"Good idea." Maggie took the notebook and flipped to a blank page. "And I thought the same thing as Zoey. I saw a couple of other guys that looked more like goons than your typical finance guys. Most of the stock brokers I know don't carry guns and they sure don't have their hugely muscled thighs and forearms busting through the fabric of their suits."

"Maybe they've beefed up their security since the money-laundering scandal," Sunny suggested.

"And maybe there's more going on at Cavelli Commerce that we first imagined," Cassie said.

Zoey scratched at the wig where it rested against her ear. "More than money-laundering, beefy security guys, assaulting their employees in the middle of the night, and murder?"

"Yeah, more than that."

But did she really want to find out how much more?

EIGHT

Zoey was surprised to see Scooter sitting on the front stoop when they returned to Edna's. "What are you doing here?"

Scooter shrugged. "Didn't have anything else to do. And I wanted to see how Operation Undercover turned out. Plus I was hungry."

"It turned out great," Edna said as she opened the front door, and they all trooped in. "We think we got what we were looking for. And I think there's some leftover pizza in the fridge. Help yourself." She grabbed the cookie jar from the counter and set it in the middle of the table. "Johnny must still be at this doctor's appointment. Let me just get the dogs."

Crossing the kitchen, she lifted the gate in the laundry room door. Havoc and Bruiser burst into the room in a doggy frenzy trying to simultaneously find someone to pet them and look for spare crumbs on the floor.

Zoey pulled off her wig and dropped it on the table. It looked like a cross between a French poodle and rodent roadkill. She sat down, and Bruiser jumped into her lap and sniffed at the wig. Maybe she thought it was someone she knew.

The door between the house and the garage opened and Johnny walked in, without the crutches. Instead he wore a dark blue boot around the bottom portion of his leg and foot. "What'd I miss? You all look like you just stepped off the stage at the community theatre." His eyes twinkled with mischief. "Or maybe you amateur detectives were up to an undercover mission."

The women all seemed to simultaneously find something else in the kitchen to look at.

"Hold on. That was a joke." His eyes darkened. "Edna, what kind of funny business did you talk these girls in to?"

"Meee?" Edna asked. "Why does everyone always assume the funny business is caused by me?"

"Because it usually is." John pulled out a chair and gestured for his wife to take a seat. "Why don't you all sit down? I'll put on a pot of coffee, and you can tell me all about it. Starting with what Shaggy is doing with his head in my refrigerator. Was he part of this? Did he drive you around in the Mystery Van?"

"No," Cassie piped up as she dropped into a chair at the table and reached for a cookie. "The Mystery Van was mine. All Shaggy—er, I mean Scooter—did was help with our costumes."

"Well you all certainly look different. I almost didn't recognize Zoey. That's quite a get-up," he said.

"You should have seen her with the wig on—she looked like a totally different person," Sunny said and nudged Zoey with her elbow. "And her Spanish accent was great."

"We needed to get into Zoey's firm to have a look around without anyone recognizing her," Edna explained. "Scooter did our makeup, and we had to make sure we all looked different. He did a great job with Zoey, but the hard part was trying to make me look like an old lady."

Maggie arched an eyebrow at her. "Yes—that *was* the hardest part."

Zoey pointed at Edna's bag. "Can I get the flash drives from your purse and borrow your laptop, Grandma? I want to check out these files to see if we got the right ones. You all can fill Johnny in while I dig through them."

An hour later, the coffee pot was empty, the story had been told, and Zoey had come up empty with the flash drives.

She groaned in frustration as she looked at the others sitting around the table. "All that work and there's nothing here. Two of these drives are completely blank. One has his monthly reports on it and the one shaped like a frog has something to do with an online video game he's playing. I've searched the one with the reports three times and can't find anything that would be deemed incriminating or evidence."

Edna patted her hand. "I'm sorry, honey. I was hoping we'd found it."

Zoey's cell phone buzzed, and her heart leapt as she saw the message was from Mac. Was her heart racing because she hoped it was news about Teddy or just because the message was from the handsome police officer?

She opened the message.

Are you still resting?

She grimaced and typed a message back. *No, I'm up. Sitting in the kitchen with the book club.*

Edna poked her. "What's that face for? Does he have news?"

"No. I just feel bad because he thinks I've been taking a nap this whole afternoon."

"Well, I've seen you close your eyes several times this afternoon."

"You mean when I blinked? I don't think a blink counts as a nap."

Edna shrugged. "Depends on how long you blink."

The phone buzzed again. *I got the mug shot of Louchenza. Sending it along. Take a look at it and try to think if you've seen this guy before or how he could be connected to the Cavellis.*

She opened the picture and stared at the photo of the doughy-faced man. *I'm sorry but I've never seen him before. I wish I were better help.*

No problem. Just watch your back and stay at Edna's.

Any word on Teddy?

No- sorry. I'll text you if I hear anything. Stay safe.

Stay safe. Good plan. She somehow thought that sneaking into Cavelli Commerce amidst armed security and wearing a disguise would not fit Mac's criteria of safety. *Thanks. You too.*

"Mac sent me a picture of the guy from last night." She passed the phone around the table. "Anybody recognize him?"

The book club studied the picture, but none of them had seen him before.

Scooter plopped back into his chair, steam rising from the triangle of pizza on his plate. He tilted his head to peer at the screen. "Hey, I know that dude. That's Jimmy Two-Fingers."

"How do you know Jimmy Two-Fingers?" Zoey asked.

"Um—well, I can tell you he's not a regular at the community theatre." He eyed Zoey. "How do *you* know him?"

"He broke into my apartment last night to try to kill me."

"Dude. Why? What'd you do to piss him off?"

"Nothing. I don't even know him."

He shook his head. "That's weird. Did they catch him?"

"Somebody did. With a bullet. He's dead."

"No way."

"Way."

"That totally sucks."

Zoey nodded. "Yeah, it does suck. Especially because I have no idea why he'd want to hurt me. It would really help me out if could tell me what you know about him."

Scooter took a bite of pizza and chewed thoughtfully.

"Look, it doesn't matter what you tell me," Zoey assured him. "There's no judgement."

He gave her a sideways glance. "No judgement?"

"Nope. None. Nada." She really needed to let up on her Spanish terms.

"Well—let's just say that besides my talents as a 'master of disguise'—I also have a degree in Herbology."

"Herbology? I don't get it."

Edna sighed. "Don't you ever watch television? I think he means he's a grower."

"What's a grower?"

"He grows marijuana. You know—pot. Ganja. Weed. Mary Jane. Wacky tobaccy."

"Yes—I know what marijuana is. Remember, I grew up on a hippy compound." She arched an eyebrow at her grandmother. "But I'm surprised you know so much about it."

Maggie reached over and pulled a piece of pepperoni off Scooter's pizza. "Really? Because we've stopped being surprised by anything your grandmother does."

"Look—you can learn a lot if you pay attention," Edna said. "Besides what I learn from cable, I'm also an informed voter, and I did my research when they wanted to legalize it in Colorado. Especially when they wanted to open a recreational shop here in Pleasant Valley."

"Okay, okay. No one's questioning your knowledge of marijuana," Zoey said, then turned to Scooter. "But what does you being a grower have to do with Jimmy Two-Fingers? Was he a grower, too?"

"No way, dude. He was all muscle. Like your granny said, weed's legal in Colorado now, and there's bucketloads of money to be made in the industry. And now that they opened the rec shop here, you'd be surprised by how much weed-traffic runs in this little town. And guys that run that much weed make a ton of dough and need a lot of muscle."

"So this Jimmy worked for one of these guys?"

"Not *these* guy—*the* guy. There's one main dude that kind of controls the show in Pleasant Valley."

"And you know this guy? Who is he? What's his name?"

"Um—well let's just call him John." Scooter looked across the table at John. "Wait, sorry dude, that's your name. Okay, let's call him Leon—wait—shit—that really is his name." He shook his head as if to clear his thoughts.

"It doesn't matter," Zoey said, although she tucked the name Leon away in her mind. "I don't know anyone in the marijuana business at all. Except you, I guess." She gave Bruiser a small bite of her cookie. "So now we know who the dead guy is, but that doesn't explain why he would come after me. What could he possibly want with me?"

"No clue. That's all I know." Scooter held up his plate. "Good pizza. Mind if I have another piece?"

Hmmm. She somehow doubted that was *all* that he knew. She pushed back from the table and set Bruiser on the floor. "I'm going to call Mac and fill him in."

"Leave my name out of it," Scooter said.

"No problem." She somehow thought Scooter was probably not his actual name anyway. She slipped into the guest room and called Mac. Her heart raced as she waited for him to pick up.

"Hey Zoey. You all right?"

The deep tone of his voice shot straight through her, and she practically swooned at the concern in his tone.

Geez. Pull yourself together girl. This isn't the seventeenth century. She needed to keep her swooning in check. Mac wasn't a knight in shining armor, he was a cop, and probably sounded concerned about a lot of people.

As much as that was true, she still sort of saw him as her knight, her protector. And just imagining him swooping her up onto his horse and riding off with her almost took her breath away.

"Zoey? You there? Are you okay?"

"Oh yeah. Sorry." She really needed to get her fantasies under control. Or at least save them for later. "I'm here. I'm fine. I just wanted to tell you we met a guy who knows Jimmy Two-Fingers."

"Where did you meet a guy like that? What's your grandmother got you mixed up in now? Are you at a biker bar?"

She laughed. "No, I'm at Edna's house. It's a guy she knows from her community theater. But he's also somehow involved in the recreational marijuana business and recognized Jimmy Two-Fingers." She felt so silly saying his name—like she was in a bad mafia flick. "Apparently he serves—or served—as muscle for the head guy in charge of the majority of the marijuana trade here in Pleasant Valley."

"Yeah, I've figured some of that out. I've been working on digging up information on Jimmy and how he might be connected to you."

"Did you come up with anything?"

"Not really. Not yet."

"Well, I guess the main guy's name is Leon."

"Leon Molloy?"

"Maybe. I don't know his last name, but surely there aren't that many Leons that are running recreational marijuana businesses."

"All of this recreational shop stuff is still pretty new, especially here in Pleasant Valley, so we keep a close watch on what's happening with it. Leon's got a shop on the west side of town, and the parking lot is always crowded. So far, he seems all above board, and his business seems legit."

"Then why does he need muscle like Jimmy?"

"There is a lot of money in marijuana. I mean a *lot*. Those businesses can bring in hundreds of thousands of dollars in cash a day."

"In cash? A day?" She had no idea.

"Yeah, and since it's only legal in certain states and not federally, the banks won't open accounts for them or set up credit card machines. So they have tons of cash and no banks to deposit it in. And it's no secret they have massive amounts of cash on site, so they've got to run tight security because their risk of being robbed is enormous."

"So where do I fit in to all of this? I'm just a lowly accountant."

"But you're an accountant for a large financial advisory firm that invests large sums of money for corporations."

"A firm that's been laundering money through a series of dummy corporations."

"That's got to be it. It makes sense that Leon would be using a finance company that may have less than stellar scruples to run some of that cash through."

She grinned. "You're pretty good at this detective stuff." Her face warmed as her mind went to what other things he might be good at.

He chuckled, and the sound of his low laughter did funny things to her insides. "Well, so far it's all just speculation. We've got to find an actual connection between Leon and the Cavellis."

"Pleasant Valley's a pretty small town. I'll talk to the Page Turners and see if they know of anything. It seems like around here, someone always knows somebody's aunt or their cousin lives next door to or they dated their brother in high school."

"Well, I'd say not to involve them, but if I know your grandmother, she's probably already made seventeen calls. Just tell them that if they do ask around, to keep it pretty quiet and don't give any details. We don't want to tip our hat that we suspect any connection to Molloy."

"Okay, that makes sense."

"All right, I'm going to get to work on my side. I'll let you know if I find anything out." He paused. "I was thinking maybe I'd stop by Edna's on my way home, if you think that would be okay. Just to check on you."

She smiled again. She couldn't have kept that smile off her face if she tried. "I'd like that."

He cleared his throat, and his voice switched back to business tone. "All right then. I'll see you later. My shift goes late tonight, so it will probably be closer to eight or nine when I get over there. Is that too late?"

"That would be perfect."

"See you then."

Butterflies tickled her stomach as she clicked off the phone. She felt like a teenager with a crush. But no teenage boy she remembered had the broad shoulders and muscled physique of Officer McCarthy.

She wondered if she should have told him about their undercover mission into Cavelli Commerce today. They hadn't really found anything, and it would probably only make him worry. Better to tell him about it tonight. In person. When he stopped by.

She checked her watch as she headed back toward the kitchen. They had several hours before he showed up. Surely the Page Turners could uncover a few things about this Leon guy by then.

NINE

Mac ran a hand across his head in frustration.

He knew there had to be something here. Some kind of connection between the Cavellis and Leon Molloy. It made perfect sense that the marijuana mogul would need a financial advisory company that would be willing to bend the rules to help him deal with his abundance of cash.

But what made sense and what he could actually prove were two very different factors.

The two odd links in the chain were Zoey and Teddy Grimes. The two accountants that worked for the Cavellis but were being hunted by Leon's head muscle. They had to be the connections. They had to be the ones who could somehow connect the financial dots that would harm both sides.

Not for the first time that day, he wished he could find Ted Grimes. He'd had his dispatcher calling hospitals and clinics around Zoey's apartment since that morning asking if they'd seen anyone fitting Ted's description or the description of the injury. But Denver was a big city, and even as she'd widened her search she'd come up with nothing.

Either someone was covering for him, or he'd gone into hiding with someone helping him that might have medical skills.

Or there was one other alternative—that Teddy was dead. That he'd been killed at Zoey's apartment and was now wearing cement shoes and sinking to the bottom of Chatfield Reservoir. But he wasn't ready to give up on the burly accountant yet. He'd promised Zoey that he would keep looking for him.

And he knew the guys in the Denver PD were looking for him, too. They'd had a couple of uniforms canvassing the neighborhoods around both of Zoey's and Teddy's homes.

They'd had a couple of hits—a neighbor had seen Teddy pull out of the garage around one that morning, and a shop owner on Zoey's street thought he saw a guy matching Teddy's description come out of her apartment building and head east on foot. If the shop owner was correct, then at least that meant Ted left Zoey's apartment alive. But so far, no one had come up with anything solid to lead them to his whereabouts.

"Hey, Officer Asshole. You want some coffee?"

Mac recognized the voice and looked up into the grinning face of Patrick Callahan. He was holding two takeout cups from Pleasant Valley Perks, and Mac reached out to take one. "Hey, Detective Dick-less. What the heck are you doing in my station?"

Pat lifted his shoulders in an exaggerated shrug. "What? Can't a guy visit an old friend in his home town?"

Mac offered him a wry grin. "Not when he just saw that old friend this morning. What's up? Did you get a lead on the case?" Maybe their hunch about Leon was correct, and Pat was in town to check up on him.

Patrick sat on the corner of Mac's desk and took a sip of his coffee. "Damn. They still make pretty good coffee over at the Perk. And did you know Stacy Hayes works over there? Remember her from Algebra? I think she was a cheerleader. Heard she's divorced now, but she still looks good."

Mac took a sip of coffee, trying to hold his patience with his old friend. "So, besides the coffee and the good-looking staff at the Perk, what are you doing in town?"

"I had a few follow-up questions for your friend, Zoey Allen. They ID'd the stiff at her apartment, and I thought I'd show her some mug shots—see if it triggered any memories about how she knows the guy."

"She doesn't know him. I already showed her a photo of Jimmy Two-Fingers, and she didn't recognize him. Apparently he was muscle for a local guy that runs the recreational weed parlor in the Valley. A guy named Leon Molloy."

"Well, haven't you been a busy little beaver today?"

Sometimes his friend really could be an asshole. And a condescending asshole at that. "Yeah, this ain't my first case. So—do you know this guy? This Leon? What can you tell me about him?"

"Not a lot. I mean I know about him. Hell, the Gazette ran a story on him and his recreational pot-shops when they first legalized the stuff in Colorado. But as far as I know, he keeps his nose pretty clean."

"It's not his nose I'm concerned about. It's his cash. How's he getting that cleaned?"

"Good question."

"You think he could be using Cavelli Commerce as a way to wash his cash? We already have the Cavellis on money laundering. When you add in that Molloy's muscle is going after the Cavelli's accountants, it seems like a logical connection."

Pat downed the rest of his coffee and tossed the cup toward Mac's trash can. "I dunno. Seems like a bit of a stretch to me, but we don't have much else to go on so it's worth looking into. Why don't we start by going over and talking to the blonde accountant?"

An uneasy feeling prickled his spine when he imagined Pat questioning Zoey. What was that about? His protective instincts kicking in? Or was he worried about Zoey meeting the brawny Irish cop who charmed every woman he knew. "You don't have to bother with that. I can take care of talking to the accountant. I already know her grandmother."

Pat narrowed his eyes and offered him a leering grin. "What? You don't want me around the blonde? What's up, Mackey? You got a thing for the hot bean-counter?"

Mac didn't need his friend giving him a hard time about Zoey. Especially because it seemed he *did* have a thing for her. Or was in the process of developing a thing for her. Maybe. Hell, he didn't know. But he knew he didn't need Pat in on whatever he was feeling. "No, jackass. I don't have a thing for her. I've just already talked to her, and it seems to me that we should spend our time and the taxpayers' money following up on *actual* leads."

Pat held up his hands in surrender, but his eyes held a knowing gleam. "All right, all right. Don't need to get all touchy about it. I got a couple of hours to burn before I gotta be back in the city. Let's go track down some bad guys."

Zoey stepped back into the kitchen, Bruiser following close on her heels. "What'd I miss?"

The cookie jar was empty, and Johnny, Edna, Sunny, and the scruffy-haired Scooter were the only ones left around the table.

"Maggie and Cassie had to leave," Sunny said. "They had something at the high school tonight that they both had to go to. They said to tell you goodbye, and they'd check in with us later."

Edna had a notebook in front of her and a pen in her hand. She tapped the pen against her chin. "We were just brainstorming, trying to come up with ideas of how this Leon Molloy could possibly be connected to you or thoughts about why he would want you dead." The notebook page was still blank. "We haven't come up with much yet."

"No, I can't imagine that you would. Because there *is* no connection. Or none that I know of. I don't smoke pot, and I don't hang out with anyone that does."

Edna grimaced. "Actually you do."

Zoey gave her a quizzical look.

"I hate to suggest it. But could this have anything to do with your parents? When's the last time you talked to Moon?"

Zoey's parents were self-professed hippies that had raised her on a commune in southern Colorado. Everything about their lifestyle was easy and free, and they lived the motto 'If it feels good, do it.' Any therapist worth their salt could tell her why she valued order and preferred things in her life to be tidy and constant. And several of them had.

"I hadn't even thought of that," she said. "I haven't talked to mom in a few weeks. Probably not since your wedding."

Johnny and Edna exchanged an intimate smile, and he placed his hand over hers.

Zoey sighed, so happy for her grandparents. "You guys are adorable. You're still such newlyweds."

Edna grinned. "I've been waiting my whole life to marry this man. I plan to ride this honeymoon as long as I can."

"All right," Sunny said. "Let's keep on task here. Otherwise Edna's going to start filling us in on her honeymoon activities and ain't nobody got time for that."

Zoey picked up her phone. "I've been meaning to call mom anyway. Just to let her know that I was okay in case she heard about the—you know—dead guy in my apartment."

"Yes, you should," Edna agreed. "Why don't you call her now, and ask her if she knows Leon or if she's had any kind of problem with him that might influence his actions toward you?"

She pushed her mom's contact and listened to an old Eagles song play as her ringback tone.

Moon picked up on the second ring. "Hello, Zoey Shining Star."

Gotta love caller ID.

"Hi, Mom. You know I hate it when you use my middle name."

"Well, you are my shining star. And I was just going to call you. You must have picked up our psychic connection."

"I'm sure that's it, Mom." Zoey didn't know how much she believed in all of her mom's metaphysical stuff, but now wasn't the time to argue.

"Are you all right? I did your cards this morning, and they seemed to suggest that danger was surrounding you."

"Well, that's what I'm calling you about." She took a deep breath. "A couple of guys kind of broke into my apartment last night."

"Kind of? Were you home? Are you hurt?" Her mom's voice was shrill in her ear.

"I'm fine, Mom. I heard them come in, and I snuck out the back window. But the thing is, when I went back with the police, we found that one of them was still in my apartment. And he was dead."

"Dead? Oh my gosh. Honey, I'm so glad you're okay."

"I'm okay. But we can't figure out why someone would break into my apartment."

"It sounds like they weren't there to rob you, but to hurt you. That would make sense."

"How could them wanting to hurt me possibly make sense to you?"

"Oh, not that they wanted to hurt you. But the reading makes more sense. I turned over a death card this morning."

"A death card?" This was getting better and better. This is why she didn't usually let her mom 'do her cards.'

"Now don't worry, the death card doesn't necessarily mean someone's going to die, but it could mean danger or signify harm."

"Well, that's a relief. I guess." Zoey was glad her mom couldn't hear the roll of her eyes. "Anyway, we may have found a small connection to the dead man with a guy here in town that runs a recreational marijuana shop. His name is Leon Molloy. Do you know him?"

"Why would I know him? We don't go to those shops. They're rip-offs. And their product is completely inferior. The blend we grow here on the commune is so much better."

Of course. She should have known. "So you don't know this guy? Never heard of him or had any dealings with him?"

"No. Nothing. He doesn't sound familiar at all."

"Okay. Thanks, Mom."

"Honey, are you safe now?"

"I'm with Gram and Grandpa Johnny."

"Somehow that doesn't make me feel any better."

"I'm fine. Really."

Her mother continued to speak as if she hadn't said a word. "What about that cute cop that was at the wedding? Mac? Why don't you call him? Maybe he can offer you some private protection."

"Gram already called him. He was with me when we discovered the body, and he's checked on me a couple of times today."

"Ahhh. That would explain the ace of hearts card–it stands for love."

She felt the heat of a blush warming her neck. "All right, Mom. I gotta go."

"Bye, honey. Keep in touch with me. I'll light a candle of protection for you. I love you."

"Thanks, Mom. Love you too."

She clicked off the phone and shook her head at the group. "No luck. My mom says there's no connection to her. She's never even heard of the guy."

Edna tapped her pen against the notebook. "Maybe you know him by sight but not by name. Do you think he has a Facebook page? Or maybe we could Google him?" She looked at Scooter for confirmation.

He shrugged. "How should I know? I grow for him—I'm not his friend on Facebook. I know if you want to see him, he's usually hanging out at his weed bar."

"What's a weed bar?"

"You know, like a regular bar, where people hang out, but instead of booze, you smoke weed."

"I've never heard of such a thing."

"Well, we've got one here in town. It's called The Joint, and Leon spends a lot of time there."

"We can't just go waltzing in to a weed bar," Sunny said. "I'm a grade school teacher for goodness sake."

"I can," Edna said. "I'm working on beefing up my bad reputation."

"Well, it's not going to help anything if *you* go in there and recognize him," Sunny said. "Zoey is the one who has to go in there."

"She can't go in there," Johnny said, speaking up for the first time. "Suppose this Leon *is* connected to all of this? That would mean he wants to hurt her. Or worse. Remember, it was one of his guys that was found dead in her apartment. This just sounds too dangerous. Why don't we call Mac and have him look into it."

"He's already looking into it," Zoey explained. "I called him and gave him Leon's name. But Sunny's right. It doesn't matter if Mac checks into him, *I* have to see him myself to know if I recognize him or know him from somewhere."

Sunny's eyes widened. "Did I say that?"

"Well, it was something like that." She twisted the edges of a loose napkin sitting on the table. "I'm the one that got us all involved in this mess. So, I'm the one who needs to help figure it out. Granted, I would normally never, ever, in a million years consider going into an establishment where the primary objective is to get stoned." She nodded at Scooter. "No offense intended."

He shrugged. "It's cool."

"But I also normally do not have thugs breaking into my apartment and trying to kill me, either. This is not a normal situation, and if I'm going to figure this out, I need to step out of my tidy little organized comfort zone and get messy. I'm not going to solve this by hiding out at my grandma's house. So, if I have to go to a weed bar to scope out a potential murderer—then that's what I'm going to do."

Good Lord—who was this person talking? It certainly did not sound like herself. It sounded like someone who was brave and tough and a little kick-ass. She only wished she felt as brave and kick-ass as she sounded.

"Okay," Sunny said. "If you can do it, so will I. I can use it as a research opportunity so if kids at school ever talk about it, I'll know what they mean."

"You're forgetting one tiny problem," Johnny said. "You can't just go in there and look around. If you go in there, you'll look suspicious if you're just standing there and not smoking pot. Are you all prepared to get stoned while you're undercover?"

"I will," Edna piped up. "I've always wanted to try it anyway. And if at least one of us is smoking, then you girls can just hold something but don't have to try it. I'll take one for the team and volunteer to get stoned."

"Oh for goodness sake." Johnny shook his head in astonishment. "This is ridiculous. And dangerous."

Edna waved a hand at him. "Oh, it'll be fine. No one's going to pay attention to an old lady like me." She nudged Scooter. "But these two are gonna need new disguises. Do you think you can come up with something for them so no one will recognize them?"

Scooter nodded. "Sure. That's probably a good idea anyway if you're trying to stay under the radar. People notice when two hot chicks walk into a bar." He ducked his head and a blush colored his cheeks. "So, I'd have to make them more average looking. Even a little on the gnarly side if you really don't want anyone to notice them."

"I can do gnarly," Zoey said. "I'll do whatever it takes to blend in. I don't want anyone there to recognize me, especially this Leon guy, or actually anyone that's inclined to kill me."

"I can do that. And just so you know, the weed bar's really mellow. As long as you're cool and don't make a big deal about anything, no one will really even notice you're there."

"I can be mellow," Edna said. "I was born mellow."

Johnny scoffed. "You haven't been mellow a day in your life." He shook his head. "It doesn't sound like I'm going to talk you out of this, so this time I'm going along. And I think we should go in separately. It'll seem more likely that an elderly couple would be on their own and that two young women would be together."

Zoey nodded. "That makes sense." She looked at Scooter. "Ready to make me unrecognizable?"

TEN

An hour and a half later, Zoey and Sunny stepped into The Joint. Scooter had worked miracles with their disguises, and Zoey felt like a different person.

This time, she had raided her grandfather's closet and came up with a baggy pair of khaki's, a long white T-shirt, and a flannel button-up shirt. She'd belted the pants with a thick leather belt and rolled up the sleeves of the flannel.

Scooter had found a wig of long straight black hair, and she'd topped it with a baseball cap pulled low over her eyes. A pair of aviator sunglasses covered her kohl-lined eyes, and Scooter had placed a temporary tattoo across the lower half of her arm. The tattoo was the word 'Courage' scrolled in curly letters and surrounded by red roses.

She glanced at the tattoo now and screwed up her own courage as she walked into the bar. Fighting her natural inclination to stand up straight, Scooter had shown her how to slouch her shoulders and change her normal stride to affect more of a trudge.

Sunny's outfit was a little more eye-catching in an effort to draw attention away from Zoey. She wore a short blue dress, torn black tights, and military boots. Her eyes were also heavily made up with the same kohl-black liner rimming her lashes. Scooter had tied another of Johnny's flannel shirts around her waist and draped a long chain around her neck. He'd given her a wig as well, this one a short brunette bob cut to cover her usual blonde wavy curls.

They made quite a pair as they slunk through the doors and scanned the room for a place to sit.

The air was thick with the sweet, acrid smell of marijuana, and Zoey blinked against the smoke that already stung her eyes. The bar had a retro look with dark paneled walls and deep red leather booths along the outer walls. Posters of classic rock musicians hung on the walls, and the center of the room had clusters of loveseats and big comfy chairs circled around low black tables.

Dusk had settled outside giving the bar itself even more of a dark and mysterious feel. She didn't know why the place made her giddy with nervousness. It was just like any other bar, except people were smoking marijuana instead of drinking.

And there was also the chance that one of the patrons possibly wanted to kill her. That could be adding to her nervousness.

The bar itself wasn't too crowded—maybe twenty people in groups of two to four clustered together. They were centered around tables covered in bongs, pipes, food wrappers, and soda cans. Some tables had the Middle Eastern-looking hookah pipes setting on them, their long hoses snaking out like Medusa's hair.

Only a few people even looked up as the women walked across the room. They slid into a booth, and a bored looking waitress wandered up and handed them menus.

"Can I get you something to drink?"

"Yes, please," Zoey answered. "Can I get a raspberry margarita—wait." She lowered her voice and tried to sound bored and aloof. And tougher than she felt. "I mean I'll take a seven and seven." It was the toughest drink she could think of.

Sunny nodded. "Yeah, me too."

The waitress sighed as if she'd been through this routine before. "We're not that kind of bar, ladies. We don't serve alcohol."

"Oh, in that case, we'll take two Diet Cokes."

The waitress raised an eyebrow. "This your first time?"

Zoey tried to shrug and come off looking cool, but Sunny had already nodded.

She tapped the menu on the table. "This shows our different blends. We sell by the gram, and you can use your own pipes, or you can buy them from us. We also offer edibles, like cookies, brownies and hard candies. If you want a little something more serious, we also offer dabs."

"What's a dab?" Sunny asked. Zoey nudged her foot under the table. They were supposed to act like they knew all this. Like they were totally used to hanging out in weed bars.

The waitress pulled a small container from her pocket and twisted the lid off. It looked like an eyeshadow pot with a small gray pool of wax in it. "A dab is like a concentrated form of high grade hash. It's pretty strong, and it'll get you real high real fast." The slightest grin touched her lips, the first sign of emotion she'd had shown. "Around here we like to say just a little dab'll do ya."

Zoey nodded her head. "Yeah, that's what I usually say, too." She tried for a jovial chuckle, but it came out as more of a weak cough. "I think we'll probably stick with the basics today."

The waitress grinned again, apparently seeing through her false bravado. "Okay then. I'll just give you some time to look over the menu."

"Thanks."

The waitress turned as the front door swung open, and Edna and Johnny stepped in.

And from that point forward, no one in the bar even noticed Sunny and Zoey.

"Would you look at this place, dear?" Edna asked Johnny in a booming voice. They both wore multi-colored Hawaiian shirts, Bermuda shorts, and Johnny wore a dark sock with a sandal on his un-booted leg. The quintessential tourists.

"We're definitely not in Kansas anymore," Johnny answered with a too-loud laugh.

"Yoo-hoo." Edna waved at the waitress. "Hi there—we're here visiting from Kansas, and this is our first time in a marijuana bar." She said the word 'marijuana' in a loud exaggerated stage whisper and used her fingers to indicate air quotation marks. "We heard you all legalized the stuff, and we thought we'd check it out." She waved at all of the patrons who were now watching them. "Hi y'all. We're Ken and Barbara. We're here visiting from a little town east of Middle of Nowhere, Kansas."

Seriously? Did Edna really pick Ken and Barbie as their aliases? Everything in Zoey's introverted personality wanted to scream to tone it down—quit drawing so much attention to yourselves.

But Edna was doing exactly what she was supposed to do. She had the attention of every person in that bar.

A table with three older bikers waved and one chuckled heartily. They all had long hair in various stages of gray and wore jeans, leather vests over T-shirts, and heavy black boots.

One raised his bong in salute. "Welcome, travelers. I'm actually from Kansas too, born and raised there and graduated from K-state." He gestured to the loveseat across the table from him and his friends. "Have a seat. You're welcome to join us."

Four kids in their twenties sat around a table smoking from a hookah, and they all broke out into fits of snorts and giggles.

Edna ignored them and crossed the bar to where the bikers sat. She nodded and offered a comment to a few of the groups as she passed. Lowering her glasses at the group of twenty-somethings, she stopped to scold them. "Shouldn't you all be in school? Is this how you represent the future of America?" This only threw the group of kids into more hysterical laughter.

She waved at another group of people and stopped in front of Sunny and Zoey's tables. She narrowed her eyes at Sunny. "You know dear, you would be much prettier if you didn't wear so much makeup." She wiggled her fingers at them as Johnny followed in her chaotic wake.

"This is very nice of you," she said, as she and Johnny sat down across from the bikers. As they had talked about earlier, she kept her back to the door and drew attention away from the bar area. "Are you all in a little motorcycle gang together?"

One of the bikers laughed out loud. He wore a red, white, and blue bandanna around his head and his hair in two long braids, Willie Nelson-style. "Lady—you are too much."

That was one way to put it. Her grandmother was indeed too much.

But she was also very good at creating a distraction, and Zoey nodded at Sunny as she slipped out of the booth. "I'm going to the restroom."

"Oh, yeah." Sunny seemed to be caught up in watching the Edna show. She snapped to attention as if she just remembered their mission. "I'll come with you."

A restroom sign pointed down the hallway behind the bar, and it seemed to be the only way to reach any other rooms so Zoey hoped they were headed in the right direction. The hallway held four doors. Two were marked with signs stating either "Dudes" or

"Chicks", one appeared to be a utility closet, and the last door had an "Employees Only- Do Not Enter" sign affixed to it.

Zoey headed for the last door. She pointed to the front of the bar and whispered to Sunny, "Keep a lookout. I'm going to check out what's behind this door."

She turned the knob, and the sound of the latch's click seemed deafening. She snuck a quick glance at Sunny, but her back was still turned and she didn't appear to have heard anything. Strains of a Bob Marley song floated on the air, and Zoey took a deep breath and pushed the door open.

The door led to another hallway, and she could see two more doors, both standing open. The voices of an old sitcom came through one door with the undercurrent of deep male chuckles and the soft sound of a whirring machine.

She'd borrowed a pair of Edna's white Keds, and one of the sneakers squeaked against the linoleum floor as she snuck down the hallway.

She froze, holding her breath as she listened for any signal that someone had heard her.

Nothing.

Slowly releasing her breath, she tiptoed forward enough to lean her head toward the door and see into the room.

Two long tables filled the middle of the room. A man sat at each table feeding stacks of money into a currency counter. The whirring sound must have been the sound of the money counters as they loaded and strapped handfuls of bills.

Fast food wrappers and empty beer cans cluttered the ends of the tables.

The men had their backs to her. Zoey tilted her head as she sought to see each man's face, trying to memorize their features and catalogue them in her mind. Both appeared to be in their mid-forties, but one was overweight with a large paunchy belly crushed against the edge of the table, and the other was lean with hardened muscles.

A grey haze filled the room as tendrils of smoke curled into the air from a myriad of cigarettes and dark brown cigars that burned in ashtrays on the tables. A large screen TV was affixed to the wall, and the sitcom held the men's attention.

The thing holding Zoey's attention was not the stacks of cash lining the table, but the silver handguns resting next to each man's hand.

Her heart-rate tripled in speed, and a thin sheen of sweat covered her forehead. She needed to get out of there.

She quickly scanned the rest of the room. A couple of shelves lined the walls holding office supplies, money straps, and plastic courier bags.

A third man of around the same age leaned against the wall, a cigarette dangling from his lip. He was tanned and wore black shorts, a golf shirt, and loafers with no socks. An expensive gold chain hung around his neck, and his dark curly hair was cut close to his head.

He pointed the cigarette and narrowed his eyes at the heavier man. "Pick up the pace, Dave. They're gonna be here in an hour, and we need to have this cash ready."

"All right. All right. I'm going as fast as I can. Gimme a break, would you, Leon? I've been here all day."

So this was Leon.

She hadn't known exactly what to expect. Maybe because of the marijuana association, she'd been expecting him to look more like the old hippies that hung around her mother's commune. More John Lennon or even someone resembling the bikers she saw in the bar.

She certainly wasn't imagining this well-groomed man who looked like he'd just stepped off the golf course.

"Hey, what the hell do you think you're doing in here?" A huge muscular man wearing a black T-shirt and jeans appeared in the doorway, blocking her view of the room. He wore a scowl on his face and a gun at his waist.

Zoey held up her hands. She tried to even out her voice, slow it down to affect the easy drawl she heard Scooter use. "Sorry dude, I was looking for the bathroom."

The man studied her face a few seconds, but for what seemed like a few hours, then pointed down the hallway. "It's back there, behind the door marked 'Chicks' not 'Employees Only'".

She backed away a few steps then turned and hurried down the hall. Her heart was in her throat at what she'd just seen. She needed to get Sunny and her grandparents and get the hell out of there.

She pushed through the door and rushed toward Sunny, who was still standing lookout at the end of the hallway.

"Your grandmother is an absolute hoot. She's got those bikers eating out of her hands." Sunny turned, and her expression changed to one of alarm as she took in Zoey's face. "What happened? Are you okay?"

She nodded. "Yeah, but we need to get out of here."

"Did you see Leon?"

"Yeah—he's here. And he saw me."

They moved quickly through the room. Zoey glanced at Johnny and gave a small nod of her head as she tossed a ten dollar bill on the table where the waitress had left their drinks. It took enormous effort to avoid eye-contact with her grandmother.

Edna was currently engrossed in a conversation with one of the bikers. He was showing her a large bong and appeared to be explaining how it worked.

As they passed by where they sat, Zoey heard her grandfather say, "Oh shucks, dear. We're out of time. We need to get on our way if we're going to get up early and see Pikes Peak in the morning."

One of the bikers passed him a pipe. "Ah, you don't have to go yet. It's still early and that old mountain will be there all day."

Edna must have got the hint, because she picked up her handbag and stood. "Oh he's just using that as his excuse. He probably needs to get going 'cause he's got a hemorrhoid that's been bothering him." She patted one of the bikers on the arm. "You know you just can't enjoy yourself when you've got troubles with the old pooper."

The biker nodded. Evidently it's hard to argue when a hemorrhoid was involved.

They passed the group of twenty-somethings on their way out the door, and Zoey was worried one of the boys was going to fall out of his chair, he was laughing so hard.

The night air had cooled off as they stepped onto the sidewalk, and Zoey was thankful for the flannel shirt. The air felt crisp and clean, and she filled her lungs with it, happy to be free of the smoke-filled room.

She checked her watch. It was getting close to eight.

They needed to get back to Edna's so she'd be there when Mac stopped by. She wondered if showing up at this establishment and sneaking into the cash-counting room fell under Mac's guidelines of trying not to tip their hat. Somehow she doubted it.

Edna and Johnny stepped out of the bar and let the door shut behind them. He turned their way. "We're headed west if you ladies would like a ride."

Staying in character, Zoey nodded her head. "Sure, that'd be cool."

They crossed the parking lot and climbed into Johnny's car.

A nervous bubble of laughter escaped her lips, and Zoey leaned forward clutching her stomach as hysterical giggles overcame her. "I can't believe you used a hemorrhoid as your excuse to get out of there."

The car erupted in laughter.

"I didn't care what she used," Johnny said. "I would have started talking about my prostate as long as we could leave."

"My head was a little spinny from all that smoke," Edna explained between giggles. "It was the first thing that popped into my head."

Edna sat in the front and seemed to be laughing quite hard. Zoey leaned forward and peered over the back seat. "Gram, are you stoned?"

"Oh no." Edna giggled again. "Well, I don't know. Maybe a little. I only did a couple of those hit thingies, but I didn't actually inhale."

Where have I heard that before?

"So what did you see?" Sunny asked. "When you went in to the back room? You said you saw Leon, and then you sure hustled us out of there quick."

The laughter in the car died, and Johnny turned toward her. "You saw Leon? Did he see you?"

Zoey nodded. "Yeah, just for a second, but I don't think he recognized me. And I'm sure I've never seen him before."

"Well, crap-cakes," Edna said. "Then this was all for nothing. We didn't learn anything."

"Not necessarily. A big guy caught me and told me to get out of there. That's what freaked me out. I *did* recognize him."

Sunny gasped. "You did? From where?"

"From Cavelli Commerce. He looked different though because he was wearing jeans and a T-shirt instead of a suit."

"Are you sure it was the same guy?"

"Yeah, I recognized the wing tattoo on his wrist."

Johnny leaned forward and started the engine. "We need to get out of here."

Before he could put the car in gear, the rear passenger door was pulled open, and the man she'd just been describing yanked Zoey from the car.

Struggling against him, she tried to scream, but he covered her mouth with his meaty hand. He pulled her toward a black SUV that was parked nearby. The engine was running and the back door stood open—waiting to take Zoey into its lair.

Flashes of information flew through her brain as she tried to remember the tips they'd learned when she took a women's defense class last year. She tried to butt her head back, but she only met with a hard muscled chest. He was so much taller than her and had her lifted completely off the ground, so the option of stamping on his feet was out. Kicking at his shins, her sneakers were ineffective.

His arms squeezed her tighter to him, his huge biceps crushing her lungs.

Her heart pounded against her chest as she tried to breathe—the panic threatening to take over as she realized there was nothing she could do.

She was powerless against his strength.

A banshee scream came from her grandfather's car as the front door flew open, and Edna emerged, a can of pepper spray held in her hands.

She shot a stream toward the big man, but he had already pushed her back so the vapor fell short of its mark.

Still the bitter spray hung in the air, burning Zoey's eyes as well. Tears fell as she squinted against the caustic mist.

"SHIT!" Her captor had released one arm to shove at Edna and now drew that arm across his eyes. "That shit burns!"

Even with one arm, he still held her immobile, and he tried to shove her into the backseat of the waiting SUV.

Kicking out her legs, she tried to push against the door frame, but he grabbed a chunk of her hair, pulling it as she cried out in pain.

"Get in the car, or I will hurt you then come back for the old lady."

Sobbing in defeat, she relaxed against him. She would never let anything happen to Edna.

He shoved her into the back seat, shifting to pull her arm against her back. Her face pressed against the expensive leather seat, and she knew it would take little effort for him to snap the bone in her arm.

Slamming the door, the SUV sped away, the whole incident taking probably less than thirty seconds.

Thirty seconds of fear and pain.

Panic rose like bile in her throat as she imagined the terror yet to come.

ELEVEN

Mac's tires squealed as he flew into the parking lot of The Joint. He was too late.

A burly man had just shoved a woman into the back of a black SUV.

He recognized Johnny's car and had seen Edna try to pepper spray the man so even though the woman had long dark hair, he knew in his gut that it had to be Zoey.

Edna turned at the sound of his tires. She must have recognized him because her arms flailed in panic as she screamed and directed him toward the SUV. Through his open window, Mac could hear her screaming to go after Zoey.

He didn't even stop. The bumper of the squad car scraped the concrete as he drove off the curb in pursuit of the black SUV. The windows were tinted so he couldn't see in the back. He knew one guy had grabbed Zoey and one guy was driving but didn't know if anyone else was inside the vehicle.

He hit the siren and pressed firmer on the accelerator. His heart beat hard against his chest, and all of his focus was on not losing the SUV.

The truck sped up, flying through a red light. A man in a red Toyota skidded sideways as he swerved to avoid colliding with the SUV. The man blared his horn and yelled a few choice words at the black vehicle.

Luckily Pleasant Valley was a small town and didn't have much traffic. They only had a few actual stoplights. He hoped the sound of his siren would have the locals getting out of the way. The last thing he wanted was for someone else to get hurt.

He couldn't let himself think about what they would do to Zoey if he didn't catch them.

Please Lord, don't let them have hurt her already.

Or worse.

No—he wouldn't go there. Couldn't go there.

She was alive when the guy shoved her into the back of the SUV—he'd be damned if he didn't make sure she was alive when she came out.

The black vehicle was slipping further away. They'd passed the city limits and were heading into the mountains. The road curved, and the SUV turned onto a dirt road. Dust flew into the window of his car as he skidded around the curve.

No other cars were around, and he knew he had to act fast so he wouldn't lose them. He pulled his gun from its holster. He didn't want to engage in gunfire, but his options were limited.

If he fired first and got a clean shot at the tire, he could hopefully disable the vehicle and have a shot at getting Zoey out of there.

He stuck the gun out the window, aimed and fired.

Damn! He missed. He fired again.

A hand holding a gun poked out the back window and returned fire.

A bullet pinged off the side of the car. Way too close.

He swerved back and forth, making his car a harder target to hit. But also making it harder to aim at the vehicle in front of him. He didn't want to take a chance at hitting Zoey by mistake.

He fired again, this time aiming for the arm sticking out the window. Direct hit! The man dropped the gun and pulled his arm inside.

Another shot. Aimed at the tires. Another hit.

A loud burst sounded as the tire blew and the SUV went into a skid. It hit the soft shoulder of the dirt road and tipped off the side.

Mac watched in horror as the car rolled upside down. He braked to a stop, his own car skidding in the gravel. Gun drawn, he raced for the overturned SUV.

The tires were still spinning, and the windows had shattered on impact. He could see the driver's head slumped against the window frame. His eyes were closed, and a nasty cut tore across his forehead. Mac prayed he was unconscious. And that he stayed that way.

A woman's arms, then the back of her head, appeared as she tried to pull herself out of the broken back window.

Mac registered the black hair and the tattooed arm. What the hell? Had he made a mistake? Was the woman in the car not Zoey?

Then she tipped her head up, and Mac saw her face. Looked into the eyes of the woman who had been filling his thoughts and haunting his dreams.

"I got you, Zoey." He holstered his gun then reached for her arms, pulling her out of the SUV.

She clung to him as he dragged her body through the window.

Almost there.

She screamed as a meaty hand reached through the window and grabbed her ankle pulling her back into the car.

Kicking against the hand, she tried to break free of its grasp.

Mac stepped forward and stomped on it, the heel of his boot crushing the man's hand. He heard a howl of pain, and the hand released Zoey's leg.

He didn't think, didn't stop to ask if she was okay. Instead, he swooped her into his arms, cradling her body against his and raced to the squad car. He pulled open the passenger door and set her inside then ran around the back of the vehicle.

A shot rang through the air, and a bullet shattered one of the siren lights.

Mac heard Zoey scream as he dropped to the ground. "Get down!"

From under the SUV, he could see a black-sleeved arm holding a gun emerge from the driver's window. Damn. He must not have stayed as unconscious as Mac had hoped he would.

Mac pulled his gun and scooted to the back corner of the car trying to shield himself as much as possible. He'd left the driver's side door of the squad car open and the engine on as he'd raced for the SUV and he sent up a silent prayer of thanks.

From a crouched position, he leaned forward, aimed, and fired off three quick shots at the SUV then raced for the door and slid into the seat. In one movement, he pulled the door shut and threw the car into gear.

Zoey had squeezed herself on to the floor of the passenger side. "Go! Go!" She screamed and covered her head as another shot hit the front window of the car. A ragged hole appeared in the windshield as the bullet ripped through and tore into the fabric of the front seat.

The tires spun in the gravel as they tried to gain purchase, then the car shot forward, barreling down the dirt road and away from the wrecked SUV.

Mac careened around the corner, turning back on to the highway and the speedometer climbed as he raced up the mountain.

He glanced down at Zoey. "You okay?"

Her face was pale and streaks of black eyeliner ran down her cheeks. A ribbon of blood had started to dry on the side of her face from a cut above her eyebrow. She pulled herself into the seat. "I'm okay."

Her voice was shaky but steady, and she reached to pull off the dark-haired wig.

Mac glanced at her quickly as he sped past a blue car. "Maybe you'd better leave it on, in case they're looking for a blonde-haired woman. I almost didn't recognize you myself."

"You didn't even know it was me? You just head into a high-speed car chase and almost get shot for all the girls?" She tried to sound funny, but her voice broke and she covered her face with her hands. Her shoulders shook as she let loose a sob.

She looked over at him. "Thank you, Mac. Thank you so much. If you hadn't shown up—I think they were going to kill me." Emotion threatened to overtake her again, and she took a deep breath.

The console was between them, but he reached out and grabbed her hand. He wished he could pull the car over and haul her into his lap. He would have given anything to take her into his arms right now and feel her solidness against him—for her comfort, as well as his own. "It's okay, Zoey. You're safe now. I'm not gonna let anything happen to you."

Anger and fear and a fierce protectiveness filled him. He knew he would do anything to keep her safe. Damn it—this was exactly what he didn't want. He didn't want to be responsible for another person. Didn't want to have her rely on him, trust in him, believe in him, believe that he would protect her.

Because he didn't know if he could. And it would hurt more to let her down. It was easier to focus on his anger. He dropped her hand. "I don't understand how they got ahold of you in the first place. You knew Leon was connected to the guy that broke into your place. What the hell were you thinking going to his bar? Were you trying to get yourself killed?"

He heard her sharp intake of breath and knew his words were probably too harsh. But he didn't care. He focused on the road and flew by another car.

"No, of course not." She twisted her hands in her lap. "You're right. It was stupid and irresponsible. We were just trying to help. We thought if we went in there in disguise that I could maybe get a look at this Leon guy—see if maybe I recognized him."

"And did you? See him, I mean?"

"Yes, he was in the back room, along with a couple of other guys. They were counting money with these machines, and they all had guns. That's when we got out of there. But they must have somehow figured out it was me, because before we could pull out of the parking lot, they grabbed me." Her voice trembled again with the memory. "They told me if I didn't go with them, they would hurt my grandmother."

His heart softened—just a little—he was still mad—but he could tell she was just as mad at herself. "Speaking of your grandmother, you should probably call her and tell her you're okay."

"Good idea." She dug her cell phone out of her front pocket. "I can't believe it didn't fall out of my pocket." She pressed some keys on the phone and held it to her ear.

"Hello, Zoey?" Edna voice boomed. She spoke so loudly into the phone, he could clearly hear her words.

"Hi, Grandma. Are you okay?"

"ME? Land's sake, child—I'm fine. I'm worried about you. Are you all right?"

Zoey lightly touched his arm. "Yes, I'm okay. Mac saved me."

"Praise the Lord. Tell Mac next time I see him I plan to kiss him right on the mouth."

Holy hell—that was not something he would look forward to.

Zoey laughed. In the time he'd known her, he knew one thing Edna could be counted on for—she could always make you laugh.

"Where are you? Is he bringing you back to the house?" Edna asked.

"No." He answered before Zoey could ask. "Tell her I'm taking you somewhere safe. And we're getting rid of your cell phone, so she won't be able to contact you." He rubbed his hand over his head. "I guess somebody should probably know where we are. Tell her to tell Johnny that I'm taking you to the place we had his bachelor party."

Zoey gave him a strange look but relayed the message.

"He's taking you to hide out in a stripper club?" Edna voice rose even higher than before.

"No, of course not." She covered the phone with her hand. "You're not really taking me to a strip club to hide out, are you?"

He shook his head. "No. But you need to have her thank Johnny for sending me that text telling me where you all were. He's the reason I showed up at The Joint when I did."

Zoey's eyes widened. "I didn't realize he'd texted you."

"Yeah, well I wish *you* would have been the one to text me. I would rather have heard from you that you were in trouble." He turned back to the road. Why had he just said that? It had been his first thought when he got the text from Johnny, but he hadn't meant to share that thought with her.

She relayed the message to Edna.

He pulled off the highway and into the lot of a convenience store. Pulling around to the back of the store, he parked and killed the engine. "Tell her you gotta go. You can call her again when it's safe."

She nodded. "I've got to go now, Grandma. I love you, and I'll call you again when I can. Don't worry about me. I'm with Mac. He'll protect me."

Her words stung like barbs in his heart. Could he protect her? His track record in that department hadn't proved too great in the past.

He held out his hand for her phone. "We've got to get rid of it, just in case they're tracking it."

She handed it to him. "That's fine. It's insured."

He got out of the car, dropped the phone to the ground and smashed it with his boot. He picked up the shattered remains and tossed them in the dumpster behind the store. "Come on," he said, opening her car door and helping her out.

She limped forward, and for the first time he noticed the tears in her pants and the smears of blood around her knee.

He wrapped an arm around her waist. "Are you okay? Can you walk?"

She nodded, a determined grimace on her face. "Yeah. I think I cut my knee trying to crawl through the broken glass of the window. I'll be okay. What are we doing?"

"We're gathering supplies. We've got about three minutes to go in to this convenient store and grab as much stuff as we can. We need food and supplies to last two or three days." He talked as they walked around to the front of the store. "Hopefully it won't be that long, but I want to be prepared."

She nodded again—placing her trust in him. "Okay. What do you want me to get?"

"I'll focus on first aid and batteries and such. You grab food. We're going to an old friend's fishing cabin—so easy stuff like bread and peanut butter, cans of soup, some coffee. He's pretty good about stocking it with basic stuff, but I don't want to take a chance on needing something he doesn't have. It's got running water and electricity, but other than that, it's pretty rustic."

"You spent my grandpa's bachelor party at a fishing cabin?"

He sighed. "He's in his eighties, and I thought he'd appreciate a few beers with the guys while sitting in a boat on the lake. And he did—he loved it. We just never told Edna what we did. He said he'd rather she imagined we were off doing something a little more wild than lounging in a boat telling dirty jokes and catching fish."

She shook her head and let out a soft chuckle. "I can imagine."

Mac's body language changed—his senses alert as he gazed through the convenience store window, then scanned the road for any suspicious cars that might be following them.

Zoey swallowed, the laughter dying in her throat. For just one second, she'd forgotten. Forgot that she'd just escaped the clutches of a man who wanted to kill her. Forgot that she was literally running for her life.

Mac opened the door and made eye contact with the store clerk. "We need to grab some supplies and get out of here quick. I need you to watch the front windows, and tell me if anyone pulls up."

The clerk was a teenage boy, probably still in high school. He jumped off his chair and scanned the front window, responding to Mac's badge and the authority in his voice. "Yes, sir."

Squinting at the boy's name tag, he asked, "Your name's Caleb?"

The boy nodded. "Yes, sir."

"Well, Caleb, we're going to need your help for the next few minutes, and it's a matter of life and death. Can we count on you to help us?"

Caleb's eyes widened. "Yeah, sure. Of course, what do you need?"

He snatched a trac-phone from a display by the counter. He dropped it and a twenty dollar bill on the counter. "Can you activate this in less than a minute?"

The boy nodded, reaching for the phone and the cash. "Sure."

Mac grabbed a basket from a stack by the door and handed it to Zoey. "Go. Grab as much as you can as quick as you can. I want to be out of here in less than two minutes."

The store was empty, and Mac grabbed another basket and started throwing things in. Band-Aids, antibiotic cream, ibuprofen, batteries, a flashlight. His mind worked quickly, assessing their situation and thinking through what they might need. He threw in matches, a lighter, a couple of toothbrushes, some toothpaste, and a bar of soap.

The store was equipped to meet the needs of hikers, campers, and fishermen as they headed into the mountains, and he was thankful it was well-stocked. Heading back up the aisle, he met Zoey at the cash register.

The teenager was already ringing up her purchases. She'd made wise choices—bread, lunch meat, eggs, bacon, butter, cheese, and a bag of coffee. The clerk rang in two cans of soup, a small carton of milk, and the trac phone. His nervous fingers fumbled the box of matches, and it fell to the ground, but thankfully didn't spill open. He grabbed it and dropped it into one of the bag with the rest of their items.

Zoey had also put in a small bottle of shampoo, two Snickers bars and a T-shirt that had been hanging on a souvenir rack by the register.

Mac ran his debit card through the reader and scrawled his signature. He handed the boy his cell phone. "After we're gone, I want you to wait thirty minutes then call the number marked PV Dispatch in that phone. It'll ring through to the Pleasant Valley Police Department, and I want you to tell them Officer McCarthy gave you his phone and a message that he has the girl and he's taking her somewhere safe. You got that, Caleb?"

The boy bobbed his head in agreement, his voice trembling a little as he repeated the instructions. "Got it—thirty minutes—PV Dispatch—Officer McCarthy—has the girl and is taking her somewhere safe."

Mac smiled and gave the boy a reassuring nod. "Good. I'll call them again later from the trac phone with more details. You just hold on to that phone and keep it safe until I come back for it. Okay? You got a safe in the back? Why don't you lock it in there?"

The clerk clutched the phone in his hand. "Okay, I will. I'll keep it safe."

"Thank you," Zoey said, her voice filled with sincerity as she reached out and touched Caleb's arm. "Thank you for helping us."

Mac had already grabbed the bags of supplies and was standing at the door, holding it open. "We're out of time. We've got to go. Now."

He gave Caleb one more solemn bit of instruction. "And if anyone comes in asking about us, we were never here. You got that, son?"

The boy nodded, his expression sincere. "Yes, sir. I never saw you."

"I'm holding you to that," he said as Zoey slipped out the door in front of him. They hurried around the side of the store toward the car.

He stole a quick glance at the road. "I just hope they haven't tracked us already."

TWELVE

Zoey carried a bag of supplies as she stepped into the old hunting cabin. The interior was dark, the only light coming from the moon shining through the front window.

A group of furniture, covered in old blankets, stood in the center of the room, clustered around a heavy coffee table. All she could think about were how many scary movies started with a woman walking into a deserted cabin in the woods where all the furniture was covered with cloths. What dangers could be hiding under those blankets?

A shiver ran down her spine. *Don't be ridiculous.* The really scary stuff had already happened to her earlier that day.

The cabin had a woodsy smell—like a combination of pine trees, dust, and moss. It also had that closed-up scent of stale air that a place gets when it hasn't been opened up in a while.

Mac followed behind her and reached across to hit the light switch. A dim bulb came on in the center of the room, giving off enough light to push the scary images of the hulking covered furniture into the corners.

She was just being silly—letting herself get spooked. It was just a cabin. Out in the woods. Isolated from everything and everyone. With a man she barely knew.

That wasn't really true. She felt like she knew Mac—like she could trust him. Even though she hadn't truly known him that long. But it was long enough, right?

He crossed behind her and set the bags on the counter.

The cabin was one big room with a large stone fireplace along the front wall. A little kitchen area filled one back corner, and a full-size bed filled the other. Her mouth went dry at the thought of spending the night here with Mac. She pushed those thoughts out of her head. She'd think about the sleeping arrangements—and that bed—later.

Right now, she needed a bathroom. And a shower. Her clothes stunk like marijuana and dirt and sweat. The kind of sweat born of fear and desperation. The man who took her wore a distinctive cologne—something expensive—and she could still smell the faint scent of it on her clothes.

All she wanted was to climb into a hot shower and stay there for an hour. Or a week. Yes, a week would be nice. She could come out when all of this was solved and over, and the bad guys had been caught. She could come out when she knew she was safe. On the drive, she had filled Mac in on everything that had happened that day, and now she just wanted to wash it all away.

She turned to Mac. "Is there a bathroom? Somewhere I can take a shower?"

He pointed to a door off the kitchen area. "There's a little bathroom, nothing fancy. But it's got hot water." He dug in the bags and pulled out the toiletries. "I saw you grabbed shampoo. I got some soap and a couple of toothbrushes and toothpaste."

She accepted the handful of things gratefully. She could have kissed him for remembering a toothbrush. Well, she could have kissed him anyway.

Down, girl. Focus. She offered him a smile. "Thank you." Heading for the bathroom, she turned back, emotions welling in her throat again. "I mean it, Mac. Thank you. For everything."

He ducked his head, his expression sincere. "No problem. And don't worry. We're safe here. At least for the next few days. We notified the station and your grandmother, and I've got tomorrow off anyway. So I think we're covered. We'll talk more about what happened when you've had time to breathe." He waved her away. "For now, go get a shower. Yell if you need me."

She stepped into the small bathroom, shut the door, and leaned back against it.

Was it too early to start yelling? Because she needed him. Needed him now.

Catching a glimpse of herself in the mirror, she cringed. Her face was a mess of dirt, smudged makeup and blood. Her skin looked pale against the black hair of the wig. She pulled it off, wincing at the hair stuck in the bobby pins.

Tugging the elastic band free, she shook out her hair. Her head hurt from wearing it up. And from the cut above her eye. Actually, everything kind of hurt right now. She peeled off her grandfather's clothes and took stock of her injuries.

Her knees were cut and a dark bruise had already started to form on the side of her leg. The flannel shirt had protected her arms from cuts, but another bruise covered her forearm where Tattoo-Guy had grabbed her and shoved her into the SUV.

Hmm. Sexy. Nothing like a few scrapes and bruises to really make a girl feel good about herself.

She unwrapped one of the toothbrushes, squeezed a line of toothpaste onto its bristles, and scrubbed her teeth. Brushing away the taste of smoke, she cupped her hand under the water and rinsed her mouth.

That helped. She turned to the tub. Now to scrub down the rest of her.

The bathtub was old and cracked, but it appeared clean. Pulling the clear shower curtain closed behind her, she turned on the hot water and stepped under the spray. All she could do was stand there as she let the water wash over her, washing the stink of marijuana off her skin and out of her hair, washing the dried gravel and blood off her legs, washing the smeared makeup from her face.

The bathroom filled with steam, and she finally picked up the soap and shampoo and washed her hair and body. The clean scent of the soap helped to revive her, and she thought about the man standing outside of the bathroom door.

She rubbed a soapy hand across her belly and breasts and imagined how Mac's hands would feel sliding across her skin. Tipping her head back, she let the water run over her hair and envisioned the feel of his hands gripping her back. He'd hugged her to him before, and she remembered how it felt to be held in his strong arms.

It felt safe.

Safe from strange men that broke into her apartment. Protected from men who shoved her into cars, intent on hurting her and the people she loved. What would have happened if Mac hadn't shown up when he did? How badly would they have hurt her?

Or worse. Would they have killed her? She could've already been dead by now. Or beaten and left for dead.

That reality, and the events of the day, came crashing down on her. Emotions welled inside of her, and she leaned against the shower wall and broke into tears.

Hugging her arms around herself, she slid down the wall of the shower, crying huge shoulder-shaking sobs as the water poured down on her back and pooled in the tub around her.

A knock sounded at the door. "Zoey, are you all right?"

She heard Mac's voice, but she couldn't answer.

The door of the bathroom opened, and he stepped in. "Aw, hell." He reached out and drew back the curtain then turned off the water. Grabbing a towel, he stepped into the tub behind her, crouched down and wrapped the towel around her before pulling her in his arms.

His feet were bare, and all he wore were jeans and a white T-shirt, which were now soaking as she leaned back against him.

She tried to pull forward. "I'm getting you all wet," she said, her voice still teary.

He drew her closer and tucked her head under his chin. "I don't care. My clothes will dry. It killed me in the car earlier when you were upset, and I couldn't do anything about it. I still can't change what happened, but I can damn sure get my arms around you and hold on to you. And I offer a pretty good shoulder to cry on."

It was a great shoulder to cry on. In fact, everything about him was pretty great. And here she was blubbering all over him. "I'm sorry. I just started thinking about today and what could have happened. I kind of freaked out."

"It's okay. I'd be more worried about you if you *didn't* freak out a little bit."

She shivered against him.

"Come on, let's get you out of the tub and warmed up." Lifting her into his arms, he carried her into the living room and sat down with her on the sofa, cradling her on his lap.

She burrowed into his chest, inhaling the clean laundry scent of his T-shirt. He'd carried her as if she weighed nothing.

While she'd been in the shower, he'd uncovered the furniture, made the bed and lit a fire. A warm glow filled the room and her earlier worries fell away. Instead, her worries now revolved around the fact that she was alone in the cabin with a ridiculously handsome cop, and she was naked except for a small towel.

He pulled a quilt from the sofa and wrapped it around her shoulders. "I'll get you some water." He slid her off his lap and crossed to the kitchen. She shifted the blanket, pulling the damp towel free and setting it on the coffee table. She twisted the quilt around her, like she would a towel, and tucked the edges in under her arms. The warmth of the fire reached to caress her bare arms.

Mac returned with a bottle of water, unscrewed the lid and handed it to her. "Have a drink. You'll feel better."

She took a sip, the water blessedly cool on her dry throat. "Thank you." She pulled the blanket tighter around her, her wet hair dripping onto her shoulders. Loose droplets ran down her back.

He grabbed the towel from the coffee table and blotted her hair. Tipping her chin up, he took stock of her injured face. "I got something for that cut. It doesn't look too bad, but let me get it cleaned up a little."

He brought over the first aid supplies and a comb. Checking the cut on her eye first, he dabbed antibiotic cream on it and covered it with a small Band-Aid. Then he sat on the sofa behind her and picked up the comb.

"Did you hit your head at all? You should probably take a couple of ibuprofen. It'll help with the pain and any swelling." He picked up a section of her hair and pulled the comb through it.

She took the bottle of ibuprofen, shook a couple into her hand, then washed them down with the water. Trying to concentrate on the task, all she think about was the feel of his hands in her hair. The slow pull as he drew the comb through to the ends, then the feather brush of the tines on her back.

Every nerve in her body was centered on the anticipation of his touch as he picked up another strand of hair and ran the comb down it. It was a simple task, one she did every day, but it was different with him. Different as his fingers brushed her skin and delicious tingles ran through her as the comb traced down her back.

Having Mac comb her hair in a dark cabin in front of a fire and wearing only a quilt was one of the most sensuous things that had ever happened to her.

Suddenly the events of the day fell away and nothing else mattered. Nothing except the feel of this man's hands as he ran his fingers through her hair.

He finished each section, then swept her hair to one side, leaving her shoulder bare. He leaned slightly forward, and she held her breath, anticipating the feel of his lips on her skin. Every part of her ached for him to kiss the soft indent where her shoulder met her neck.

He was so close, his breath tickling her shoulder. But instead of his lips, his fingers lightly brushed her shoulder and moved down to the bruise on her arm.

His voice was soft, barely above a whisper, his lips close to her ear. "I'm sorry he hurt you. I wish I could have gotten there sooner."

She turned her head, just enough to bring her lips within an inch of his. "You're here now."

He dipped his head, not toward her lips, but instead pressed his forehead to her shoulder. Saying nothing, he sat like that for a moment, his hand resting gently against her hip, the soft cotton of his T-shirt touching her bare arm.

Taking a deep breath, he pulled back and knelt in front of her. He touched her leg, his voice low and serious. "Let me take a look at your knee. I figured you cut it when you were crawling through the broken glass trying to get out of the car."

She swallowed, trying to follow his switch in behavior. A minute ago she thought he was going to kiss her, but now he was back to business, applying antibiotic ointment and Band-Aids to her scraped knees.

Except her feelings were anything but business. Every touch of his hands on her leg sent shockwaves of sensation running through her. Knowing she was naked under the blanket and having his hands brush her thighs was torture.

She caught her breath—aware of his every movement. The way the denim of his jeans felt as his hip bumped against her leg. The corded muscles of his forearm as he pressed the bandages to her knee. Every brush of his fingers.

Edging forward, the blanket slipped further up her thigh. A slight part of her legs, and Mac froze.

He clamped his hand on her thigh and looked up at her, an expression of doubt in his eyes. His voice was husky as he said her name. "Zoey. You've been through a lot today. I don't want to take advantage…"

That was exactly what she wanted. She wanted him to take advantage—of *every* part of her.

Twice.

She reached up, laid her hand on his cheek. "I have been through a lot today, and if it's taught me anything, it's that life is short. And we have to take advantage of every moment that we have. I spend so much of my time controlling my life, keeping everything in neat, tidy boxes. But right now, I want to live. To experience life. I want to feel." She leaned closer, and the blanket slipped a little more. "I want to feel you."

He hesitated. Only a moment. Then he leaned forward and brushed his lips against her shoulder. Exactly as she'd been wishing he'd do.

Another kiss. This one a little higher than the first. She tipped back her head, giving him full access to her throat. His hand reached up, cradling her neck as his fingers slid into her hair.

Every nerve tingled with anticipation as his lips laid a slow, fiery trail along her neck. She sighed and arched against him as his other hand slipped around her back, his fingers splayed along her waist.

He pulled back. Looking into her eyes, she only saw her own want and need mirrored in his expression. His gaze dipped to her mouth, and he grazed his thumb along her lower lip.

She swallowed, her mouth growing dry. He drew near, desperately close, his breath against her lips. Her body sang with the electric heat of ache and need.

Then, finally. The slightest touch. His lips grazed hers, and she felt his body tense, felt the desire radiating from him. Another kiss. Once more. Again. Lightly.

His lips were soft, teasing, then pressing down, capturing her lips with his. Then more. Fevered. His hand clasped her cheek as he took her mouth in an onslaught of passion.

It was the most amazing kiss of her life. Breathless, and aching to touch him, she wrapped her arms around his neck, pulling him tighter against her.

He moved closer, into the spot between her parted legs, and she wrapped her legs around his waist, drawing him nearer still. She couldn't get close enough to him.

Could he feel how hard her heart was beating against her chest?

This was so unlike her. Unlike any other time she'd been with a man. She liked to plan out how a date would go, make the decision ahead of time if he was a man worth getting undressed for. And if he made the cut, it was always civilized, in a bed, after having taken her clothes off and neatly folded them in a chair.

Now, she wasn't even wearing clothes. Or makeup. Her hair was wet, and she was barely wearing a quilt while she wrapped her legs around the hard muscled body of a man who made her feel sexy and wanton.

And it was amazing.

Mac pulled back, his breath ragged as he slid his arm around her and gently laid her back on the sofa. Slowly, deliberately, and without taking his eyes off of her, he loosened the blanket from around her chest. Spreading it open, his gaze burned like licks of fire as he took in her full nakedness.

The cool air in the cabin caressed her heated skin, and her nipples puckered under his hunger-filled stare. She fought her natural inclination to cover herself; instead she reveled in the sensation of feeling wanted and desired.

Her back arched slightly, like a magnet being pulled toward him, her body pleading for his touch. Who was this vixen taking over her body? She didn't know, but she liked it.

And she loved the reaction she was getting from him. Tilting her head, she pursed her lips as she playfully flirted with him. "Are you going to frisk me now, officer?"

He chuckled, a low throaty sound, and a slow, naughty grin curved his lips. "I did bring my handcuffs."

She gulped. Okay. Maybe she wasn't ready to get that adventurous.

He laughed again, as if sensing her sudden unease. "How about for now I just take you into my custody?"

She smiled. Now that she could handle. "How about for now, you lose the shirt?" She blinked, looking up at him from under her lashes. "And the pants."

He pulled the still-damp T-shirt over his head, and she gulped at the hard toned muscles of his chest. Undoing the button of his jeans, he unzipped them, pushed them over his hips, and let them fall to the floor.

Lord have mercy. He was wearing black boxer briefs, the cuffs snug around his powerfully built thighs.

He knelt on the sofa, lowering himself onto her body. "Are you sure you're okay with this?"

She nodded, not trusting her voice. The weight of him was wonderful, and his body fit against her like they were two pieces of the same puzzle. Wrapping her arms around him, she pulled him down and kissed him.

Kissed him with everything she had, conveying her feelings through the intensity of her passion. And he met that passion, running his hands along her body, skimming her skin, caressing, stroking.

Dipping his head, he kissed her neck, her throat, her chest. Sliding her taut nipple into his mouth, he swirled his tongue around the swollen tip, then sucked it tight between his lips.

She moaned in pleasure, feeling the sensation rippling through her, gripping the folds of the blanket in her fists, as he teased one breast, then the other.

He explored her body with his hands and his mouth—touching, tasting, discovering what made her sigh, or moan, or cry out in pleasure.

"I need you." His voice gruff against her ear. "God help me, I want you so bad."

"Then take me," she said, her words coming out in quick pants.

He stood and lifted her from the sofa, carried her to the bed and laid her gently on the cool sheets. "Hold on." He rummaged in the night stand, coming up with a box of foil-covered condoms.

She gave him a questioning look.

"I told you, my buddy keeps this place pretty well stocked. And he's single." He ripped a package open, covered himself, and slid into the bed next to her. Brushing her hair from her face, he smiled at her. "I like you better as a blonde."

She grinned. "Good, that wig was terribly itchy."

His features sobered, and he touched her cheek. "You are so beautiful."

The warmth of a blush crept up her neck. He made her feel beautiful. "I bet you say that to all the girls you rescue and bring to your secret fishing cabin," she teased.

He shook his head, his expression still serious. "No. I don't. I've never brought a woman here at all. The only thing I've ever done here is go fishing with the guys." He smiled. "I'm really just a boring guy that spends most of his nights working out or watching television."

"You're anything but boring," she said. "I haven't been bored a single second that I've been with you."

"Just wait. You'll see how dull my life is once this whole thing with the Cavellis is over." He stopped and cupped her cheek. "And it will be over."

"I know." Her voice was soft. She believed him. And she knew he would protect her.

She also knew that, in her eyes, nothing with Mac would be considered dull. She ran a hand up his muscled bicep, loving the chill that she elicited from him.

He touched the temporary tattoo that Scooter had put on her arm and traced the letters of the word 'Courage' with his fingers. He gave her one of his naughty grins. "I like your tattoo."

She laughed. "I only wish it were true."

He tilted his head, giving her a questioning look. "What are you talking about? It's totally true. You're one of the most courageous women I know. You're testifying against one of the richest guys in Denver. And you've been going undercover trying to catch a killer. That's pretty brave in my book."

"I don't feel very brave right now." She gazed up at him, whispering the words. "In fact, I'm scared to death. Scared that I'm already in this too deep. That I already care about you too much. That you're going to break my heart."

Pulling her close, he spoke into her ear, his breath sending warm sensations down her spine. "I'm scared, too." He stroked the backs of his fingers down her neck, then laid a soft kiss at the base of her throat. "You're all I've thought about these past few weeks. I can't seem to get you out of my mind."

"I've thought about you, too." She bit her bottom lip and stared at his chest. "And I've thought about this."

"This?" He dipped his head and grazed her lips. A teasing kiss followed by a deeper one. He pulled her under him, settling between her legs and running a hand down her arm, the curve of her waist, the side of her leg. "How about this?"

A delicious shiver raced up her spine and she arched into him, her tender nipples skimming against his chest. "Yes," she breathed the word.

He pulled her body tight against him and she wrapped her legs around his waist. His hips moved in rhythm with hers as he sought her lips, taking her mouth in hunger and desire.

A log fell in the fire, and a shower of flickering embers spun into the air. But neither noticed, the flames of their passion burning so hot they created their own sparks.

THIRTEEN

Mac cracked an egg against the side of the cast iron skillet, and it sizzled as it hit the hot grease. A stack of bacon threatened to tip over on a plate next to the stove.

The morning sun filled the cabin with a golden glow, and a ray of light fell across the bed where Zoey slept.

Lord, she looks like an angel.

His angel.

No. *Not* his angel. She was his for the night. Maybe for the short time they spent at this cabin. But this morning, reality had set in. She had looked at him last night like he was a hero. Her hero. Like he would be the one to save her. Protect her.

And he knew that wasn't true. He couldn't protect her, and he couldn't bear to see the look in her eyes when he let her down.

She rolled over, and a sigh escaped her lips. Her hair spread across the pillow, and he remembered the way the silken strands had felt against his bare skin the night before. She was so damn beautiful.

Maybe he could pretend. Pretend to be her hero. Just one more day.

They could stay at the cabin. Lock out the rest of the world. He could keep her safe for one more day.

He scooped the fried eggs onto two plates and set them on the small kitchen table. Grabbing the coffee pot, he filled a cup for her, then topped off his own.

"Smells delicious." She sat up in bed, patting her hair, which was now a tangled mess around her head.

"Breakfast is ready."

She climbed from the bed, pulling the sheet free and wrapping it around her, toga-style. "I'm starving. You were the best workout I've had in months. I must have burned two thousand calories." She laughed, her smile reaching her eyes.

And his heart fell.

That was it. In that moment as she crossed the bare planks of the wood floor, with her long legs and her pink toenails, with the sheet from the bed trailing behind her, he knew. He knew he was in love.

It had been so long since he'd felt it, he wasn't sure he would recognize it again. But it was there, unmistakable, undeniable. He loved this woman.

He cleared his throat at the emotion settling there. "Good morning, beautiful."

She stepped close to him, laid a soft kiss on his cheek, then grabbed a piece of bacon and stuck it in her mouth. Closing her eyes, she chewed the bacon and moaned in ecstasy.

Geez, he must be in love. He was getting hard just watching her eat breakfast. "Good?"

Her eyes popped open, and she laughed. "Yes. Delicious. Best bacon I have ever tasted." She dropped into the kitchen chair, picked up her cup, and took a sip of the hot coffee. "This is perfect. Thank you. I didn't expect you to make breakfast for me." Pulling the plate to her, she dug into the eggs.

"I wanted to. And I was up anyway." He sat down across from her and grabbed his fork. He was up in more ways than one. Focusing on his own eggs, he stabbed at them with the fork and shoveled a bite into his mouth.

He'd put on his jeans and T-shirt from the night before, and suddenly realized her clothes were still filthy and crumpled on the bathroom floor. Lucky for him. He was happy to have her half-naked all day. Hell, he'd be happy to have her completely naked all day.

He grinned. "That sheet looks good on you."

"I'm glad, because other than the souvenir T-shirt I bought at the convenience store, I have nothing to wear today."

"I think there's some laundry detergent up here. We can wash your clothes in the sink and lay them on the porch. They should dry in the sun today."

Her voice teased as she flirted shamelessly with him. "But then what will I do until they dry? I'm practically naked."

That was it. He couldn't take it anymore. "Not naked enough," he said as he stood and scooped her from her chair.

She squealed in delight as he carried her to the bed. "I thought you were hungry."

"I am." He nuzzled his face into her neck. "Hungry for you. In fact, I'm starving."

He pulled the sheet away and rolled her onto her stomach. Trailing his fingers down her back, he brushed her skin, stopping to cup his hand on her waist. Leaning down, he kissed her shoulders, then her spine, working his way down to the small of her back.

She squirmed under him as he lightly drew the tips of his fingers up her legs, starting at her ankles, tickling her thighs, then caressed her bare bottom. Eliciting a moan, he grinned then stood to peel off his clothes.

Rolling over, she grinned up at him, her gaze wandering from his face down to his legs.

He shook his head at her. "You know I still might have to arrest you?"

Her eyes widened in mock fright. "Me? Why?"

He offered her a slow grin. "Because a body like yours has got to be against the law."

She laughed. "Oh, boo. That was terrible." She crooked a finger at him. "Come here. How about I let you show me your gun?" She giggled at her own terrible joke.

He laid down next to her, and she touched his cheek, her expression turning serious. "You know, you already broke the law in my book."

He tucked a strand of her hair behind her ear. "Oh yeah? What'd I do?"

Her voice was soft, almost a whisper. "You stole my heart."

Damn.

Her words went right to his own heart. He leaned forward, touching his forehead to hers and looking into her eyes. "You don't have to steal mine. It already belongs to you."

She caught her breath, catching her bottom lip with her teeth, and he almost came undone.

Pulling her to him, he kissed her—hard—crushing her mouth with his as he feasted on her lips. Sliding his tongue between her lips, she moaned against his mouth. She tasted like bacon and coffee, a heady combination, and he knew she was the only breakfast he needed.

In fact, she could be his breakfast, lunch, and dinner. He couldn't get enough of her. Touching her, tasting her, feeling her squirm and move under him.

The rest of the world fell away, and all that mattered was this moment, this time spent with her in his arms. He forgot about everything else. Everything but her.

Zoey snuggled against him, her head resting in the crook of his shoulder. They'd been in bed all morning, and her body was spent and sore. But in the best possible way.

She was learning his body, discovering where he liked to be touched, what made him sigh or moan. She liked those spots the best. In fact, she liked all of his spots. His abs were flat and toned, his skin tanned, and everything about his body turned her on.

As much as she was learning his body, there was still so much she didn't know about him. And she wanted to know it all. Wanted to hear all of his stories. She ran her fingers down his chest, tracing the tattoo of a cross that covered a white puckered circle of scar tissue on his right pec. "This looks like a bullet wound. Have you been shot?"

His body tensed. "Yeah. A couple of years ago. That's why I came back to the Pleasant Valley PD."

She could tell there was more to the story, but she didn't want to pry. Okay, she did want to pry, she wanted to know the whole story, but she didn't want *him* to think she was prying. "You don't have to talk about it if it makes you uncomfortable."

He sighed. "It does make me uncomfortable. In fact, it makes me mad as hell."

She shrank back against his angry words.

But his arm wrapped tighter around her shoulders, and he pulled her against him. "Not mad at you. Mad at the situation. But I should tell you about it. I *need* to tell you about it. I just don't want it to change how you feel about me."

"What do you mean?" She tipped her head up to look at him. "I'm not going to feel differently about you because you were shot. That's ridiculous."

"It's not the fact that I *was* shot. It's *why* I was shot." He stared up at the ceiling, as if the answers to life's problems would appear on the cracked and faded surface.

She snuggled closer, offering her support by entwining her body with his. "Tell me."

"It was back in Chicago. It happened on a gorgeous fall day. Chicago can be an ugly city, but I remember thinking how pretty it looked that day, with the leaves changing and the heat of the summer finally cooling off. We were on foot patrol that day, my partner and I."

He stopped and ran a hand over his face, rubbing his temples, as if he suddenly had a headache. "My partner was a girl named Ashley, and she was like a little sister to me. We'd been partners for a couple of years. She'd been assigned to me right out of the Academy, and we just hit it off. She was a great girl, funny and sweet, but she swore like a damn sailor." He smiled at the memory of her.

"Were you in love with her?" Zoey asked, but she wasn't sure she wanted to know the answer.

"What? No, it wasn't like that. In fact, she was engaged to another cop, a guy one precinct over. They'd gone to the Academy together. No, I wasn't in love with her. But I did love her. She was one of the best friends I've ever had."

Zoey picked up on the 'was' in his statement, and a feeling of dread settled over her. Somehow she knew this story wasn't going to have a happy ending. She stayed quiet, waiting for him to tell her the rest.

He cleared his throat, as if this part of the story was harder for him to tell. "We were on the south side that day. Normally, we liked to walk through the neighborhoods. It was good for people to get to know us. To feel safe around us, like we were really part of the community, and not the enemy. And everybody loved Ashley. She had this big laugh, and she hugged everybody. Even homeless guys whose clothes stunk and whose hair hadn't been washed. She didn't care. She was a good person." His voice broke, and he paused.

She picked up his hand and held it in hers.

"It was a Thursday, around lunchtime. Just a normal day. We'd stopped at a sidewalk vendor and grabbed a couple of dogs. Isn't that stupid? I remember eating those hot dogs, walking down the sidewalk. Ash was making some stupid joke, laughing, and we came around the corner of this alley and a group of guys were standing there doing a drug deal.

"It happened so fast. I guess one of them thought they'd been set up and started accusing the others of being narcs. One kid took off running, then everybody started pulling out guns. We both dropped our dogs and reached for our weapons, but it was too late. One of them grabbed Ashley and held a gun to her head. I had my pistol pointed right at him. An easy shot. I remember the look in Ashley's eyes, pure terror. She was a tough girl, but nothing prepares you for that moment that you think you're going to die."

"That must have been so scary."

"Yeah, the scariest part was that these gang members were mostly teenagers. Tough little shits that thought they were bad-asses, and they were totally unpredictable. This guy holding onto Ashley couldn't have been more than fifteen. Just a damn kid. And she knew it. She was trying to talk to him, settle him down. She was holding onto his arm—the one he had wrapped around her neck—and I remember there was a streak of yellow mustard across the back of her hand.

"She was shaking her head at me. She wanted me to drop my gun—thought we could talk it out. I should have known. Those kids were hot-heads. They didn't think. And this guy was just a kid. The gun he was holding barely fit in his hand. I should have reacted. It was my job to protect her. She was my partner." His voice caught, and he took a shaky breath.

"What happened?"

"I still don't really know. There was a sound, probably a car engine back-firing. But it must have spooked one of the guys because he fired at me. It took like three seconds. He missed the first time, and I fired back, but he got me with the second shot. They were running away, firing as they ran. I was going down, still shooting at them, but the kid holding Ash fired, too. I saw her fall, knew she was dead, then everything went black."

Zoey covered her mouth with her hand. "Oh, no. I'm so sorry."

He cleared his throat again and closed his eyes against the memories. "The bullet went straight through my chest, but I must have hit my head on the concrete when I fell. Somebody had called an ambulance, and I woke up later that day in the hospital. Ashley was dead, and so was the kid that grabbed her. He must have got hit in the crossfire. So she died for nothing."

He looked down at her, tears filling his eyes. "You understand? She died for nothing. I could have saved her, but I didn't. I didn't save her because I didn't take a shot at that kid. That kid—who died anyway."

Her heart broke at the pain in his eyes. But it also swelled with love for him. He was this tough cop who didn't seem to be afraid of anything, and he was sharing his deepest hurt with her. A wound that shattered not only his bones, but his soul.

"I'm so sorry." She touched his arm.

He pulled it away, pulled away from her and sat up on the edge of the bed. "I don't want you to be sorry for me. It was my fault. I could have saved her. And I didn't. She died on my watch."

She sat up, afraid to touch him. "It wasn't your fault. It just happened. It certainly doesn't change the way I feel about you. I still feel safe with you."

She was about to say, *I still love you*, but he turned to her, a mixture of pain and anger in his eyes. "Don't you get it? You're *not* safe with me. I can't protect you."

He pushed off the bed and crossed to the sink, his anger and misery rising off him like steam. He grabbed his mug of coffee, took a drink, then hurled it across the room. It hit the door of the cabin, shattered and the pieces fell to the floor. He turned away from her, bowing his head in defeat as he gripped the sides of the counter.

Zoey scrambled from the bed, mindless of her nakedness, and rushed to him. She threw her arms around his chest, clinging to his back, and trying to convey her love through the strength of her embrace.

It probably wasn't the right time. She'd always imagined professing her love to a man over candlelight and champagne. But her life hadn't been going at all how she'd planned, and falling for Mac was like nothing she'd imagined. To hell with her plans.

Her tidy life had been blown to pieces, and he had proved to be better than anything she had ever imagined. Gathering her courage, holding on to him, she spoke the words against his bare back. "I love you."

He slammed his fists into the counter, his body simmering with anger, as he spoke between gritted teeth. "I don't want you to love me."

She stood her ground. Dipping under his arm, she squeezed between him and the counter. Gripping his shoulders, she looked up at him. "I love you, anyway."

He reached down, picked her up, lifting her onto the counter and pinned her there with his body. "Don't you get it? I don't want you to love me. I don't want to be your hero. I can't protect you. I'm already crazy in love with you, and I couldn't bear it if anything happened to you. I swear I couldn't live with myself if you got hurt while I was supposed to be protecting you."

She took his face into her hands and wrapped her legs around his waist. In all of that, all she'd heard was that he'd just said that he was crazy in love with her. Speaking slowly, enunciating each word, she tried to express their heartfelt meaning. "I. Love. You. Anyway."

He stared at her—hard—anger and pain evident in his eyes.

Not giving an inch, she stared back and repeated her declaration, this time in a softer voice. "I love you."

He released his breath, shaking his head, then pulled her to him, crushing her mouth in a kiss filled with fury and carnal desire.

She clung to him, her hands gripping his back as she returned his kiss. Pressing herself into him, she pinned him in the circle of her legs.

Passion and want tore through her as he seized her bottom, tipping her toward him and filling her. He took her, fast and hard, moving with her in a fierce rhythm of animal need.

Love and arousal swirled inside of her, a mixture of intense affection and a wanton lust. She cried out, holding on as he took her to the edge of desire. Then he said her name, and she was lost, tumbling over into ecstasy.

And she knew in that moment that no one else would ever measure up to the depth of feeling she shared with him. He had ruined her. Ruined her for any other man.

Fourteen

Zoey sat at the kitchen table, the sunset framed in the front window of the cabin. Mac was putting together a light supper of soup and grilled cheese sandwiches. They'd missed lunch, instead spending the time in bed.

She'd finally taken the time to wash her clothes and hang them over the deck chairs on the front porch. While they dried, she wore the white T-shirt she'd bought at the convenience store and a pair of black bikini underwear. It was probably boring to some, but she still preferred plain cotton bikini underwear.

Although last night with Mac had inspired her to try something new. When this was over, she might go back to Vickie's Secret and purchase more than just a clearance pair of pajamas.

Mac stood at the stove, stirring the soup that simmered in a battered saucepan.

"You sure I can't do something to help?" she asked.

"You could grab us some water."

She hopped up, crossing to the cupboard and filling two glasses with water. "This makes twice that you've cooked for me. I'm impressed." She put the glasses on the table.

"Don't be too impressed. Grilled cheese and fried eggs are the extent of my repertoire."

"Aww—now you're just trying to dazzle me with your fancy French words."

"Oui, mademoiselle." He gave her a smoldering debonair look and twirled an imaginary moustache.

She laughed, enjoying this silly side of him. "I had no idea you were so cultured."

"There's a lot of things you don't know about me. I'm like a man of mystery."

She stepped up behind him, sliding her arms around his waist. "You're like a mystery that I'm sure having fun solving. You know my grandmother is practically a detective, and yesterday she told me she was working on her psychic abilities. Maybe I got some of that from her."

He turned, still in the circle of her arms, and grinned down at her. "You know, talking about your grandmother kind of kills the flirty atmosphere."

She laughed. "True. What do you think we can do to get it back?"

He leaned down, nuzzling her neck. "I've got some ideas."

"I like your ideas." Sighing, she tilted her head back, enjoying the feel of his lips on her skin. "So, I did realize something earlier today that I don't know about you. Even though I've called out your nickname several times this weekend, including once when you were having your way with me on the kitchen counter, I don't know what your actual first name is."

He chuckled. "What if I told you it was Neville or something awful—would you have still screamed out that name?"

She gave it a try, clutching his shoulders, and crying out in mock-ecstasy. "Oh—oh—Neville –yes." She broke into giggles. "Yeah—it doesn't have quite the same ring to it."

"No, I guess not." He dropped a quick kiss on her lips then stepped away to check the sandwiches. "My first name is actually very boring. It's Michael."

She tried out the name. "Michael McCarthy. I like it."

He shrugged. "It's a good Irish name." Sliding the sandwiches onto a plate, he set them on the table. "There's quite a large Irish community in Pleasant Valley. A bunch of us went to St. Paul's together. Like Pat Callahan, the cop I was telling you about that's down in Denver and helping us with this case. And Shawn Murphy, he's the guy that owns this cabin. He and Pat and I used to come up here a lot when we were younger, but I haven't actually been back up here in a long time. I'm glad he didn't move the hidden key."

"Me, too." She scooped the soup into bowls, carried them to the table, and sat down across from him.

He handed her a napkin, and she put it in her lap. "Dig in," he told her.

She took a bite and savored the crispy crust, the smooth flavor of the melted cheese. "Mmm. You do make a mean grilled cheese." Her napkin slipped from her lap, and she bent forward to grab it.

The sound of a gunshot ripped through the air at the same time the glass of the front window exploded. A bullet hit the back of her chair, splintering the wood in the place where her head had been moments before.

Terror filled her as Mac grabbed her and pulled her to the floor. He tugged her body with his to behind the sofa as another shot rang out and a bullet shattered her glass, spilling water across the table.

She held her breath, listening. The only sound in the cabin the dripping of the spilled water as it ran off the table and hit the floor. "How did they find us?" she whispered to Mac.

"I don't know." He looked around the room, his gaze falling on his gun hanging in its holster off the closet door. "Stay here."

In a crouch, he moved quickly across the room, grabbing his shoulder holster and ducking into the bathroom. Another bullet hit the bathroom door, the sound of the gunshot getting closer.

Zoey screamed as the door to the cabin burst open, kicked in by the solid boot of the intruder.

Two men rushed in, both dressed all in black and wearing rubber masks of past president's faces. One appeared to be Nixon and the other Ford.

She felt unprotected and exposed where she hunkered behind the sofa. Her mind faltered, confused by the strange masks and the presence of the two men, but her body reacted, scooting around the edge of the big sofa.

Time slowed down, each second magnified, as one of the men pointed his gun at her head.

Before he could shoot, the bathroom door flew open, slamming against the wall.

The shooter turned as Mac flew from the bathroom, his gun held out in front of him. A gunshot exploded in the room as he fired at the taller assailant.

The first man went down. The second, the one in the Nixon mask, ducked right, hitting the ground and crawling toward Zoey.

The man on the ground scooted toward the kitchen and fired back at Mac.

Mac retreated back into the bathroom. "Run, Zoey," he yelled.

Mac fired again. She heard a startled cry and the sound of the other guy's gun falling to the cabin floor.

She scrambled forward, trying to stand.

Taking a step forward, she screamed as a hand clutched her ankle.

Kicking out, trying to free her foot, panic rose in her as she saw the assailant twisting his arm to point his gun at her.

A heavy statue of a bronze fisherman held magazines down on the battered coffee table, and Zoey grabbed the statue and threw it at the man holding her leg. It hit him in the cheek, and with a grunt of pain, he released her leg.

Crawling forward, she got to her feet and raced for the open door of the cabin. Stumbling down the stairs of the porch, she ran for the dense wooded trees circling the cabin.

"Go after her," she heard the one in the kitchen yell.

Rocks bit into her bare feet and brittle shrubs scraped at her legs, as if they were trying to slow her progress. Ignoring the pain, she sprinted through the woods, trying to put as much distance between herself and the masked men as possible.

She heard several gun shots, and sent up a silent prayer that Mac was okay.

Dusk had fallen, and the canopy of the trees blanketed the forest in darkness. Though thankful for the extra cover the darkness provided, it also hindered her progress. She couldn't see what lay in the path in front of her, and she stumbled over rocks and exposed tree roots.

The door of the cabin banged open, and she heard the pounding of large feet as someone ran into the forest after her.

She ducked around a large evergreen and crouched to the ground. Her heart beat frantically against her chest as she cocked her head, listening for the sound of who had followed her into the woods.

Covering her mouth, she tried to catch her breath, tried to quiet the sound of her labored breathing as she gasped for air.

Terrified, she knew the man who'd exited the cabin was one of the masked assailants. If it was Mac, he would have called to her by now.

"Come out now, and it'll be quick. If you make me hunt for you, I'll make it slow and painful," she heard a voice say. It was hard to tell how far away he was, but she heard him clearly. "Come out, you stupid bitch."

A memory slammed into her, taking her breath away. She'd heard that voice before. In her apartment the night the two men broke in. His words came back to her—*somebody needs to teach this stupid bitch a lesson.*

She peeked out from behind the tree, trying to see where the voice had come from. The guy in the Nixon mask stood at the edge of the trees. He was the one who had been in her apartment.

And he wanted her dead.

Her mind raced with the possibilities of escape, but nothing seemed viable.

She peered around the tree again. The man moved forward, his black clothes causing him to fade into the darkened forest.

Tilting her head, she listened for a twig to snap or a scrape of gravel. Her eyes scanned the trees for movement. A slight breeze blew through, rustling the leaves of the aspen trees, and drawing her attention to the flashes of movement.

How long could she stay here, crouched behind this tree? How long before he made his way in this direction and ferreted her out?

Her white T-shirt had to shine against the darkened forest, but what could she do? Grabbing a handful of dirt, she rubbed it across the fabric of the shirt.

Staying low, she tried to get her bearings. Was she safer trying to make her way out to the highway or back to the cabin? How far had they traveled to get back here? Five minutes or ten? She couldn't remember.

Gazing up at the trees, she couldn't tell which direction the road even lay. What if she ran into the woods and went the opposite direction of the road? Or worse, got lost.

No one even knew they were out here. Except her grandfather, who thought she was safe with Mac, and the guys who were trying to kill her.

How the hell did they find her anyway?

She clutched her arms around herself, her stomach churning in fear and desperation. She couldn't stay crouched behind this tree forever.

A twig snapped.

The sound happened so quickly, she couldn't tell which direction it came from. Was he to the right or the left of her? Behind her or already in front?

She searched the dense trees for any sign of him, listening for another sound, trying to hear anything over the frantic beat of her heart.

Another twig snapped.

Closer. It sounded like it had come from the right.

What should she do? Should she try to run? Take her chances?

If she could hear his steps, surely he'd be able to hear and track her if she went barreling through the trees trying to run away.

Relief flooded her as she heard the far-off sound of a siren coming up the mountain. Had Mac called them? Did that mean he was okay? Then why wasn't he out here, helping her?

Maybe it was a hiker—someone that had heard the gunshots. But that could mean that Mac was hurt—or worse. She couldn't let herself think that. Couldn't go there in her mind.

Focus on getting out of here. Finding a place to hide.

She heard a man's voice swear. He must have heard the sirens, too.

He was getting closer. She had to do something.

A huge fallen log lay in the path about twenty feet ahead of her. If she could make it to the log, she could take cover behind it. Maybe burrow under it. It was better than hiding in plain sight, squatted down behind a tree.

Taking a deep breath, she sent up a prayer, and took off running. A stone tore into the bottom of her foot and the rocky path attacked her bare feet.

She heard the sound of running behind her, but she didn't look back. Couldn't look back. Could only look forward, focus on her destination—the fallen log. If she could just get behind it.

A gunshot rang out, and the wood splintered on the tree next to her. The shot hit about the same height as her head, and she ducked and kept running.

The sirens wailed in the distance. They had to be almost there.

If she could just get to the tree. It was so close.

She reached out her hand—another gunshot ripped through the air—this time accompanied by a stinging burn in her left arm.

The shot spun her sideways, knocking her off-balance, and she pitched forward.

Her head cracked on the side of the tree stump as the ground came rushing up to meet her.

This was it. This was how she was going to die—barefoot, in the middle of the woods, wearing a dirty T-shirt that advertised Bud's Bait and Tackle.

Please God—let Mac be okay.

She prayed for Mac as the darkness closed in, and she sank to the soft moss-covered floor of the forest.

FIFTEEN

The low beeping of a machine and the smell of antiseptic stole into Zoey's consciousness. The beep had a solid rhythm, reminding her of a heartbeat.

She blinked, trying to open her eyes. Dust motes floated in the air as sunlight streamed through the window and onto the white sheets of her bed.

Sunlight? Her bed? What?

She struggled to sit up. What happened? Where was she?

It was obvious she was in a hospital—but where?

The last thing she remembered was being at the cabin with Mac, eating grilled cheese, then—the door slamming open—the terrible masked men—running through the forest—the sound of gunshots…

Terror seized her, and a scream clawed at her throat.

She tore at the sheets, fighting to get her feet off the side of the bed. She had to get out of there. She had to find Mac.

Oh God—Mac!

"Whoa. Whoa. Hang on there, honey." Edna walked into the room and hurried to her side. "You're okay, Zoey."

She set the coffee cup she'd been holding on the table next to the bed and wrapped her arms around Zoey's shoulders. "You're all right. You're in the hospital. And they've got a policeman stationed right outside your door, so no one's going to hurt you again."

"I don't care about me. Where's Mac? Is he alive?" She clawed at her grandmother's sleeve. "Please, is Mac okay?"

A sad look crossed Edna's face. "Yes, he's okay. At least he's not in the hospital."

"What happened? Where is he?"

"He was knocked out at the cabin. I guess he had called 9-1-1 before he blacked out. He said he woke up when the police got there, and you were gone. He remembered telling you to run, and he helped the police search for you. He was the one who found you at the base of the tree. You were passed out and bleeding. You'd been shot in the arm. But you were lucky, the bullet only grazed your shoulder so you're going to be fine."

She looked down at herself. Her left arm was bandaged and sore. A line of dried blood crusted down her inner arm. "In the arm? I was shot in the arm? Then why did I pass out?"

"They think you fell and hit your head on the base of the tree when you were hit. That's probably what saved you. The gunman most likely thought that he'd killed you."

Fragments of memory were coming back to her—the rustling of leaves—the deep smell of pine. "Most likely? How do you know? Did they catch him?"

"No. He was already gone by the time the police arrived. That's why they think that—they figured he must have thought you were already dead—otherwise he would have stuck around to finish the job."

That sounded right. He'd been pretty determined. She couldn't imagine him giving up unless he thought he'd completed the job.

"What about the other guy? Is he dead?"

"No. Mac said there'd been another man and that he'd thought he shot him. There was blood on the floor, but by the time Mac woke up, he was gone, too."

That still didn't explain what happened to Mac.

"Gram, what's going on? Where is Mac? What are you not telling me?"

Edna shook her head. "To tell you the truth, honey, I don't know what the holy heck is going on. He *was* here. He stayed by your bedside all night. Then this morning, he said he had to get out of here. That he couldn't take you getting hurt on his watch. He said to tell you that he was sorry, and this was all his fault. And something about how he'd warned you that he couldn't protect you, and that this deal with the two of you just couldn't work."

She lowered her voice and gently touched Zoey's arm. "I'm sorry, but he said to tell you not to call him and not to expect to hear from him. It was all completely out of character. I've never seen Mac like that. It all sounded like a bunch of hooey to me, but he said you'd understand."

That was crazy. How could he think her getting shot was his fault? Or that he could have stopped it?

She looked around the room for her things—her purse, her clothes, her phone. Then she remembered she had nothing. Her purse was still at her grandmother's house, her phone was crushed and broken at the bottom of a dumpster, and her clothes were probably still on the front porch of the cabin.

"Do you have your phone, Grandma? Can I borrow it? I've got to call him. I need to talk to him." Her voice carried a desperate plea, even to her own ears.

Edna dug her phone out of her purse. "Of course. You can try. But he hasn't answered any of my calls or texts. I don't think he wants to talk."

She took the phone, pressed the contact number for Officer Mac McCarthy and listened to the phone ring. His voicemail picked up, and she almost wept at the sound of his voice. "Mac, it's Zoey. I'm calling you from my grandma's phone. I'm still at the hospital. Please call me. I need to talk to you. Don't do this. Don't leave me like this. I love you."

She clicked off the phone and handed it back to Edna, who wore a surprised expression on her face. "So a few things might have changed with Mac since I saw you last. We've gotten—closer."

"Yes, I gathered that."

Before Zoey could say more, the door to her hospital room opened, and the Page Turners book club strode into the room. Cassie and her niece Piper carried a huge bouquet of colored balloons and a plastic container of cookies.

Maggie carried a take-out tray filled with coffees, and Sunny's arms were filled with magazines and a stuffed teddy bear holding a heart that read 'Get Well Soon.' They must have been out of bears holding hearts that said 'Sorry you got shot and your new boyfriend ditched you'—because that sounded more like the get-well bear she needed.

Her grandfather brought up the rear, a beautiful vase of flowers clutched in his hands. He set the flowers down and hurried to Zoey's side. Well, hurried as much as a man in his eighties wearing a boot on his foot could. "I'm so glad you're okay. You scared us to death."

She loved that Johnny seemed so tough, and yet was so tender with her and her grandmother. "I'm okay, Grandpa. Have you talked to Mac?"

He shook his head, the same sad look shining in his eyes that had been in Edna's. "I'm sorry, honey. I haven't talked to him since he left this morning." He pulled a new cell phone from his pocket and handed it to her. "I did manage to get a new phone for you. It's one of those trac phones, but at least you'll have something if you need to make a call."

She hugged him to her. "You're the best. Thanks so much." She lowered her voice so that only he could hear. "I appreciate the flowers and balloons, but this is the best thing you could have brought me."

He winked and gave her a knowing nod.

Then the Page Turners took over the room. Everyone talked at once—asking questions, throwing out theories, exclaiming over Zoey's condition, or trying to feed her.

She turned down three offers of cookies, an offer of cake and one of a sandwich. Edna offered to go get her a milkshake. They all wanted to please her.

But she wasn't hungry. She wasn't thirsty. And as much as she loved ice cream, no milkshake was going to fix the tear in her heart that Mac's leaving had caused.

After several hours of hanging out, Zoey feigned exhaustion and finally convinced the Page Turners to leave. The room was blessedly silent as the door shut behind them, leaving only her and Edna in the room. Johnny had left earlier, heading home to put his leg up and to feed and take care of the dogs.

Zoey covered her head with her good arm. "How long am I going to have to stay here?"

"I'm not sure. At least overnight again. Hopefully the doctor will release you when he does his rounds in the morning."

She looked down at the hospital gown. "I don't even have any clothes."

"Oh, I took care of that." Edna pulled a plastic shopping bag from inside of her cavernous purse. "The nurse told me when they brought you in that all you were wearing was a T-shirt and underpants, so I grabbed you a few things. It's not much, but I stopped at Target and got you some yoga pants, a top, a bra and some underwear. I found these little sneakers just so you'd have some shoes to wear out of here. And I bought you a few basic toiletries, too." She pulled the items out of her bag as she talked and set them on the bed.

Zoey picked up the travel size bottle of shampoo. She was ready to use her own shampoo, in her own place. She missed her apartment. Although she wondered if it would feel different now. Now that a dead guy had bled all over the foyer floor. Would she ever feel safe there again?

Now wasn't the time to worry about that. She needed to concentrate on getting out of the hospital. Getting out and finding Mac. If she could just see him, talk to him, she knew she could convince him not to leave her.

She dug through the other items on the bed, holding up a black lace bra and a three-pack of packaged undies. Or what some would call undies—she called them dental floss. "Grandma, I'm in the hospital, not going on a date. Why did you get me thong underwear?"

Edna shrugged. "Just because you're in the hospital doesn't mean you still don't want to feel pretty. Besides, I assumed that's what all the young ladies wore nowadays. Although personally, I've tried them, and they feel like I'm walking around with a wedgie all day."

She winced as she imagined her grandmother in a pair of thong underwear. Now she'd never get that image out of her head. "Well, I don't wear them either, unless it's with a particular outfit that I don't want my panty-lines to show."

"Sorry, honey. You'll just have to put up with wedgieville until you get out and can buy your own undies."

"Thong undies are better than no undies, I guess." She pulled a pair from the pack and grabbed the toiletries to head for the bathroom, then realized she was still tethered to the IV stuck in her arm. She rang for the nurse.

"Can I get the IV removed so I can take a shower?" she asked the nurse that replied to her call.

"Have you been drinking liquids? Or eaten anything?" the nurse asked.

Zoey nodded. "I've been drinking water all day, and I had half a sandwich earlier." She'd finally given in to the pressure of the Page Turners and eaten part of a sandwich and a cookie. "I'm really feeling fine. I'd just like to take a shower."

The nurse nodded and removed the IV tube. She left the needle in her arm and taped the plug to the side of her elbow. "I can't remove it all the way until you're released, but this will let you take a shower. Just don't stay in there too long. You hit your head pretty good last night, and your body's been through a lot of trauma. You might think you're doing fine, but you don't want to push yourself by trying to do too much too quickly. There's a nurse call-cord in the bathroom if you need me. I'll bring you a fresh hospital gown."

Free of the IV cord, she climbed out of bed and shuffled to the bathroom. Her feet hurt from the cuts and bruises she'd inflicted on them from running barefoot through the woods. Her legs were a patchwork of damage, scratches crisscrossing minor cuts and scrapes.

But the injuries to her body were nothing compared to the pain in her heart. What was Mac thinking? Why hadn't he called?

She brought the trac-phone with her into the small bathroom. She'd programmed Mac's number into it from Edna's phone earlier and sent him a text giving him her new number and asking him to call her.

With her arm still bandaged, Edna had to help her wash her hair, but she could otherwise get soaped up and dried off. She put on the bra, the thong underwear, and the fresh hospital gown the nurse had dropped off. She might still be in the hospital, but at least she was clean and had washed the dried blood off her skin.

Edna helped her climb back into bed and combed out her hair. It brought back memories of Mac combing her hair the night before, and her heart ached.

Why was he doing this? She understood that he felt guilty about not being able to protect his partner, but he *had* protected her. That first man was going to shoot her in the face if Mac hadn't kicked down the door and fired first. He's the one who'd yelled for her to run.

And the *main* difference between her and his past partner was that she was still alive. She hadn't died on his watch. She'd only been shot in the arm. It was practically a flesh wound.

A flesh wound that hurt like hell right now. She grimaced as she adjusted her body on the hospital bed.

"Is your arm hurting?" Edna asked, already heading for the hallway. "I'll have the nurse bring you some ibuprofen."

The nurse returned with Edna a few minutes later and handed Zoey a paper cup with two capsules inside. "This will help with the pain."

Would it help with the pain of her broken heart? Did the nurse have any magic pills for that?

She took the medicine and leaned back on the pillow. Edna eased herself down into the chair next to her bed. It was obvious her grandmother was running out of steam.

Zoey picked up Edna's hand. "Why don't you go on home, Gram? I'll be fine here. I'm just going to go to sleep."

Her grandmother waved a hand away. "No, I'm fine. I can stay."

"Grandma, don't be silly. You were here last night. You need your rest. Besides, there's a cop sitting outside my door. Nothing's going to happen to me. I'm just going to sleep." It wasn't the cop she wished was sitting out there, but at least it gave her a little peace of mind that she was being watched over.

Edna finally relented. She gave Zoey a squeeze before she left. "I'll be back first thing in the morning. You just rest now. And don't worry, I'm still on the case. I'll figure this out yet."

"I know you will. Good night."

She *was* tired. She could barely keep her eyes open, but thoughts of Mac kept her from drifting off.

The new cell phone was right by her pillow. She checked it again. No messages.

She typed another text to Mac. *Please answer me. I need to know that you're okay. That we're okay. I don't blame you for this.*

She held the phone to her chest, praying for his response. Her heart leapt a moment later when the phone buzzed.

It was a message—from Mac. *But I blame myself. I couldn't protect you and it's killing me. I can't go through this again. I won't. I trust the guy at the hospital who is watching over you. I wish things could have been different. Please don't text me again.*

Each of his words was like a fresh slice to her already fragile heart. He couldn't mean it. Were his wounds so deep from what happened with Ashley that he would deny himself his own happiness in order to not put himself in the position of protecting someone he loved again?

She closed her eyes, tried to block out the hospital and the pain in her arm. And in her heart.

She finally fell into a fitful sleep, but woke with a start several hours later. Her heart was racing as if she'd had a nightmare.

Struggling to sit up, she wondered what had caused her to wake so suddenly. The room was dark except for the dim light above her bed. She checked her phone. It read 11:45 PM. Almost midnight.

The door to her room was open a crack, and she heard voices from the hall.

"Are you sure? She's sleeping right now. Nobody's in there with her." She thought she recognized the voice of the cop who had been stationed outside of her door.

"Yeah. I'm sure. You can take a breather. Grab a smoke. We'll stay here and keep watch for a bit."

She *knew* she recognized that voice. It was Mac. He'd come back for her after all.

Maybe he thought he could show up in the middle of the night—just to keep watch over her while she was sleeping.

She threw back the covers. He wasn't getting away this easy. He needed to face her and tell her if he wanted out.

The nurse had reconnected her stupid IV and the cord tangled in the sheets. She didn't care, she'd drag the dang IV pole with her—she just wanted to see him.

She tugged the cord free, stood up next to the bed. Her legs were still shaky. She pulled the pole to her then froze as she heard the voice that spoke to Mac.

"I can't believe that guy still smokes. Doesn't he know those things will kill you?"

Her heart hammered against her chest. That voice. She would have known it anywhere. It was the one haunting her nightmares.

It was the voice of the same man who had broken into her apartment, who had hunted her down in the woods then shot her and left her for dead.

Terror and confusion seized her. Where could she hide? She had to get away. Why was Mac talking to her assailant? She stood frozen in place, listening to them talk.

She heard Mac chuckle, and her stomach churned at the reasons that he would be laughing with the guy who tried to kill her.

"The main thing is that now we're here and in charge of watching her. Now we can take care of her ourselves."

Bile rose in her throat, and she covered her mouth to keep from getting sick. What the hell was going on? What did he mean by 'take care of her'? Was Mac in on the plan to get rid of her?

That didn't make sense. He was alone with her at the cabin. If he wanted to harm her, he could have. Instead, he'd spent two days in bed with her. She wanted to gag. Had she been having sex with a guy who wanted her dead? Sharing her most intimate thoughts? And telling him she loved him?

It had seemed so real. Could he really be that good of an actor? Had that all been an act? A ploy to keep her off-balance? To make her feel safe until the masked guys could get there and actually kill her?

No. That couldn't be. He'd told her that he loved her. She'd bared her soul to him.

An icy realization hit her. He'd told her he loved her, then broke it off with her as soon as they left the cabin.

Questions tumbled through her mind as she tried to make sense of this. Is that why he was still alive and hadn't actually shot either of the assailants? Had that all been a charade to make it seem like he was on her side? Maybe he hadn't even been knocked out. Maybe he hadn't come to her rescue because he wasn't planning to rescue her at all.

She'd thought he'd been the one to call 9-1-1, but it could have easily been a tourist or someone driving by that heard the shots, then he just took credit for it.

None of this made sense to her. Her head pounded from a sudden headache, and she held onto the side of the bed to keep her knees from buckling.

She'd trusted him.

"Geez, you're in a pisser of a mood tonight." The assailant talked to Mac with a familiarity, like he knew him well.

"Give it a rest, Pat. This isn't easy for me. I don't want to hurt her, but I have no choice."

Pat? That was his name—the man who had shot her. Why did that sound familiar? Someone had just been talking about a guy named Pat or Patrick.

It was Mac. He'd told her Pat was a guy he knew from high school, another cop that was helping him on the case. And that Pat had been up to the fishing cabin with him.

She thought he was taking her somewhere safe—to a deserted cabin that no one knew about. Except him and the guy who was trying to kill her. Had that been the plan? To take care of her at a place that they both knew? A place that was secluded and surrounded by woods.

But they were cops—sworn to protect people. This didn't make sense. Her mouth went dry as she thought of the other possibility. They were police officers, so they would know how to hide a body and not leave any evidence.

"Don't be such a puss about it," she heard Pat say. "Just do it quick—it's easier that way."

Fear shot through her. She had to act. Now.

She couldn't stand here, frozen in place, and wait for them to take care of her.

She peeled back the tape and yanked the IV needle from her hand.

Son of a bitch!! That hurt! They always made it look so easy in the movies.

Blood seeped from the spot where the needle had been and she wiped it on the sheets.

Her gaze darted around the room, looking for a place to hide. Not the bathroom, that was too easy. Could she squeeze into one of the closet cabinets? No—too tight. A large recliner sat in the corner of the room. Edna had slept in it the night before.

Zoey tiptoed across the room, trying not to make a sound. She crouched behind the recliner, using the curtain from the window as extra camouflage.

Just in time. She held her breath as she heard the door to her room open.

"What the hell? Where is she?" Pat's voice sounded angry.

She heard Mac enter the room. "What do you mean? Did you check the bathroom?" She heard him open the bathroom door then slam it shut. "She's not in there."

"Maybe that cop's already been taking some smoke breaks, and she took off when he was on one."

"Let's check the nurse's station."

She heard both men leave the room, their shoes thumping on the linoleum as they hurried down the hall.

Squeezing out from behind the recliner, she grabbed the sneakers Edna had left on the counter as she raced to the door and peered out. She could see them at the end of the hall talking to a nurse. At the other end of the hall was a steel door, leading to the stairwell.

This would be her only chance.

Taking a deep breath, she slipped through the door and sprinted for the stairwell.

"There she is."

She heard Mac's voice then the pounding of their footsteps as she raced for the door. Pulling it open, she fled into the darkened hallway.

Stumbling down the steps, she'd gained a full floor before she heard the stairwell door fly open. But she was barefoot, and they wore shoes. It wouldn't take long for them to catch her.

She pulled open the door to the next level and ran into the hall, calling out for help. Who was going to help her? They were the police. Why would anyone believe they were trying to harm her?

The lights were dim in the hallway corridor, and she fought the terror that built in her chest. The nurse's station was at the other end of the hall, but she didn't see anyone at the desk. Small town hospitals didn't have the staff that large cities did, but still—where was everyone?

The elevator across from her dinged, and she whipped her head toward it. The doors opened, but it was empty. She took it as a sign and raced for the open doors.

Once inside, she hit the button to close the doors, repeatedly smashing it as she prayed for the doors to close before they found her.

The stairwell door opened, and Mac appeared. He saw her and ran for the elevator. "Zoey. Wait."

"No, please. Just let me go." A sob tore through her as the doors slid together.

He reached an arm out to stop the doors, but his expression changed as he must have seen the terror in her eyes.

The doors shut, and she fell to her knees. The numbers of each button lit up as she pressed all of them in hopes it would buy her some time if they didn't know what floor she got out on.

She rode two floors, two incredibly long fear-filled floors. Pulling on the sneakers, she held her breath as she waited. The second time the doors opened, she got out. This floor was also quiet. She raced across the hall and ducked into the first patient room she came to.

Thankfully the bed was empty.

Leaving the lights off, she ran around the bed, grabbed the phone and sank to the floor. The linoleum was cold against her practically bare bottom—stupid thong underwear—and she pulled the hospital gown around her as she started to shiver.

Shivering was a sign of shock. She took a deep breath, trying to calm down. She just needed to get out of here. Needed to call someone she could trust. Lifting the phone, she dialed her grandmother's number.

"Hello? Is this the hospital? Is my granddaughter all right?" The caller ID must have shown the hospital's number.

"Grandma, it's me, Zoey."

"Speak up, honey. I can hardly hear you."

"Gram, they're here. They're trying to kill me." Her voice broke. "I think Mac's in on it."

"What? Where are you?"

"I'm hiding in a patient room. It's on the sixth floor. Hold on." She checked the number on the phone she was holding. "It's room 632."

"Listen, honey, I'm right outside the hospital. I couldn't sleep because I just kept feeling something was wrong so I was coming back anyway. You stay where you are—room 632—and I'll come find you. Leave it to me. You just stay put."

The line went dead, and Zoey clutched the phone to her chest. Edna was coming. Great. Her salvation was coming in the form of an eighty-something year old woman with arthritis and a bunion on her right foot.

She tugged the blanket from the hospital bed and wrapped it around her. As silly as it might sound to some, she had faith in her grandma. Edna had gotten herself and others out of tighter fixes than this before.

She just had to wait.

What seemed like an hour later, but was probably only about ten or fifteen minutes, the door to Room 632 gently pushed open and a soft voice whispered, "Zoey? Are you still in here?"

Recognizing Edna's voice, she scrambled from behind the bed and threw her arms around the elderly woman's shoulders. She wanted to cry, to release the tension of the last half hour that she'd been running and hiding from the man she'd thought she loved.

But she knew she couldn't lose it now. She had to keep it together a little longer. At least long enough to get out of the hospital. "Grandma, I've never been so glad to see you in all of my life."

Edna patted her shoulder. "I'm glad to see you too, honey. And I'm awful glad you're okay. I found us some disguises and it's a good thing, because with that gown, the rest of the hospital is able to see you, too."

"Disguises? Why would we need disguises?"

"I was listening when I walked into the hospital. They're talking about a missing patient and organizing a room-by-room search. You need to put these on, and we've got to get you out of here." Edna handed her a pile of blue scrubs. "I borrowed these from the surgical supply closet."

"Good thinking. How'd you get into the closet?" She quickly pulled the scrubs on.

Edna was putting on a pair of scrubs over her clothes. "I've found that if you walk with purpose and act like you know what you're doing, most people don't even question you." Edna shook out a white lab coat and put it on over the scrubs. She handed Zoey a surgical mask and cap. "Here put these on over your face and hair. Then we're just going to walk right out of here."

"What if they see us? What if Mac recognizes me?" Her voice caught. "Grandma, I've been such a fool. I thought I loved him, but it turns out he isn't who he said he was. He was talking to the guy that's been trying to kill me. I heard them talking and recognized his voice and not only is he a cop, he's a friend of Mac's. They've been friends since they were kids."

"You're right, that doesn't sound good. But it doesn't mean that Mac was in on the plan to hurt you." Edna turned Zoey and secured the surgical cap and mask around her head. "I'm a pretty good judge of character, and I have a hard time believing Mac would want to hurt you."

"I wouldn't have believed it either. Except I heard him say it himself. He said he was there to 'take care of me' and that he 'didn't want to hurt me.' And his friend told him just to do it quick and that it would hurt less. Does that sound like the conversation of a man not in on the plan?" She spoke through the mask, her breath condensing against the fabric.

Edna drew her lips together in a tight line. "I don't like it, but I'm still trying to keep an open mind until I can talk to him myself."

"Well, I don't care if I ever talk to him again." That was a lie. She did care. She cared too much.

Edna pushed her discarded hospital gown under the bed. "Right now, we need to focus on getting you out of here." She pulled her own cap and mask on, using the cap to hide her curly gray hair. She turned to have Zoey tie the strings of the mask. "We'll have to take the elevator down, at least to the second floor. Then we can get off and take the stairs the rest of the way. We can slip out one of the side doors on the main level."

Zoey opened the door a crack and peered into the hallway. It was empty. She could see the elevator doors from where she stood. "You go push the elevator button. If you get one and it's empty, then hold the door and I'll come get in."

"Got it." Her grandmother slipped from the room and pushed the elevator button.

She closed the door behind her, except for a small crack that she could see through.

The elevator binged, and Zoey held her breath. The doors slid open, and two women stood inside. They held white vending machine coffee cups and both looked tired and worn out.

"I forgot my stethoscope," she heard her grandmother say as she waved the elevator on. "I'll catch the next one."

Forgot her stethoscope? Seriously?

The elevator dinged again, and this time it was empty. Edna held the door open with her foot and waved Zoey forward.

She crept from the room, her heart pounding as she waited for Mac or Pat to come charging through the stairwell door. But they didn't. She made it safely into the elevator and scooted to the back corner as Edna pushed the button for the second floor.

Only four floors to go. Fifth. Fourth. Third. The doors slid open on the third floor and a middle-aged couple stepped on. They nodded at Edna, who stepped in front of Zoey.

Geez. Where were all of these people when she was looking for help a half an hour ago?

The doors quietly slid together. Just as Zoey was releasing her breath, a male arm reached into the elevator, holding the doors from closing. They slid apart and the other cop, Mac's friend, Pat stepped on.

Zoey froze. She clasped the back of Edna's coat, clutching the fabric between her fingers as she ducked her head and tried to shrink behind the smaller woman. She felt Edna tense and knew that she'd figured out who he was.

Trying to relax, she dropped her hands to her side. Grabbing Edna must have reinjured her IV wound and to her horror, a single drop of red blood hit the elevator floor.

She couldn't breathe, couldn't move. What if someone saw it and asked if she was okay? The last thing she needed was any attention drawn to her. Moving her foot the slightest bit, she covered the drop of blood with her shoe.

Pat hadn't noticed. Sneaking a glance at him, his attention was still on the elevator door. Funny, he didn't look like a killer.

He was dressed in plain clothes, jeans and a black zip-up sweatshirt. He could have looked like a regular guy, if it weren't for the badge hooked to his belt and the gun he wore at his hip. He faced forward, his body bouncing with nervous energy as he waited for the elevator to open on the next floor.

She looked up at him again, tried to study him, to memorize what he looked like. To learn the features of the man who had tried twice now to kill her.

He'd failed twice, but she sure as hell didn't want to give him another chance tonight.

The door opened on the second floor, and Pat got out.

Standing still, Edna made no movement to follow him, and Zoey followed her lead. The elevator doors slid shut, and she let out her breath. "That was him," she whispered.

"Yeah, I gathered that," Edna whispered back. "It took everything I had not to grab his gun and shoot him myself."

She wasn't as brave as her grandmother. She just wanted to get out of there.

One more floor and they'd be on the main level. They'd wanted to avoid that floor just because they knew it would be more populated. But when the doors slid open and they stepped off along with the other couple, they saw the lobby was fairly deserted.

"I still don't think we should just walk out the front door." Keeping her voice low, Zoey directed her grandmother down the nearest hallway. "Our best bet is to sneak out a side door."

"Agreed. There should be one at the end of this hall."

They made it safely to the door and peered through. The exit led into the parking lot, and Zoey could see her grandmother's car. They were almost there.

She looked down at the words written on the red bar across the door. "Emergency Exit. Alarm will sound."

Just great. That's perfect.

"Sometimes they just have the warning and nothing happens when you actually open it," Edna said.

"What happens if this isn't one of those times and the alarm does go off?"

Edna shrugged. "Then we run like hell."

It was as good a plan as any.

They pushed through the door, wincing as the alarm shrieked a piercing warning.

Then they ran like hell.

SIXTEEN

Mac shook his head as he stood in Zoey's deserted hospital room.

What the hell was going on with her? Why had she run?

And why the hell had she looked so terrified of him when he tried to catch her in the elevator?

He called the number of the trac-phone she'd given him earlier that day. A ring tone trilled, and he spotted the phone tangled in the sheets on the hospital bed.

She doesn't even have her phone with her.

Peering closer at the bed, he saw a smear of blood and the end of her IV tube dangling from the bag, the clear tape still on it as if she had ripped it from her arm.

What had made her leave this room in such a damned hurry that she tore the IV needle from her arm and left her phone behind? She wasn't even wearing shoes.

Something had to have happened to scare the hell out of her. Had she gotten a call or a threat of some sort? He checked the recent calls on the phone, but the list was empty.

What was going on? And why would she be scared of him?

Why didn't she just come out of her room and talk to him?

Unless something or someone was keeping her silent.

Or too terrified to come forward.

He thought back over his conversation with Pat as they stood outside of her room. He'd been an idiot and admitted to Pat that he'd had a thing for Zoey but that he was breaking it off with her.

He remembered telling Pat that he didn't want to hurt her and Pat advising him to do it quickly. Could that be it? Did she think he *really* wanted to hurt her? There had to be more to it than that.

He'd expected to get some type of reaction from her after he'd broken things off and told her to not call him again. But he was expecting sadness or for her to be pissed off at him. There was no reason for her to be *afraid* of him.

"We can't find her anywhere." Pat walked into the room. "We've checked all the rooms. She must have gotten out of the hospital. Somebody said they thought they heard one of the side door alarms go off. So it's likely she's already gone. You have any idea where she might be headed?"

He was fairly certain she would head for Edna or one of the Page Turners. Although how she'd get there with no phone and in only a hospital gown, he had no idea.

Plucking his phone from his pocket, he tried Zoey's grandfather first.

"Hello." Johnny picked up on the first ring. Usually when someone gets a call after midnight, it takes them a few minutes to answer and their voices often sounded groggy with sleep. Johnny's voice was alert and held no hint that he'd just been asleep.

"Hey, John. It's Mac. Have you heard from Zoey?"

"Heard from her? What do you mean? She's supposed to be in the hospital, and hopefully sound asleep. Why? Is something going on? Is she all right?"

"I'm not sure. We think she took off. She's left the hospital. I just wondered if you had any idea where she went or if she'd shown up over there."

"No, I haven't heard from her. But why would she leave the hospital? And in the middle of the night?"

"That's what I'm trying to figure out."

"Do you think one of Leon's guys got ahold of her?"

He could hear the panic in Johnny's voice and tried to calm him down. "Honestly, I don't know what the hell happened. The last time I saw her, she was running down the hall and got into an elevator. I didn't see anyone chasing her, so I don't know what she was running from."

Unless it was me.

"That doesn't make sense."

"I know. How about Edna? Can you check with her? See if she's heard from Zoey."

"Um—she's not here."

Isn't that interesting? "Where is she?"

"She said she couldn't sleep and was going to head back to the hospital to be with Zoey."

"Well, I haven't seen her either."

"Do you want me to come down there?" Johnny offered. "I'm up anyway. Damned heartburn."

"Nah. I'm gonna head over to the station, check on a few things. Keep me posted if you hear from Zoey. Or Edna." He had an idea that might at least give him a place to start.

"Will do. Same goes with you."

Mac clicked off and turned to Pat. "Listen, I'm gonna head over to the station. I want to check on something. Are you good staying here in case she turns up?"

Pat shrugged. "Sure. If I get tired of waiting, I might cruise around, look for a blonde chick running down the road in a hospital gown."

"Let me know if you find her."

Fifteen minutes later, Mac walked into the Pleasant Valley Police Department. Only a few people were on the night shift and the department felt hushed compared to its normal bustling noise.

He checked his desk phone, just in case he had any messages, before winding his way over to the dispatcher. "Hey Rosie, how's my favorite lady? Can you check to see if I died tonight, cause you sure look like an angel to me."

Rosie was in her late fifties and had been with the department for over twenty-five years. Not much happened around this town that escaped her notice. She was also used to Mac's charm and only somewhat immune to it. She waved a hand in his direction. "Oh, stop it. What do you want?"

"I need you to track a cell phone for me." He was sure it wasn't a coincidence that no one seemed to know where either Zoey or Edna were, but he was fairly certain they were together. Zoey might not have *her* phone with her, but if she were with her grandmother, they might be able to get a hit on Edna's phone. "The name is Edna Allen Collins."

Rosie arched an eyebrow. "Oh Lord, what's that woman got herself into this time?"

"I'm hoping she's with her granddaughter, Zoey Allen. Zoey ripped out her IV and left the hospital tonight, and I have a bad feeling about what could have happened that would have made her run like that."

"Poor girl." Rosie shook her head and punched some keys on her computer. "Give me a minute here, and I'll see what I can find."

He tried to think through the possibilities of what could have spooked her. Maybe she got a call on the phone in her hospital room. Maybe one of Leon's guys threatened her that way. "Hey Rosie, you know everybody. What can you tell me about Leon Molloy?"

"The happy grass guy? I know he's the one who brought that damn recreational marijuana to our town. Opened up a bar in town where people go just to smoke that stuff. His poor mother is so embarrassed, she won't even talk about him at church anymore. If someone asks her, she just walks away."

"You go to church with Leon's mom?"

"Sure. Maybe if you showed up for Mass a little more often, you would know her, too. Although she used to go to Sacred Heart. She's only been at St. Paul's for the past five years or so."

Mac ignored the barb. "What can you tell me about Leon or his family?"

"Oh, I don't know. She moved to town in the late eighties, early nineties. Single mom, had just the one boy, Leon. She'd been married to an Italian guy down in Denver, apparently a real schmuck. I think she was his third marriage, because I remember he already had kids with one of his earlier wives."

"An Italian guy?"

"Yeah, I always forget his name. I know it reminded me of an Italian pasta, like Tortellini, or Cavatelli, maybe."

"Cavelli?"

Rosie snapped her fingers. "Yep, that's it." A look of dawning realization crossed her face. "Isn't that the name of the finance company that Zoey's the key witness in? The one with the money-laundering thing?"

He'd been looking for a connection between the Cavellis and Leon Molloy and it had been right under his nose. They had to be half-brothers. "What else do you remember about Leon?"

"Oh, he was a pretty quiet kid. A little pudgy. Kept to himself. I remember he had one kid that he hung out with sometimes, a neighbor or something." She thrummed her fingers on the desk as she tried to recall the name. She looked up and grinned. "Oh, I know who it was. So do you. He worked in this department several years ago, and I think you knew him from St. Paul's. It was Callahan. Patrick Callahan. As a matter of fact, he was here—yesterday, I think—I'm pretty sure I saw him talking to Royce."

Patrick Callahan? His heart stopped in his chest. Pat couldn't be mixed up in all of this. That didn't make sense.

He fought the notion, but a few things started to click into place. The only two people who knew where he'd taken Zoey was her grandfather and his partner, Royce. There was no way Royce would have said anything. Unless he'd been talking to another cop, one that had known Mac since high school.

Pat would have known exactly where to find the cabin and how to go down the back roads to avoid the police coming up the pass.

This couldn't be right. Pat couldn't be involved. He'd just been with him, helping him to stand guard in front of Zoey's room.

Oh, no. What if that was it? What if Zoey had recognized Pat's voice and that's what made her run? And if she had heard them together, that might have been enough to spook her.

"I got a hit on that phone," Rosie said, breaking into his thoughts. "But it's weird. It says she's at the Community Theatre downtown. I know that Edna Collins is kind of kooky, but there's no way she's trying to see a play in the middle of the night."

SEVENTEEN

Zoey looked around the deserted parking lot as she and Edna pulled up in front of the Pleasant Valley Community Theatre. "What are we doing here?"

"Hiding." Edna pulled a can of Mace from her purse and slipped out of the car. "Come on. It's easy enough to figure out where I live—I'm still in the phone book for goodness sake—so it's not safe for us to go back there. And I don't want to put any of the other Page Turners at risk by going to them. This was the best place I could think of."

Zoey followed her grandmother. "How are we going to get inside? Don't they lock this place up?"

"Yeah, but it's still summer, and someone's always leaving a window open."

They made their way along the side of the building checking for open or unlatched windows.

"Bingo. Found one." Edna pointed at a basement window that was open a crack. Popping the screen off, she tugged the window all the way open. "All right. In you go."

Zoey peered through the glass. It looked like the room was an office and had a credenza against the wall under the window. If she could squeeze through, she should be able to stand on it instead of having to drop straight into the room.

The window was barely above ground level, and she sank down and poked her legs into the open window. Wiggling through, the opening was snug on her hips, and she figured she was about one cheeseburger away from not fitting.

Worried she was going to have to ask Edna if she had any Vaseline in her purse, she twisted sideways then made it through

Thank goodness. Turning onto her stomach, she tried to locate the credenza with her feet.

Finding it with her toe, she gave another push through and found herself standing on the cabinet. She looked through the window at her grandmother. "Okay, I'll go find a door and let you in."

"I'm not coming in with you."

"What? Why not?"

"I'm going home to get Johnny. I'm worried that someone might show up at our house. So I'll get Johnny and come right back, then we'll figure out what to do from there."

Zoey looked around the office, her eyes trying to adjust in the dark. "Do you want me to wait here?"

"No, I wouldn't. I'd go up to the theatre. Just go left in the hallway and take the stairs up. It's in the back so you could probably turn on a light, and there's more comfy furniture up there. Why don't you try to rest until we get back?"

"Maybe I'll just stay here." The thought of stumbling around in the darkened theatre was less appealing than waiting in the sparse office. She peered up at her grandmother, knowing that she usually prepared for any situation. "Do you happen to have a flashlight?"

"Oh, yeah. I'm sure I've got one in here somewhere." She dug through her large purse then passed the whole thing through the window. "Here, just take my whole bag. You should be able to find anything you need in there."

She reached for the purse. "Thanks."

"Okay, honey. I'll get back as soon as I can." Edna waved and disappeared into the darkness.

Zoey took a deep breath. She dug through Edna's bag and found the flashlight. Switching it on, she shone it toward the door and followed the beam out of the room. Turning left, she followed the hallway to the stairs.

Images of axe-murderers filled her head as she peered up the bare stairwell. She swallowed her fear and ran up the stairs as quickly as possible.

Gasping for breath, she pushed through the door and into the foyer. Wow, she needed to up her cardio routine—that run up the steps had almost killed her. It probably didn't help that she was in a creepy building in the middle of the night and scared that someone actually did want to kill her.

The theatre was to the left and she stepped through the heavy velvet curtains. Shadows filled the dark theatre, and her pulse raced as she swung the flashlight over the row of seats.

The soft sound of her footsteps were absorbed into the thick carpet as she moved down the aisle toward the stage. Her imagination ran wild with thoughts of ghosts or spirits that could be haunting the old theatre. Every creak and groan of the building had her spooked and jumpy as she stumbled up the steps of the stage.

Thankfully the curtain was open, and she walked behind the stage and found a panel of light switches. She released her breath as she flicked the switches and found one that lit up the backstage area. She left the lights off in the auditorium area just in case they could somehow be seen from outside.

Having the lights on scattered most of her spooky notions, and she forgot her fears as she wandered through the props and costumes of the latest production of the theatre. It was evident from the costumes and the ruby slippers that they were putting on *The Wizard of Oz*.

She ran her hands along the costumes of the Cowardly Lion and the Scarecrow, and she marveled at the beautiful gossamer blue dress of Glenda the Good Witch. Layers of sparkling tulle and satin made up the gorgeous gown.

The backstage was full of painted and decorated sets that could be easily rolled on and off the stage. She dropped onto a patchwork quilt covered bed that appeared to be in Dorothy's bedroom and grunted as she realized the 'bed' was actually a piece of plywood. She wouldn't be resting on that.

Looking through the sets, she wandered past the yellow brick road, the Tinman's cottage, and a tiny village that she assumed was where the Munchkins lived. The sets were beautifully painted, and she admired the detailed artwork. Caught up in the aspects of the production, she roamed the backstage area, entranced with the sets and the props of the play.

Sinking into a chair in front of a makeup table, she rested Edna's big purse on her lap. She felt wired, her senses on overload from the mixtures of running through the hospital and landing in the city of Oz.

There was no way she was going to rest. Even if Dorothy's bed had turned out to be made of feathers and down.

She opened Edna's purse, glancing through the jumbled assortment of things that her grandmother felt she needed to carry around with her. Edna had some pretty good stuff in there—a couple of candy bars, tissues, mints, a romance novel, a first aid kit, a notebook with pen, antacids, a makeup bag, dental floss, lipsticks, her high-heeled stapler, assorted medications and her wallet were some of the more normal items one might find in a purse.

But Zoey didn't know how many other old ladies carried brass knuckles, a can of Mace, a can of Pepper spray (*what? In case she ran out of Mace?*), a switchblade (*seriously, Grandma?*), plus a Swiss army pocketknife, a blood pressure cuff, and a small bottle of hand sanitizer.

She grabbed one of the candy bars, unwrapped the top, and took a bite. Pulling out the romance novel, she settled back in the chair and checked out the story.

But the words on the page couldn't hold her attention. She was too antsy, too keyed up. Plus, she didn't really want to read about a romance when her own love-life was currently in such terrific shambles.

Her gaze kept coming back to the beautiful blue dress, with its sparkling bodice and glimmering skirt. Wouldn't it be great to click her heels together three times and have all of this over? Or better yet, to have never had it happen in the first place?

But if it had never happened, she would have missed out on one of the best nights of her life. The night with Mac. She wished the Wizard were here now so she could ask him if what had happened with Mac had been real or just an act. Except the Wizard himself had actually turned out to be just an act as well.

Wasn't anything in her life real anymore? What could she even count on?

Was it too much to ask to have a good witch or even a fairy godmother float down in a sparkly blue dress and help a sister out?

She set Edna's things on the counter and crossed to the dress, as if the sparkles were pulling her forward. Brushing her fingers across the satin, she had the sudden insane urge to try the dress on.

What could it hurt? Edna would take at least twenty minutes to get back, and she was driving herself crazy with thoughts of Mac. Maybe trying on the dress would take her mind off her troubles, just for a minute or two.

She pulled off the scrubs and stepped into the blue gown. It fit perfectly. Smoothing the front of the dress across her waist, she caught a glimpse of herself in the makeup mirror. The gown was gorgeous. She glanced at the glittering ruby red shoes on the prop shelf.

Did she dare?

In for a penny—in for a pound her grandma liked to say. Although what the heck that actually meant, she wasn't exactly sure.

Right now, it meant she was trying on the shoes.

She got them down and stepped into them. They were a tad too small, but she didn't care. Pinched toes were the least of her concerns. She turned in a circle, letting the magic of the costume fill her.

Except she didn't believe in magic. That was her mom's department. Moon believed in magic and the stars and spells and potions. Not her. She was too practical for all that nonsense.

She was the sensible one, level-headed and rational. She certainly didn't believe in charms and magic.

But what if she did? Just this once.

What if she let go of all that sensible logic and just let herself believe? Believe in shooting stars, in good witches and fairies, in magic.

Just this once.

She took a deep breath, looked down at the ruby red slippers, and clicked her heels together three times. Her voice was soft, barely a whisper. "There's no place like home. There's no place like home. There's no place like home."

"What the hell are you doing?"

She jumped as a male voice spoke out from the darkness.

It was Mac.

But how? It couldn't be. How could he possibly have found her?

Maybe magic was real after all.

EIGHTEEN

Mac blinked at the beautiful vision in blue and tried to make sense of what he was seeing.

The parking lot had been empty when he'd arrived, but it hadn't taken too much skilled detective work to track the movements of two people and discover the recently scuffed dirt in front of the open basement window.

He'd crawled through and after a few minutes of searching the theatre, discovered the lights on in the backstage area. He'd expected to find Edna and her granddaughter behind the curtain, but the surprise was on him.

He sure as hell hadn't expected to find Zoey wearing ruby red slippers and a sparkling blue gown. The dim lights shimmered off the sparkles in the dress and she looked—well, magical. That was the only word for it.

The only way he could describe the way she turned to look at him—with love shining in her eyes like she couldn't believe he was here. And here to save her.

As worried as he'd been chasing her down, he couldn't help the corners of his mouth as they lifted in a grin. She looked so beautiful. His chest tightened at the ache of love and responsibility he felt for her, and in that instant he knew. He knew that his earlier behavior was bullshit. That there was no way he was going to let this woman go.

That he would do anything—lay down his own life—to protect her.

He would do anything to see her look at him like that. Like that very moment.

Except that moment changed, and her expression went from love to terror. "How did you find me?"

"I tracked Edna's cell phone." He took a tentative step toward her.

Her eyes were wide with fright. She looked like a deer caught in the headlights. A beautiful deer wearing a twinkling blue dress.

She took a step back, holding her arms out in front of her as if to ward him off. "Stay away from me. Don't come any closer." Her eyes darted to a handbag on the counter.

He recognized the bag as Edna's and knew it could contain any number of items she could use against him. "Zoey, what's going on? Why are you acting like you're afraid of me? Why did you run from me in the hospital?"

"As if you didn't know." The shelf next to her held props, and she reached toward the closest item, coming away with an oil can.

He hated that answer. Why did women always think they already knew? And what the hell was she planning on doing with that oil can? Fixing a squeaky hinge? "I *don't* know. Why don't you tell me?"

"I heard you talking. Outside my room in the hospital. I heard you say that you were there to take care of me."

He took a step closer, and she threw the oil can at his head. He deflected it with his forearm. *Shit*. She had a great arm. At least the one that hadn't been shot. "Yeah, of course I said that. I *was* there to take care of you. I tried to stay away, but I got worried that one of Leon's men would show up and try to hurt you."

She grabbed for another prop, this time coming up with a giant lollipop. She threw it tomahawk style, but it fell way short of its mark—his head. "One of Leon's men did show up. You. And I *heard* you say that you had to hurt me, then your so-called friend told you to do it quick." She lobbed a picnic basket at his head.

"He's no friend of mine."

She stopped, her arm raised, her hand poised to throw what appeared to be a large yellow brick. "Why not?"

"Because I think he's somehow involved in all of this. I think he may have been one of the men who came out to the cabin to attack us."

She lowered the brick, her eyes full of suspicion and doubt. "I know he was."

He'd figured as much. "How do you know?"

"Because I recognized his voice. I'd heard his voice twice before. Once in my apartment the night the two men broke in, and once in the woods, right before he shot me. When I heard him talking outside my hospital room, I knew it was him right away. But I couldn't figure out why he was talking to you."

"We've known each other since we were kids, but I hadn't seen him much the last couple of years. And I had no idea he was connected to this. In fact, now that I think about it, I've seen him more in the last few days than I have in the last year. And now it makes perfect sense. He's been digging for information on this case all along."

"And you've been giving it to him."

His shoulders slumped, and he let out a heavy sigh. "Yeah, I guess I have. I guess I'm an idiot. He called me earlier tonight, offered to take me out for a couple of beers. I was in a shitty mood, so I went. I had a few too many and started talking about you and how much I liked you. And how I'd just broken your heart."

He snapped his fingers. "Actually, he was the one who suggested we go to the hospital to check up on you. He must have known I could get him close to you. And I led him right to your door. That son of a bitch."

Zoey took a tentative step toward him. "How do I know if I can believe you or not?"

He shook his head and stared at her in disbelief. "Seriously? If you truly believe that I could hurt you, then maybe we didn't have the connection I thought we did."

"I didn't want to believe it, but what was I supposed to think? You were outside my room chumming it up with the guy who has been trying to kill me and talking about hurting me."

He grimaced. "I guess I can see your point." He moved a little closer. "Zoey, please believe me. I had no idea Pat was involved in any of this. If I'd known he was the one who tried to hurt you, I would have killed him myself. I still might."

She set the brick down and approached him warily. Stopping in front of him, she looked up into his eyes, as if searching for answers there. "You also conveniently broke things off with me right after I'd been shot."

"I'm sorry about that."

"Why? Why did you leave the hospital without talking to me? Why did you tell me not to call or contact you?"

"You know why. It was tearing me up that I hadn't protected you at the cabin. We'd just been talking about all of that stuff with my old partner, so it was on the surface, like a wound I'd just picked open. And then those guys broke in, and it was like I had to live it all over again. I couldn't do anything to stop them. And you ended up getting shot. Just like her."

"No, not just like her. She was shot and *killed*. I was shot in the arm. And just barely." She peered up at him, a grin tugging at the corners of her lips. "It's really only a flesh wound."

His expression stayed sober, and he lifted a curl of her hair and pushed it behind her ear. "I couldn't bear it if something had happened to you. I know we haven't known each other that long, but I felt a connection with you from the first time I met you. I couldn't stop thinking about you. About wanting to be with you. The last few days have been amazing. Well, not the running for our lives part, but the part when we were together. I don't usually let people in so quickly, but with you it was different."

"Different? How?"

"You walked in and completely captured my heart. After I met you, I knew I didn't stand a chance against falling for you." He looked into her eyes. "I am in love with you. Utterly hopelessly in love with you."

She reached up and touched his face. He caught his breath, and a sensation of desire ran down his spine.

"I am utterly hopelessly in love with you, too."

He bent his head forward, touching his forehead to hers. "I know. That's why I couldn't take a chance on you getting hurt. I'm sorry for the way I went about it, but I cared about you too much to risk having you get hurt because of me."

"You leaving hurt much worse than the bullet that grazed my arm. I can recover from that. I can't recover from you breaking my heart." She peered up at him. "Listen to me, Michael Mac McCarthy, I don't need you to step in front of a bullet for me. I don't need you to protect my body. I want you to protect my heart."

She leaned forward, her lips grazing his cheek as she spoke softly into his ear. "If you want to protect me, then do everything in your power to not break my heart again. You can shield me from insults and harsh words. You can defend me against feelings of self-doubt, and you can shelter me from stormy days. But you can *protect* me by guarding my heart. By loving and cherishing me. That's what I need from you. To protect my heart."

She kissed his cheek, then grinned up at him. "And I also need you to protect me from spiders. I hate spiders."

He laughed. Sliding his arms around her waist, he pulled her to him. The blue gown crinkled against his chest. "I can do that. I'm excellent at killing spiders." He leaned in, and captured her mouth in a kiss.

A sudden thought occurred to him, and he pulled back. "Where's Edna?" He ducked his shoulders as he searched the darkened theatre around them. "She's not going to come after me with a loaded gun, is she?"

Zoey laughed. "No. She dropped me off and went to pick up Johnny." Her laughter died as her expression sobered. "Edna was worried Leon's guys would go after them to get to me, so she dropped me off, then went to pick him up. They're coming back for me."

He grimaced. "Damn it. I'm sorry any of you are involved in this. And I feel like an idiot that I trusted that guy. That I didn't see through him earlier."

"It's not your fault. How could have possibly known? And up until tonight, he may not have even realized that we meant anything to each other." She ran her finger lightly along the edge of his chin then softly touched his lips. "And you do mean something to me."

She leaned in, replacing the pad of her finger with her lips against his. A tender kiss, but filled with meaning. "You mean everything to me." She deepened the kiss, pressed herself into his chest as she wrapped her arms around his neck.

The tightness in his chest loosened as he gave himself to her. Gave his heart. No conditions, no restrictions. His breath came in ragged gasps as he spoke between kisses. "I love you, Zoey. With everything in me. I belong to you, heart and soul."

"I love you, too." She pulled him into a tight embrace.

He pulled back, cupping her chin in his hand and tried to convey his feelings in his gaze. "I mean it. I'm in this thing. When I'm with you, I feel like I'm home."

She blinked. "There's no place like home," she uttered softly before he kissed her again.

NINETEEN

Zoey felt his kiss all the way to her toes. Her pinched toes.

She kicked off the ruby red slippers. They had already worked their magic. Now they were just hurting her feet. And she didn't want anything to distract her from the way Mac's lips felt against hers.

His arms wrapped around her waist, pulling him to her. The dress cinched around her waist, and her breasts practically popped free of the low-cut bodice. Who would have thought a sparkly dress with poofy sleeves could make her feel so sexy?

He wore jeans, a snug black T-shirt, and black motorcycle boots, and he was so damn handsome, he almost took her breath away. The sleeves of his shirt stretched around the hard muscles of his biceps, and she ran her hands up his arms, awed by their strength.

Looking down at her, his gaze lingered on her lips, and her knees threatened to buckle with the intensity of the emotions she felt for this man. Everything about him and their relationship had been messy and chaotic, so unlike the structured way she led her life. But she was okay with it.

In fact, she found that she was starting to like it. To enjoy a little chaos and spontaneity. Being with him also felt daring and exciting in a way that an organized sock drawer could never compare to.

He kissed her neck, her throat, then the tops of her breasts. Soft, sweet, agonizingly slow kisses that she felt all the way to her core. She caught her breath, clutching his back as ripples of desire coursed through her. She wanted him, needed him.

It didn't matter that a few hours ago her heart had felt like it had been shattered into a million pieces. He'd found a way to repair it. And it felt whole again.

He drew back and grinned at her. "I've never kissed a princess before."

She laughed. "I'm not actually dressed as a princess. I'm dressed as a witch."

"Oh, well, I *have* kissed one of those before."

"Very funny. This dress belongs to Glenda the *Good* Witch. From *The Wizard of Oz*."

"Ah, that makes sense now why you were holding that yellow brick." He smiled. "Thanks for not throwing that one at me, by the way."

She laughed again. "It was made of styrofoam. I don't think you were in too great of danger."

He narrowed his eyes and tightened his hold on her waist. "I feel a little like I'm in danger now. It scares me how much I care about you."

Caressing his cheek, she laid a gentle kiss on his lips. "I know. Me, too."

"Do you think if we follow the yellow brick road, the Wizard would grant me a wish?"

She peered up at him, her voice soft. "What's your wish?"

He offered her a naughty grin. "For Glenda to take her dress back."

"But then I would have nothing to wear." She batted her eyelashes innocently at him.

"Exactly." He leaned in and took her mouth in a hungry kiss. He held her cheek gingerly with one hand as he ran his other through her hair, then cupped the back of her head.

She loved the way he kissed her, gentle and forceful at the same time. She parted her lips, letting his tongue in, letting him taste her. Heat curled in her belly. She wanted him. All of him. And she wanted him now.

He reached his hands down under her bottom, lifted her against him, then set her down on the makeup table. She wrapped her legs around his waist as his hands skimmed under the dress, his fingers lightly caressing her skin.

His kisses became more fevered. Pulling her closer, his hands slid along her thighs and under her rear, then stopped. His lips curved into a grin and he spoke against her mouth. "Are you not wearing any underwear?"

She laughed. "I am. But just barely."

His hands slid up and found the elastic band of the thong undies. He gave it a gentle tug. "I can fix that."

Before he had a chance to fix anything, the melodic tones of "*All About That Bass*" filled the air.

Mac chuckled. "Is that your phone?"

"No, it's my grandma's." Edna's bag sat beside her. She dug through it, looking for the phone, as she tried to catch her breath.

"Of course it is."

Finding the phone, she checked the display then held it to her ear. "Hello. Grandpa?"

"Zoey, are you all right?" her grandfather asked.

"I'm fine, but I'm worried about you. Where are you? Did Grandma find you?"

"Yes, we're right out front. Can you let us in?"

"I'll be right there." She hung up the phone and looked up Mac. "My grandparents are outside." She slid off the makeup table and rearranged her dress as she started down the stairs of the stage. "Come on."

She raced up the auditorium aisle, out of the theatre, and hurried to the front doors. Praying they didn't have an alarm connected to them, she pushed one open, and her grandparents slipped inside.

"I'm so glad you're okay." Johnny folded her into his embrace. He smelled like toothpaste and that blue soap that he used.

Edna gave her a quick hug then eyed her suspiciously. "What in the world have you been doing? Your face is all flushed, and your hair is a mess. And why the hell are you wearing that dress?"

Mac stepped out of the theatre behind her. "She...."

Before he could say anything, Edna pulled a can of pepper spray from her pocket and held it out toward him.

"Get back. I'm not afraid to use this. I won't let you hurt my granddaughter."

Geez—how many cans of defensive spray did Edna have? Was she buying it in bulk at Costco? Zoey held her arms out in front of Mac. "It's okay, Grandma. He's not trying to hurt me. It was a misunderstanding. He didn't know it was his friend that tried to kill me."

Edna lowered the pepper spray. "Oh, good. I told her you couldn't be in on this. I always liked you. It'd be a shame if I would've had to shoot you."

Mac arched an eyebrow at her. "I'm assuming you mean with the pepper spray?"

Her grandmother looked at the floor. "Uh—yes, of course that's what I meant. It would be a shame if I had to shoot you with the pepper spray."

"I agree. That would be a shame."

"Well, now that we know you're not in on this crazy scheme," Johnny interrupted. "What are we going to do about it?"

"First we're going to find someplace safe," Mac said. "Then we're going to devise a plan to catch the sons of bitches."

Edna nodded. "Agreed."

"But where are we going to go that's safe?" Zoey asked. "They know where my grandparents live so we can't go back to their house. And I don't want to risk showing up at any of the Page Turners."

Mac shook his head. "No, and I don't think it's safe going back to my place either. Pat knows where I live." He touched Zoey's arm and looked down at her with an expression of concern. "But we can't stay here. You need to get some rest. You look tired, like you're about to drop."

Oh, good. That's just the look she was going for. Nothing more attractive than looking dead-tired. "I'm okay."

"I hate to state the obvious," Johnny said. "But if we're looking for a place that's anonymous where you can also rest, we should just check into a hotel."

Edna nodded. "Good idea. The Travel Inn is out by the highway and it has parking in the back so my car would be hidden. Plus, that's where Scooter works the night shift. He'd probably let us check in under an assumed name."

For once, Zoey was glad her grandmother watched so much crime television. She would never have thought of that. Although at this point, she could barely think at all. Suddenly all of the stress of the day settled on her shoulders and she *was* tired. So incredibly tired. "Yeah, that sounds like a good idea. Let's go."

"Are you going to wear that dress, Cinderella?" Edna asked.

She looked down at the sparkly dress and her bare feet. "I probably shouldn't. Otherwise whoever's playing Glenda's going to be pretty upset when they go to look for their costume. Give me a minute to change."

Five minutes later, the small group headed for Edna's car. Zoey had changed back in to the scrubs and collected her grandmother's purse.

She and Mac climbed into the back seat amidst a frenzied greeting from Havoc and Bruiser. The two little dogs climbed all over them, licking their faces.

Edna pulled the front door closed. "We didn't know what else to do. We couldn't leave the dogs alone at the house."

"It's fine." Zoey cuddled the little poodle against her chest.

"All right, let's go. I'm just going to leave my car here for now," Mac said. "The fewer ways Pat can trace me, the better."

Johnny pulled out on the road and headed for the hotel.

Mac fingered the cotton scrubs shirt she wore. "I can see now how you two slipped out of the hospital without anyone noticing."

Edna was still wearing the white doctor's lab coat. "Don't worry. I'll return these to the hospital later. We didn't steal them. I just borrowed them for a bit." She pointed to a plastic sack sitting in the seat next to Zoey. "I brought you some more clothes again. You need to start calling me Amazon the way I deliver."

"How about if I call you my life saver? Seriously, Gram, you may have actually helped to save my life tonight. And thank you for the clothes."

Her grandmother reached over the seat and patted her leg. "I love you, honey. I would do anything for you. I also brought you some prescription ibuprofen that your grandpa had left over from when he broke his leg. They'll make you tired, but they'll help with the pain."

Zoey had been trying to ignore the dull throbbing pain in her arm. A headache had been threatening in her temples, and she dug through the bag and found the bottle of capsules.

Edna passed her a bottle of water, and she took two, then leaned back against the seat and closed her eyes. She smiled as she felt Mac take her hand, the warmth of its solid pressure giving her reassurance that everything would be okay.

Ten minutes later they pulled into the parking lot of the Travel Inn. Johnny parked the car behind the hotel, and he and Edna offered to go and get them checked in. "You stay here. We'll be right back."

Mac handed him some cash. "I'll keep an eye on her."

The pills had made her drowsy, and Zoey could have curled up in the back seat and slept until morning.

Her grandparents returned a few minutes later. Mac opened the back door and handed Edna the two dogs then grabbed the rest of the bags.

Johnny opened the back door of the car and helped Zoey out. "Scooter was on duty at the desk, and he must think pretty highly of your grandmother. He let her register as Nancy Drew and gave us a *Two for the Price of One* deal on the room. I don't know if he's allowed to do that, but I handed him your cash, and he gave me two keys to adjoining rooms. And he called me 'dude' like five times."

Zoey smiled. "Yeah, he likes that word." She leaned on her grandfather as they made their way through the back of the hotel to their rooms.

Mac unlocked the doors and let them in. She heard him tell her grandparents that they'd see them in the morning as she headed for the bathroom.

Turning on the light, she caught a glimpse of herself in the mirror. *Oh geez.* She was a mess. A purple bruise colored the side of her forehead, and her eyes looked sunken and fatigued. Her face was pale and drawn, and her hair was mussed.

Grabbing a wash cloth, she wet it and washed her face. The cool water felt good. But the medicine coupled with the events of the day had completely exhausted her.

"You okay?" Mac asked as she stepped out of the bathroom a few minutes later.

She nodded, not able to muster enough energy to actually answer. Stumbling to the bed, she toed off her shoes, pulled back the covers, and sank into the mattress. She felt Mac slide into the other side and pull her against his solid body.

He smoothed her hair and laid a soft kiss on her cheek. "Just sleep. You're safe with me."

As she drifted off, she felt safe. Safe in his arms.
For now.

TWENTY

Zoey blinked her eyes open as she heard muted voices coming from the room next door. Disoriented, she looked around the motel room, trying to decipher where she was. Another blink, and it all came back to her.

Sitting up, she saw she was alone in the room. Mac's side of the bed was empty. She got up and trudged to the adjoining door of the neighboring room.

Pushing it open, the smell of breakfast hit her as she took in the room full of people. Edna, Johnny, Mac, Sunny, Jake, Cassie, and Piper were seated around the motel room. The two dogs were curled together on the bed, and a spread of breakfast sandwiches, juice, and donuts covered the small dinette table.

"Good morning, sunshine." Mac poured her a cup of coffee from a box on the table and crossed the room to place it in her hands. He grinned down at her. "You awake?"

She took a sip of the warm coffee. "Not yet. But I'm working on it. What's going on in here?"

"Edna called me this morning and told me what was going on," Sunny said. "We brought breakfast and some supplies."

"I told them not to come," Edna said. "But they insisted."

Cassie handed her a plastic sack. "I brought you some things. Why don't you take a shower and get dressed. You'll feel better after a shower and some breakfast."

Zoey looked into the bag and wanted to weep at Cassie's thoughtfulness. The hotel would have shampoo and conditioner, but Cassie had brought her a razor, scented body lotion, a few hair products and a new toothbrush and toothpaste. Just what she needed to feel like a human again. "Thank you."

Mac guided her into the bathroom. His chin carried the scruff of a day's worth of beard, but he smelled like soap, and she assumed he must have already showered. He wore the same jeans as the night before, but had changed to a soft faded blue T-shirt. "Jake loaned me a clean shirt. And he and Sunny brought clothes for your grandparents. They're really good friends. They all are."

She nodded. "Yes. They are. So are you."

He smiled at her. "Thanks. Do you need a really good friend to help you take a shower?"

She grinned back. "Yes. But it's probably not the best idea with my grandparents and half the book club in the next room. If you could just help me cover up the bandages on my arm, I can probably handle it myself."

He helped her pull the shirt over her head, being careful to avoid her injured arm. It might have been sexy standing in front of him in her lacy bra if it weren't for the myriad of bruises and scrapes covering her arms and torso.

"I'm a mess," she said, looking down at her battered body.

"A beautiful mess." He gave her a quick kiss, then dumped the items in the plastic bag onto the corner of the tub and secured the plastic around her bandaged arm. "This will have to do for now. It won't hurt if it gets a little wet. I don't trust taking you back to the hospital today. But Sunny also brought over some fresh bandages and I'm fairly skilled at first aid, so I'll redress your arm when you get out."

"Thanks." She took another sip of coffee, letting the caffeine work its magic. "I won't take long, and I'll be careful of my arm."

"Take as long as you like. I'll be right outside if you need me." He pulled the door shut behind him.

Turning on the water, she dropped the rest of her clothes and stepped under the warm spray. The combination of the hot water and the shower products revived her, and she felt so much better as she pulled back the curtain and reached for a towel.

Her heart filled as she saw her clean clothes, a bottle of ibuprofen, a fresh cup of coffee, and a donut sitting neatly on the counter. Mac seemed to know exactly what she needed.

The donut was a great start, but what she needed now was to figure out a way to get her life back. To catch these guys that were after her, and to find a way to feel safe again.

As she got dressed and brushed her teeth and hair, she had a feeling that Edna was in the next room devising such a plan.

She was right.

Ten minutes later, she stepped back into the adjoining hotel room and sat on the edge of the bed next to her grandmother. "Well, have you got it all figured out yet?"

Her grandmother pursed her lips. "We're working on it."

Cassie wrapped a breakfast sandwich in a napkin and passed it to Zoey. "We know we've got to find a way to catch all of these guys together. We need to prove that this Pat Callahan is in on this, too. That he's the one who tried to kill you." She winced when she said the word 'kill'.

Zoey took a bite of the sandwich. The combination of egg, bacon, and cheese was the perfect thing she needed to get her strength back. It seemed bacon was the answer to a lot of problems. "What if I arranged a meeting with him? Wore a wire and got him to admit he was the one who shot me?"

"Use yourself as bait, you mean?" Mac asked. "Not a chance. There's no way I'm letting you put yourself in danger like that."

She bristled at the command and his directive that he wouldn't "let her" do something. But she knew it was coming from a place of protectiveness, not conceit. And frankly, facing Pat Callahan again scared the living daylights out of her.

"If anything, I should face him and try to get him to talk," Mac suggested.

"No way," Jake said. "You can't even talk *about* him without waves of anger coming off of you. He'd know right away you were onto him. And I'm afraid if we let you in the same room with him, you'd end up killing him yourself."

"True."

"We need someone that he would trust," Zoey said. "That is already part of their world and wouldn't cause suspicion."

A knock sounded at the door, and they all froze.

No one was supposed to know they were there.

Mac pulled his gun from its holster and gestured for Jake to open the door.

Jake crossed the room, his muscles tense as he pulled open the door.

"Hey, dudes. I just got off my shift and wanted to check on Zoey." Scooter sauntered into the room, oblivious of Mac and Jake's vigilance. He spied the breakfast items on the table. "Hey, are those donuts from that bakery down on Main? I love their chocolate glazed ones."

"Help yourself," Piper said, passing him the box.

Zoey looked around the room, watching as each person realized the weed-smoking gold mine that had just wandered into the room. "Oh, Scooter. We were wondering if you might be able to help us with something."

"Sure," he answered around a mouthful of donut. "What's up?"

"We've discovered the identity of the guy who was sent to kill me, and we think he works for Leon Molloy."

Scooter's mouth dropped open. "*Kill* you?"

"Zoey was kidnapped outside of The Joint the other night," Mac explained. "I got her back, but Leon's guys found us again and shot Zoey."

"In the arm," she said. "I'm fine."

Scooter wiped his mouth on the back of his hand. "Look, I just grow grass for the guy. I'm not involved in any kidnapping or shooting at anyone. Do you think I had something to do with this?"

"No, of course not," Edna said. "We're not accusing you. We just want to know if you'd be willing to help us catch the guys that are involved."

He shrugged his bony shoulders. "What would I have to do?"

Mac sat next to him on the side of the bed. "Have you ever seen a guy around Leon that's about my height and age, maybe a little taller, kind of a tough blond-headed Irish guy?"

"You mean Pat?"

Mac nodded. "Yep. That's exactly who I mean. Did you know Pat's a cop? A dirty one, evidently."

"You're shittin' me. Dude. No way."

"Way. And we need to find a time and a place that we can catch Pat and Leon together."

Scooter picked up another donut, apparently more at ease now that he knew he wasn't in trouble. "That's easy. It'll be tonight. They transfer cash and crops every Saturday night. They all meet at one of the grow houses, and these big guys take cases full of cash. They also pick up product and take it to the recreational stores to restock them."

"What do mean by big guys? Do you know who they are?"

"No, but they're the same guys every week. And I've seen them at the weed bar, too. I can't figure them out though. Sometimes they're dressed like body guards, and sometimes they wear business suits."

"Business suits?" Zoey asked. She gave Mac a knowing look. "Like the guys at Cavelli Commerce. That's got to be where the discrepancies in the audit were coming from. There were large sums of cash being deposited into dummy corporations."

"Leon is half-brothers with the Cavellis," Mac told the group. "That's the connection we've been looking for. The same guys must be working for both Leon and the Cavellis." He looked at Scooter. "What else do you know about these guys and what they do?"

Scooter shrugged. "Not much. It's not like we sit around and talk to each other. I know they're the muscle, like the security guys. Leon packages up all the cash that he can't deposit in the banks, and they guard it and move it like the armored truck guys. It's like they transport the cash."

"But where do they transport it to?"

Scooter shrugged again. "I don't know. Someplace in Denver. Some financial company. I think the guys are related to Leon somehow. Like his step-brothers or cousins or something. Must be the guys you're talking about."

"What time do they usually make the transfer?"

"Um, they usually meet around nine or so. Leon likes to get home in time to watch the news."

Zoey leaned forward. "So, we need to catch them in the act. Maybe we could have Scooter wear a wire?"

"No," Edna said. "That's too dangerous. We need to get some kind of surveillance equipment in there. I saw a show once where they prosecuted a robber because he got caught on the family's nanny cam."

"Gram, we can't put a nanny cam inside of a grow house. They might be a little suspicious if a teddy bear were sitting on the table with them."

Mac held up his hand. "Hold on. Edna might be on to something. Not necessarily a nanny cam, but something similar. If we could get some kind of recording device in there, we could prove that they were the ones that came after Zoey."

"What about the money-laundering? Don't we want to get that evidence as well?" Edna asked.

"Yeah, that would be great, too. But if we can get them for the murder of Jimmy Two-Fingers and the attempted murder of Zoey, that would be enough to put them away for a long time."

"So, you *do* want to catch them with a teddy bear?" Scooter asked.

"No," Jake said. "Teddy bears are old school nanny cams. They have so many more sophisticated cams now. We have several down at our PI office. They put spy cams in potted plants, clocks, DVD players, and even cereal boxes."

"That's great," Zoey said. "But we still can't have Scooter waltz in there with a potted plant or a DVD player. What's he going to do? Ask if anyone wants to watch a movie? Or see if maybe they're in the mood for some Cinnamon Toast Crunch cereal?"

"Dude, I love Cinnamon Toast Crunch," Scooter said. "I'm always in the mood for cereal."

"I think Jake's got the right idea. We don't have to use a potted plant. They have other things. Things that are so common, you wouldn't even notice them. I've seen spy cams in a bottle of water. What could you get your hands on today, Jake?"

Jake rubbed his chin. "I'd have to check with my partner, Finn, but I know we've got some different ones we've used on surveillance jobs before. We've got the bottle of water one you were talking about. And a coffee cup. We've got some watches and a ball cap."

"Those would work," Mac said. "It would be easy enough for Scooter to carry a bottle of water and a coffee cup in with him. Then we could have a couple of recording devices in place. Would you be up for that, Scooter?"

He nodded. "Sure, that doesn't seem too hard. I could wear a baseball cap too, if that would help. Then I could try to look at whoever was talking."

Edna rested a hand on his Scooter's shoulder. "We don't want you to do anything that's going to put you at unnecessary risk."

"I work for guys that are killing people," he said. "I think helping to catch them and finding another rec distributor is going to be a pretty good risk for me."

"I agree," Mac said. "These guys are into way more than just recreational grass. You're better off working with someone else anyway."

"Aren't we overlooking an important piece of this, though?" Zoey asked. "We're talking about how dangerous these guys are and yet, we're going after them with a water bottle spy-cam, a few guys, and a book club. Shouldn't this be where we call in the authorities? Or get some help from the police department?"

Mac grimaced. "Ordinarily I would say yes. But I don't know how deep this thing goes. I would never have believed that Pat would be in on this. I don't know how many other guys in my department could be on the take from these guys. Damn it, I just don't know who to trust."

"I can help with that," Jake said. "I've got some guys that I used to work with in the FBI that I'd trust with my life."

Mac picked up Zoey's hand. "It's not my life that I'm worried about."

Twenty-One

Mac pulled the nondescript van up to the curb outside the warehouse. The exterior of the van was faded and had a blue logo advertising Joe's Plumbing, but the inside was state of the art. Jake and Finney used the van often in their private detective agency work.

Jake had also contacted some of his friends in the FBI, and they were setting up around the perimeter of the warehouse. Between the money-laundering and the attempted murder, the Feds were more than willing to step in and help on the case.

They'd also brought some sophisticated listening devices of their own and were each wearing a headset that connected to Jake inside the van.

The warehouse was on the edge of town, a large brick building with a steel garage door on one end and an entry door on the side. Scooter had drawn them a crude schematic of the layout of the grow house so they had an idea of how things were set up inside. The plants and tables were toward the back, away from the doors and the loading area, which worked out well as it would hopefully keep the growers out of harm's way.

Mac had detailed how the plan should go and given Scooter specific instructions to drop and crawl under the tables as soon as the team entered the building. There would be a couple of other growers working that afternoon, but Scooter was sure they would follow his lead when the time came.

Mac was a little worried about their reaction time, especially if they sampled their stock as they worked, but Scooter had assured him that no matter how stoned he was, if armed men entered the building, they would all be able to drop and hide.

It was his normal routine to show up at the grow house midafternoon, so Scooter had gone over earlier and taken the spy-cam equipment with him. Mac wasn't too excited that a major part of their plan hinged on the capabilities of a guy who was most likely baked and had been wearing his shirt inside out.

He turned off the engine and twisted in his seat. Zoey and Edna sat next to Jake in the back of the van. It wasn't his choice to bring them. He would've much rather had them stay at the hotel, away from the danger. He wanted them somewhere that he didn't have to worry about their safety, but no amount of talking could have convinced either of them not to come.

Johnny had agreed to stay behind with the dogs and the other Page Turners. Edna had him on speaker on her cell phone, and he was instructed to call the police, or God forbid, an ambulance, if anything went wrong.

"What now?" Zoey asked. She looked better.

He'd redressed her arm earlier that afternoon and had talked her into taking some more ibuprofen and sleeping for a few hours. The combination of rest and some food had done wonders for her.

She wore black yoga pants, a snug black T-shirt, and her hair had been pulled into a long ponytail. It looked like she could have been an average woman headed to the gym. Except for the bruises on her face and arms and the bandages covering a gunshot wound across her shoulder.

"Now we wait," Jake answered. The back of the van was equipped with a long bench and a small chair pulled up to a built-in counter covered with several computer monitors and what looked like stereo components. He turned on the monitors and flipped several switches on the components. "If Scooter did what we told him to, he should already have the spy cams set up in the warehouse."

The monitors flickered to life, and they saw three separate angles of the inside of the warehouse. Two were static images, and one was bopping up and down as it focused in on a large leafy marijuana plant.

The receivers clicked on, and a soft humming sound emanated from one.

A louder humming sound accompanied by sporadic song lyrics came from another. "Whoa-oh. Livin' on a prayer."

Zoey chuckled. "Is that Scooter singing?"

They leaned forward.

The camera in Scooter's cap moved up and down to the beat. "Oh-h, we're half-way there—it doesn't make a difference if we're naked or not."

Mac grinned. "That's Scooter's poor attempt at singing. He's completely butchering the lyrics. Did he just say 'naked' or not?"

The group in the van burst into laughter. And not mild chuckling. Side-holding, tears-running-down-the-face laughing as they sang the massacred lyrics again.

It felt good to laugh. It probably wasn't even that funny, but the laughter was good. For all of them.

Their laughter died as a black SUV turned down the street and pulled up to the warehouse. Mac counted three men, including Leon, as they got out and walked to the door.

Another SUV and a dark blue Mustang pulled in behind the first vehicle.

Mac gestured to the cars. "That's Pat's Mustang."

They watched as Pat climbed from his car. Two large muscled men exited the second SUV. The taller of the two had a sling wrapped around his arm.

Zoey stared at Pat. "So, that's what he looks like. He looks different when he's not wearing a Nixon mask." She pointed to the guy with the sling. "And I'm sure that's tattoo-guy, the one that grabbed me. He must have been the other guy at the cabin. The one that you shot. That's probably why he's wearing that sling."

Mac nodded. "I'll bet you're right."

The men headed into the warehouse, and they appeared on two of the monitors.

Mac watched as they shook hands and greeted each other.

"Shh—quiet. Can you turn it up a little, Jake?" Edna asked. She leaned forward, staring at the screen with rapt attention. She was enjoying herself a little too much. He was surprised that she hadn't offered to bring popcorn.

Although her giant hand bag was at her feet. He wouldn't put it past her to have a bag of the stuff inside her purse.

He turned his attention to the screen as Jake raised the volume on the speakers and flipped on the recording device. Scooter had done a good job placing the spy cams. They could clearly see and hear the men.

Pat moved toward Leon with his hand outstretched. "Hey man, good to see you."

Leon rebuffed his gesture, an angry look on his face. "Don't 'hey man' me. I'm not in the least bit happy with you."

Pat's face turned angry, then sullen. "What's your problem?"

"My problem is that I gave you a job to do, and you can't seem to be able to accomplish it. All you had to do was take care of one skinny little bookkeeper."

Zoey's eyes widened. "That's it. They're talking about me."

"At least they called you 'skinny'," Edna whispered.

"Shhh." Mac scolded them with a finger to his lips.

"It's not my fault," Pat said, sounding like a spoiled child. "She must have had help getting out of the hospital."

"That's not my problem. My problem is that I gave you a direct order to get rid of the girl and yet, Zoey Allen is still alive."

"Look, I already shot the bitch once."

"In the arm. That doesn't shut her up or keep her from testifying. Next time try shooting her in the mouth."

Mac looked at Zoey. Her face blanched pale. "I think we've heard enough."

Jake held his arm up. "Hold on. If we hang tight, we may be able to get something about the money."

The big garage door went up, and one of the black SUVs backed in to the loading area of the warehouse. Two of the guys opened the hatch and started loading large tubs into the back end.

They could see the other men in the background as they passed briefcases and large tubs between them. One of them opened one of the cases and held it out for Pat's approval.

Pat nodded, and they set three identical silver briefcases next to him.

Fortunately, when the case was held out for Pat, they had a perfect view on the monitor of the stacks of cash filling the case.

"See if you can zoom in on that money, Jake." Mac asked. "Can you tell if those are hundreds or twenties?"

Jake zoomed in on the monitor and squinted at the camera. "I can't see the bills clearly, but they're strapped in purple bands which would be two-thousand straps. That's generally how they strap twenties. Hundreds or fifties would be in brown or gold straps. So my guess would be those are twenties, and there's got to be at least a hundred thousand dollars in each case."

"Holy smokes," Edna said. "That's a lot of moola."

"From what Scooter said, they transport the marijuana in the plastic tubs so I'm assuming that's the weed they're moving."

Edna nodded. "That's a lot of grass, too."

Leon held up his hand. "If I can't trust you with taking care of the girl, maybe I shouldn't trust you with my cash."

"Give me a break, Leon," Pat said. "I've been transporting money to the Cavellis for over a year now, and we've never had a problem. You know you can count on me. Who took care of Jimmy when you thought he was skimming from you? Me. You know you can count on me."

Leon nodded. "Yeah, but that Jimmy thing is still unresolved, too. The plan was for you to pin Jimmy's death on the girl. All wrapped up neat and tidy. As far as I can tell, nothing is wrapped up at all. All you've done is create a shit-storm of problems."

"Lay off me. I'm the one risking my neck and my job here. Not everything always goes according to plan. I said I'd get rid of the bookkeeper, and I will. I just need a little more time. I can get Mac to tell me where she is and take care of her tomorrow. He'll help me out. He trusts me."

"Not anymore I don't." Mac spit the words out, anger and humiliation filling him. His gut burned with fury and shame that he'd been conned by someone he'd considered a friend.

"I think we've got enough," Jake said. "Are you ready to take him down?"

"Yeah, let's do it." Mac turned to Zoey and Edna. "I need you both to stay in the van. I can't concentrate on my job if I'm worried about you."

Zoey nodded, her eyes wide with concern. "We will. But be careful, please. I don't like worrying about you, either."

He tightened the straps on his flak vest and checked the monitors again. "Yeah, I think we're good. We don't want to take a chance on them finishing up and leaving. Let's do it."

Jake spoke into the headset attached to his ear. "Let's move in. On my go."

Mac opened the back of the van, and he and Jake stepped out. He turned back to Zoey. "Stay here. Lock the doors. We're gonna get these guys."

"Be careful." She reached for his hand.

He pulled her toward him, leaning in and taking her mouth in a passionate kiss. His hand dug into her hair, cupping her head as he tried to convey the deep love he felt for her. Tried to express his feelings through that one kiss.

She clung to his arms, kissing him back with fervor and emotion.

He pulled away, catching his breath. "I love you," he whispered, then pulled his gun out and spun toward Jake. "Let's do this."

Jake nodded, voicing another set of instructions to the FBI team. Guns drawn, they ran across the street and slowly approached the warehouse doors.

Motioning with his hand, Mac pointed to the open doors.

Jake nodded and spoke into the headset. "Move in. Now."

The next few minutes were pandemonium, as Jake and Mac charged into the warehouse from one side and the FBI team stormed in from the other.

Mac's trained eye took in all the details at once. He saw Scooter and two other scruffy guys hit the floor and crawl under the tables. He saw a couple of Leon's guys hit their knees with their hands raised and a couple of others took off running.

He made eye contact with Pat—just for one second—but that one second told him that Pat knew. Knew Mac had found out that he was dirty. That he had betrayed their profession. And their friendship.

In the next moment, two things happened that changed the entire course of the plan. The first was that one of the security guys pulled a gun and fired at an FBI agent, starting an explosion of gunfire. The second was that Pat ducked behind the SUV and ran out the back door of the warehouse.

Mac dove for cover behind a table covered with plants as erratic gunfire filled the room. "Stay down," he yelled at Scooter and the other growers that were cowered under the tables toward the back of the room.

A bullet struck one of the five gallon buckets that held a plant on the table in front of Mac. Dirt seeped to the floor next to his foot.

He had to get out of here. He had to follow Pat.

Scanning the room, he saw Jake across from him, behind the wheel of the SUV. "Jake," he yelled. His friend turned, and caught his eye. He pointed toward the door. "Cover me."

Jake nodded and sent two shots in the direction of Leon's men.

Bent over, Mac stole from behind the table and ran for the side door. A shot exploded near his head, and the glass of the door shattered as he pulled it open and slipped outside.

That was too damn close. His heart pounded in his chest. He tried to catch his breath as he flattened himself against the wall and searched the darkened street for his former friend.

He had to find Pat.

Had to find him before he found Zoey.

Twenty-Two

Zoey peered out from behind the vehicle and yelled to Edna. "We've got to get back in the van."

Her grandmother was wedged between the curb and the wheel of an old sedan parked on the street across from the van. Edna covered her ears with her hands. "Not until they stop shooting."

Mac had given them one instruction—stay in the van. But had her grandmother ever followed instructions in her life? No.

Everything seemed to be going so well. They could see the FBI charge in on the monitors and some of Leon's men drop to their knees with their hands raised.

"I've never seen an actual bust before," Edna had said, excitement in her tone.

"You can see one right now. On this monitor." Zoey had tapped the screen. All of her attention had been focused on watching for Mac to be okay and listening for the men to be taken into custody.

She was so focused, she hadn't reacted quickly enough when her grandmother opened the door of the van and climbed out. Yanking the headphones from her ears, she'd stumbled out of the van. "Grandma—get back here. We're supposed to stay in the van."

Edna had made it halfway across the street when the gunfire started and instead of running back toward the van, she had run forward and ducked behind the wheel of the car.

The car was a little ways up the street from the van, so at least Zoey could see her grandmother from where she crouched behind the van. The door had closed behind her as Zoey got out, and when the gunshots started, she'd taken cover behind the vehicle.

Her heart raced as she prayed for Mac to be okay.

Glass shattered, and she leaned forward in time to see the side door open and Mac come running out. He flattened himself against the building. He was probably only twenty feet from where Edna hid behind the car.

Zoey took a tentative step forward, reaching out a hand to signal. "Mac, over here."

His head jerked toward her, and their eyes met.

A look of fear crossed his face seconds before a large arm clamped around her neck, and Zoey was yanked off her feet.

"You've caused enough trouble for me, you stupid little bitch." The voice was gravelly in her ear, filled with anger and tension, and she froze at the feel of the cold hard steel of a gun as it pressed to her temple.

She would recognize that voice anywhere. Pat must have somehow escaped from the warehouse.

Kicking her feet, she screamed for Mac and clawed at his arm. He was a big guy, taller than Mac even and strong as an ox. He carried her with little effort, her body pinned against his by the strength in his forearm.

He backed in to the alley next to the van. "I'm not letting you go again."

Terror washed over her, filling her every pore. This was it. He was going to kill her.

She couldn't breathe. Couldn't think. Her body started to tremble, and she recognized that she was most likely going into shock.

Stop it! She had to think. Had to figure out how to get herself out of this situation. Remnants of her self-defense class came back to her, and she plotted how she could gouge, bite, or kick at the opportune moment.

"Let her go." Mac appeared at the edge of the alley, his gun drawn and pointed at Pat's head.

"What the hell, Mac?" Pat's voice held an edge of panic. "You're gonna pick this bitch over me? We've known each other since high school. What happened to bros before hos?"

She didn't care how long they'd known each other. This 'ho' wasn't sticking around for the high school reunion.

"You stopped being my 'bro' when you turned your back on me and the department." Mac's tone was hard as steel. "I never figured you for a dirty cop, Pat."

"I'm not dirty, man. Marijuana's legal in Colorado. I'm just helping out an old friend. Like I thought you were. You know being a cop doesn't pay shit. I'm just trying to earn an extra buck."

As he talked, his voice took on a more desperate plea, as if he realized what an awful situation he was in. His arm also tightened around Zoey's chest, squeezing the air from her lungs, and he dug the end of the gun into her forehead.

"No amount of cash is worth killing for." Mac took a tentative step forward. "Just let her go, Pat."

Pat shook his head. "I can't. I've got a job to do."

"So do I." He inched a little closer.

Zoey could see the determination in his eyes. "Mac, this isn't like before. He isn't a kid. He's a killer." She knew he had to be reliving what happened with his old partner. A hostage situation, a gun pointed at the head of someone he cared about. She hoped her encouragement would fuel his resolve.

"Shut up." Pat yanked her a step backwards, squeezing her arm where she'd been shot and sending shocks of pain through her.

She was running out of time. She had to do something. And do it now.

She narrowed her eyes at Mac, sending him a message with every fiber of her being. If there truly was any psychic ability in her family, she prayed Mac was getting her thoughts now. "You've got this, Mac. You can do it."

He nodded his head, just the slightest movement. His jaw was set, and his lips pressed together in a firm line.

"I said shut up." Pat wrenched at her body again, and she knew this was her chance.

Maybe her only chance.

She opened her mouth and bit down on his arm.

He yowled in pain, loosening his grip, and she stamped down on his foot as hard as she could while ramming her elbow backwards into his stomach and flinging her head back into his jaw.

A jolt of pain shot through her head at the impact with his jaw, but she had to fight. She struggled to get away, clawing at his arm with her fingernails.

He shifted, trying to get a better grip on her as she fought to break free. The butt of the gun cracked against her skull, and her teeth knocked together as stars formed in the air in front of her eyes.

Balling up her fist, she hammered it backwards as hard as she could, trying to hit him in the balls. She must have got close because he pitched forward, a groan of pain escaping his lips, and she twisted free of his grasp.

A shot rang out, the deafening sound ringing in her ears, and Pat clutched his chest and crumpled to the ground beside her.

He reached for her leg, his fingers skimming her ankles. She kicked at his hand and sprinted toward Mac, her feet flying as she raced to get away.

He was already running toward her, and he grabbed her in a fierce hug. After squeezing her tightly against him for just a moment, he pushed her behind him. "Go get Jake and the FBI guys. I'm gonna cuff this asshole."

"He's still got a gun," she said, as she ran to the end of the alley. She could see her grandmother standing next to Jake on the sidewalk as the FBI marched the handcuffed men out of the warehouse.

Sirens wailed in the distance—an ambulance probably on its way now.

"Jake, we need you," she yelled then turned back toward Mac.

She saw him kick Pat's gun away, then lean forward, pressing his knee into the other man's side. Pat howled in pain and swore at Mac.

Ignoring his screams, Mac pulled Pat's arms back and slapped a set of cuffs on them as Jake came running into the alley, his gun drawn and ready.

He ran to Mac's side. "You got this bastard? How can I help?"

"Just stay here with him. He had a gun on Zoey, and I shot him."

Jake nodded. "Good. You did the right thing. If you hadn't, I'm sure he would have killed her." He gestured toward the warehouse. "We got the rest of them. They shot one of my guys, but only hit him in the leg. We've got an ambulance coming, so I'll keep an eye on this guy until they get here."

"Thanks." Mac stood and walked toward her.

With no hesitation, she ran into his arms. "You did it. You saved my life."

He held her tightly against him, and she could feel his hands shaking against her back. "I couldn't bear it if anything happened to you. I came around the corner and saw him with a gun to your head, and I swear my heart stopped."

"So did mine. I was terrified. I knew this time he was really going to kill me."

He looked down at her, brushing back her bangs and examining her forehead. "You've got a cut on your head where he hit you with the gun."

She shrugged. "Add it to the list. My poor body is so scraped and bruised. But I don't care. I'm alive, and that's all that matters. I'm alive because of you."

He smiled. "You're alive because your grandmother insisted on you taking self-defense classes. You had some pretty great defensive moves there."

She laughed, more from nerves than from anything actually being funny. "I was running on total instinct."

"Well, your instincts were good. You got away from him just enough to allow me to get a clean shot."

"Zoey. Oh my Lord, are you all right?" Edna appeared in the alley, rushing to her granddaughter's side.

Zoey let go of Mac and hugged her grandmother. "Yes, I'm fine. Thanks to Mac."

Edna drew Mac into their hug. "I'm just going to hold on to both of you for a minute. I was so scared. This was nothing like it appears on TV. I was so terrified I almost wet my pants."

Zoey grinned. "I'm glad you're okay, too."

Flashing lights accompanied by sirens filled the air as two squad cars and an ambulance pulled onto the street in front of the warehouse. Policemen and first responders poured from the vehicles.

Zoey pointed toward the chaos. "You'd better go talk to them."

Mac nodded. "You gonna be okay? I want an EMT to take a look at your head."

"Okay, fine. But let them take care of the more critical stuff first." She pushed him forward. "Go on, we'll be fine."

He kissed the top of her head, then let her go and hurried toward the squad cars.

Edna pointed to a guy standing alone on the sidewalk in front of the warehouse. "There's Scooter. Let's make sure he's okay."

They crossed the street to where Scooter stood. "You okay?" Zoey asked.

In an uncharacteristic display of affection, Scooter grabbed Zoey and pulled her into a tight hug. "Dude," was all he said, before he released her and shoved his hands into his pockets. He cleared his throat as if he were overcome with emotion. "The other grow guys took off before the cops showed up, but I wanted to make sure you were okay. I heard that Pat grabbed you."

She smiled. "Thank you for staying. And for worrying about me. I'm all right. Pat did grab me, but Mac shot him."

"Is he dead?"

"No. At least not yet."

"Dude."

"Yeah."

Edna wrapped a comforting arm around Scooter's shoulders. "You did good in there. They couldn't have pulled this off if it weren't for you. You placed the cameras in perfect spots."

Scooter ducked his head in modesty. "That part was easy. I didn't know they were gonna start shooting at each other, though. I wasn't prepared for that."

"No, I don't think anyone was," Edna said. "But we're just glad you didn't get hurt."

"Thanks, Mrs. C." He looked around at the clusters of people dealing with the aftermath of the raid. "What do we do now?"

Zoey leaned against the side of the building. "We wait."

It took several hours for them to clear out Leon's men and catalogue the evidence in the warehouse. Another ambulance had arrived, and both Pat and the injured FBI agent had been taken to the hospital.

A fireman had examined Zoey's forehead and applied a butterfly bandage to her cut. She agreed to check in at her doctor's the next day.

Johnny had arrived, along with the majority of the Pleasant Valley police department. They probably hadn't seen anything this big in years and must have called the whole department in.

Zoey had insisted that Edna head back home with Johnny and get some rest. Her grandfather had agreed, and Edna had finally relented. She left Zoey with her bag again, though.

It was a good thing, too. With a dull throb pounding in her head, Zoey had dug through the bag and discovered more ibuprofen in the bottom. She downed three capsules with a small bottle of water she'd also found. She wished she'd had this bag with her earlier. She could have used her grandmother's Taser on Pat.

It was after midnight, and Zoey slumped in a hard plastic chair next to the warehouse wall. Spotting Mac, she thought he looked even more tired than she felt.

The cops had set up tables and been collecting and cataloguing evidence in brown paper sacks. The sacks were lined up along the tables, their tops half-opened or crumpled in an attempt to close them. Her OCD was flaring up as she itched to organize and straighten the bags.

Mac crossed the room and dropped into the chair next to her. She handed him the bottle of water, and he took a swig.

She grinned. "It's really bugging me the way those bags are disorganized and only half-closed."

Mac laughed, resting his arm along the back of her chair. "Well, normally we staple or tape them shut, but someone forgot to bring the tape. Next time we do a raid, we'll add that to our supplies list."

She reached for Edna's bag. "Never fear. Edna's bag is here." She dug through the bag, remembering she'd seen her high-heeled stapler from work still inside. Finding the pink stapler, she pulled it from the purse. "Look what I found. My stapler from my office. Edna still had it in her bag." She snapped the stapler closed for emphasis, but it wouldn't close.

"Oh great, it's jammed. Something from Edna's purse probably got stuck in it." She opened the back of the stapler and gasped.

Instead of staples inside the chamber, a small device connected to a USB port had been inserted into the space where the staples usually fit. It was smaller than a dime, and she dug it out with the edge of her fingernail. "I think this is the flash drive from Teddy. In fact, I'm sure of it. I know this will have his evidence on it."

A feeling like a vise squeezed her chest. In all the conversation overheard tonight, no one had said anything about Teddy. And she still hadn't heard from him. She sent up a silent thank you to him for the flash drive and prayed that he was hiding somewhere and okay.

Mac held up the drive. "I'll bet you're right. I've just never seen one this small." He stood up. "Jake's got a laptop in the van. Let's take it over and see if anything's on it."

They hurried across the street and climbed into the back of the van. Jake was inside, working on the recorded pieces and sending them electronically to the FBI and the police department. "What's up, guys?"

Mac held up the tiny drive. "We think this is the flash drive we've been looking for. We were hoping to plug it into your laptop and see if anything's on it."

Jake took the drive and plugged it into the USB port of his computer. "Cool. I've heard they're making these tiny flash drives now, I've just never seen one."

A window opened on his screen with a list of dates. Jake clicked on the top date, and lines of information filled the screen. Data detailing funds deposited and cash transfers, corporate names, and dates.

This was it. The evidence they needed to put the Cavellis away for money laundering and fraud. Teddy had done it.

"I can't believe I've had the evidence with me this whole time. I grabbed my stapler when we went into Cavelli Commerce the first day the body was discovered in my apartment. It's been in my grandmother's hand bag this whole time."

Mac grinned. "We should have learned by now. When you need something, you should always check Edna's purse for it first."

She laughed. "Oh, my gosh. That is funny, but also kind of true." She rubbed her tired eyes. "What I need right now is about ten hours of sleep. Think we can find that in there?"

Mac rubbed her shoulders. "No, but I think we've done enough that we can call it a night. I'm going to email this information to the judge, and he can issue a warrant for Cavelli Commerce first thing in the morning. Let's go back to my place, and we can catch a few hours of sleep and a shower, then we'll take down the Cavellis in the morning."

Jake passed him the flash drive. "Sounds good. I just made a backup copy in case anything happens to this one. You guys head on home. I'll stay here and finish up."

Zoey leaned in and hugged Jake. "Thank you. We'll be in touch in the morning." She stepped out of the van.

Scooter had given her grandparents a ride home so Johnny could leave his vehicle for them. She crossed the street to the car while Mac told the other cops they were leaving.

Teddy had come through with the evidence they needed. Now she just hoped they could find him.

And that he was still alive.

Twenty-Three

Zoey stood in the lobby of Cavelli Commerce. It was just past nine in the morning, and Mac had just served Salvatore Cavelli with a search and seizure warrant and had informed him he was under arrest for money-laundering and fraud.

The whole thing took less than ten minutes. It would take the FBI ten days to thoroughly search the company property and records, though.

Zoey looked around at the building where she'd worked for the last two years. It looked like an average company with gray carpet on the floor and muted landscape paintings on the walls. It was hard to believe it had become a front for a multi-million dollar money-laundering scheme.

Mac had tried to convince her not to come. Told her that she didn't need to be there. But she wanted to be. Wanted to see Sal escorted out in handcuffs. And she wanted another chance to search Teddy's desk to see if she could find any clue as to where he might be hiding.

She slipped down the hall, hoping the accountant's offices would be empty. They weren't. A pretty woman wearing a snug skirt and high heels was digging through the drawers of Teddy's desk.

"Can I help you with something?" Zoey asked, as if she still worked there and could help with anything.

Startled, the woman jumped and let out a little shriek. She turned around, her hand clutched to her chest, then let out a sigh of relief. "Oh, it's you, Zoey. Thank goodness. I about had a heart attack. What are you doing here?"

Now that she could see her face, Zoey recognized the woman as Megan, Sal's receptionist. But what was Sal's receptionist doing looking through Teddy's desk. Was she searching for the flash drive? Trying to destroy it before the evidence came out about her boss. "I could ask you the same question. What are you doing here? And why are you going through Teddy's desk?"

She looked like a deer caught in the headlights. "Um, I was just looking for something."

One of the financial advisors poked his head into the office door. "Hey, we've got to get out of here. They're evacuating the offices."

Dang. There went her chance to search Teddy's desk.

She fell into step behind Megan, heading for the lobby of the firm. All of the employees were being herded out toward the elevators. She spotted Mac and waved.

He looked so official in his uniform. And ridiculously handsome.

They'd both been so worn out last night that they'd fallen into bed and gone right to sleep. But waking up in the circle of Mac's arms had felt like heaven. So had the half hour they'd spent in bed after they woke up and the twenty minutes they'd spent in the shower together after that.

Her lips curved into a goofy grin as he walked toward her.

"What are you smiling about?" he asked.

"I was just thinking about this morning."

His face lit with a naughty grin, and he leaned in to whisper in her ear. "Yeah, well all I can think about is tonight."

Holy hot man-in-uniform. Fingers of desire trickled up her spine as his breath tickled her neck. "Now I'm thinking about that, too."

He chuckled and dropped a quick kiss against her neck. "I have about another hour before I'm finished up here. Can you find something to do for a while, then we can head back up the mountain together?"

She'd have to since they'd ridden down to Denver together. They'd dropped off Johnny's car that morning, and she'd grabbed a fresh pair of clothes. It felt good to be wearing jeans and a pretty floral top instead of the workout clothes and disguises she'd been wearing the past few days. "Sure. There's a Verizon store across the street. I'll go over and get a new phone then wait for you at the coffee shop downstairs."

"Perfect."

An hour later, Mac exited the building. She'd only been waiting a few minutes. She had a new iPhone and a tray of iced coffees next to her as she sat at an outdoor table in front of the coffee shop.

He smiled as she handed him a cup. "How lucky am I? A beautiful woman *and* a cup of coffee waiting for me."

She tipped her chin up and placed a soft kiss on his cheek. "If you think this feels lucky, wait until we get back to your place."

He laughed and wrapped an arm around her waist. "Let's go."

Halfway up the mountain, her new phone buzzed with a text message from an unknown number. Her heart leapt to her throat as she read the message out loud to Mac. "I just got a text that instructs me to come to a specific address on the south side of Denver and it says to bring Bruiser."

"Who's it from?"

"It's got to be from Teddy. Don't you think?"

"Either that, or it's a trap. And somebody is still out there that wants to hurt you."

She hadn't even considered that possibility. She'd thought she was safe, now that all the bad guys were locked up. Her face must have looked stricken, because he picked up her hand and squeezed it.

"Hey, I'm a cop. I always assume the worst. But we can hope for the best. Let's go pick up the dog from Edna's, and I'll go with you to this address. Just in case."

"That sounds good."

They drove to Edna's and picked up the little white poodle.

"Havoc's going to be sad to see his friend go," Edna said. "They've become quite the little pals. Maybe I need to get a poodle."

Johnny shook his head. "We do not need a poodle."

Edna shrugged. "What does that have to do with anything?"

Zoey chose not to enter into the argument, instead she hugged her grandparents and carried the little dog out to the car.

Forty-five minutes later, she and Mac pulled up outside of a brick two-story home. The neighborhood was upper middle-class, with manicured lawns and new cars in the driveways.

"This is the address." She studied the house. "It sure doesn't look like a trap."

They crossed the lawn and rang the doorbell.

The front door swung open, and Zoey couldn't have been more surprised to see Megan, the pretty receptionist from Cavelli Commerce.

She stood back and motioned for them to come in. "Follow me."

Zoey stepped in to the house. Could this be a trap after all? Why had Sal Cavelli's receptionist summoned them to her home?

They followed her through the kitchen and into a large living room.

A tousled mane of curly brown hair was visible above the headrest of a recliner. A video game was on the television and she could see a controller held in a pair of large hands. Her heart leapt as a man's voice asked, "Hey babe, could you bring in some chips on your way back?"

Zoey's heart filled with joy as she recognized the voice. And so did the little poodle. It whined and wriggled in her arms as the man in the recliner spun toward them.

"Teddy!" Zoey rushed forward, dropping to her knees by his chair. "Oh my gosh, you're alive."

He grinned and pulled her and the little dog into a bear hug. Bruiser climbed up her shoulder, trying to get closer to lick Teddy's face. "Yes, of course I'm alive. Not kickin' much. But alive."

She smiled back, so happy to see his face. "But how? What happened? What are you doing here?"

He looked up at Megan with affection in his eyes. "I needed help, but I knew they'd be looking for me at a hospital. I hid out most of the night trying to figure out what to do. Then I remembered that Megan's sister was a doctor so I called her at work, and she picked me up and brought me here. Her sister came over and stitched me up. I was lucky the damage wasn't worse. And I was lucky to have Megan to take such great care of me for the last several days."

From the smile he and Megan exchanged, it appeared that she'd become more than just his nurse.

He cuddled the dog to his chest. "I can't tell you how glad I am to see this little girl, though. Thanks so much for taking care of her."

"Of course, but how did you know I had her?"

"I was worried about her and sent Megan over to pick her up. She said she found your note on the refrigerator saying you'd taken Bruiser. I knew she was in good hands with you."

"But how did you get away that night? When we went back in the morning, one of the guys was dead in my living room, and you were nowhere to be found. I was so afraid they'd found you and killed you." Her voice faltered with emotion.

"I'm sorry. I couldn't tell you where I was. I couldn't tell anyone. I saw on the news that they found that guy dead in your apartment, and I didn't know what to think. I can assure you he was alive when I left."

"But how did you get out of there?"

"A combination of adrenaline and luck, I guess. I heard them searching your apartment, and I could tell they were in your office, so I tried to make a break for it. I stepped out of your bedroom and could see the door was standing open. But evidently only one guy was in your office, and the other one was standing in the living room between me and the door. I used to play football in high school—offensive lineman—I don't know if I ever told you that. But my old football days came back to me, and I tucked in my shoulder and charged the guy. I knocked him to the ground, then ran out the door. I heard the other guy yelling, but I didn't stick around to hear what he said. I just kept running."

He must have noticed the badge clipped to Mac's waist because he looked up at him. "I might still have a pretty good tackle, but I assure you I didn't kill that guy."

"Sorry. This is my friend, Mac," Zoey said, introducing him to Teddy and Megan. "He's a police officer with the Pleasant Valley PD, and he helped catch the guys that did this."

"I know you didn't kill him," Mac said, after shaking Teddy's hand. "His partner shot him. Evidently he'd been skimming off the company's dollar. He was supposed to get rid of him and Zoey both and make it look like Zoey was the one who shot him. Two birds with one bullet."

Teddy's face paled, and he rested his hand on Zoey's arm. "Geez. Thank goodness you got out of there."

Zoey took his hand. "No. Thank you. You saved me. I would never have gotten away if you hadn't warned me. You saved my life, and I can't thank you enough."

Teddy grinned. "You risked yourself to take care of my dog, so we'll call it even." He looked up and winked at Megan. "And hey, it all worked out pretty good for me. I kept trying to win this gorgeous girl over with coffee and my witty charm, and I guess all it really took was getting stabbed in the gut."

Zoey laughed. She squeezed his hand, then stood to go. "I'm so happy for you." And she was. She was filled with a deep affection for this big teddy bear of a guy who had risked his own life to help her. "We'll let you rest. We can talk more later. I'm just so glad you're all right."

He set the dog on the floor, pushed up from the recliner and pulled her into another bear hug. "I'm glad you're all right, too."

She looked up at him. "Hey, we found the evidence. That was pretty smart hiding the flash drive in my stapler."

He chuckled. "I'd hoped that you'd found it. I tried to hide it in plain sight. Megan's been sneaking into my office looking for a pink stapler the past several days. When she said she couldn't find it, I had a feeling that you'd somehow gotten hold of it."

"I did. It was on my old desk. That's probably why she couldn't find it. The cleaning people must have put it back. Plus, I took it that first day. And we used that evidence to arrest Sal this morning. It was everything we need to put the Cavelli brothers away."

He gave her a high five. "Yes. Score one for the bean counters."

She laughed. "All right. We're gonna go. You rest. I'll call you later this week." Before she left, she gave Megan a quick hug. "Thank you for taking care of him."

Megan grinned. One of those goofy grins that revealed her feelings for Teddy clearly on her face. She shrugged. "It worked out for me, too."

Zoey's steps were light as they left the house and climbed into Mac's car.

She turned to him with a smile. "I feel good. Like everything's really going to work out."

He chuckled then picked up her hand and brushed his lips across the back of her knuckles. "So, where do we go from here?"

"Do you mean where are we going to drive to in the car or do you mean where do *we* go from here?"

He shrugged. "Take your pick."

She let out a deep sigh. "Gosh, I guess I have some big decisions to make. I can tell you that I'm moving out of that apartment. There's no way that I'm sleeping in that bed again, and there's not enough bleach to get the blood of a dead guy off my floor."

"Where will you go?"

"Welllll, I've been thinking about moving up into the mountains—to Pleasant Valley. I know my grandparents would love that, and I've found something of interest that I'd really like to explore there."

He chuckled. "Is that right?" He gazed out the front window of the car for a moment, as if weighing his thoughts, then turned back to her, sincerity in his eyes. "As long as you're making big decisions, I have another one for you to consider."

Her pulse quickened and butterflies formed in her stomach. "You do?"

"I do. But hold on." He got out of the car and ran around to her side.

The butterflies in her stomach went crazy as he opened her door and bent down on one knee. He grinned at her, that adorable handsome grin that did funny things to her insides.

He picked up her hand. "I've never done this before, so I wanted to do it right. I know things have been crazy the past few weeks and we haven't known each other all that long, but I can't imagine my life now without you in it. And I feel like my heart knew you the minute we met. It recognized you as the woman I wanted to spend the rest of my life with."

He took a deep breath. "Zoey Allen, will you marry me?"

Stunned, she sat speechless, not knowing what to say. This is *not* how she did things. She was a planner. She made lists. She weighed consequences. She didn't jump into spontaneous choices.

He smiled. "I can see your wheels turning as you're trying to formulate a decision. I know your hands must be itching to create a spreadsheet or at least make a list. But there's no formula or equation when it comes to love. I know you like things neat and orderly, but love is messy and crazy and spontaneous. It doesn't fit into a tally column of pros and cons. It just is."

He pressed her hand against his heart. "The only thing I know is that my heart belongs to you. We don't have to get married today, or even tomorrow. But I want you to come home with me. To let me love you and make you laugh every day. To let me make you breakfast and grilled cheese sandwiches for the rest of your life."

"You do make a pretty mean grilled cheese sandwich." She grinned, her heart soaring. "I do like things organized, but in the last month, my life has gone from calm to chaotic, and it's been the best, most frightening, most wonderful month of my life. I don't need a spreadsheet to know that I love you with all of my heart, and all I want is to get tangled up in a beautiful messy life with you. Yes. I will marry you."

A gorgeous smile filled his whole face, and he stood up and pulled her from the car, crushing her against him in a tight hug.

Then he kissed her, tenderly, sweetly, and with so much love she felt like her heart would break. He pulled back and brushed her bangs from her eyes. "I love you like crazy."

"I love you, too." She grinned up at him. "Just so you know, I'll probably have your sock drawer and your spice cabinet organized before the end of the week."

"I've recently been thinking my socks needed more organization."

She laughed. "And you know I'm going to plan the hell out of our wedding. Like down to the last cupcake."

Laughing, he dipped his head, speaking between soft kisses. "Yes, I know. Good thing I like cupcakes."

A fierce and overwhelming love filled her, and she wrapped her arms around his neck and pressed against him.

He pulled back, cupping her chin in his hand and gazing into her eyes. "Let's go home and get messy."

THE END

Check out all the adventures of the Page Turners book club:

Another Saturday Night and I Ain't Got No Body
Book 1 of the Page Turners Series
On Amazon

Easy Like Sunday Mourning
Book 2 of the Page Turners Series
On Amazon

Just Another Maniac Monday
Book 3 of the Page Turners Series
On Amazon

Be the first to find out when the newest Page Turners Novel is releasing and hear all the latest news and updates happening with the Page Turners book club by signing up for the newsletter at: Jenniemarts.com

If you enjoyed this book, please consider leaving a review!

If you enjoy small town contemporary romance with hot cowboys-
Try the Hearts of Montana series.

In **Tucked Away** (Book 1 of The Hearts of Montana series), Charlie Ryan is a city girl who inherits a farm in small town Montana and when she gets there, she finds a lonely teenager girl, a goat named Clyde, a hunky cowboy, and a place she finally feels like she can call home.

ONE

A bead of sweat trickled down her back as she stared into the cold brown eyes of her captor. A gold ring pierced his nostril. He snorted, his breath forming a circle of condensation on the window. She laid on the horn again, hoping this time to scare the beast away. He stood there, unfazed, staring at her and swatting flies away with his tail.

"Nice bull." Keeping her voice low, she pulled on the handle and gently pushed open the car door a fraction of an inch. The huge black bull, roughly the size of a small pickup truck, pawed at the ground, then put his head down and rammed the side of her bright red rental car.

She let loose a scream of terror and frustration. The car held all of her worldly possessions, packed in a few liquor store boxes and a couple of Louis Vuitton suitcases, her last shred of dignity tucked into one of the side pockets.

Charlie Ryan had spent the last hour trapped in a car that reeked of stale French fries, her silk blouse clinging to her damp back, desperately rethinking her decision to drink that large iced tea. Why had she ignored the sign reading, *last services for 200 miles*? Who knew that meant gasoline? She thought it meant *cell* service, and her phone had died hours ago as she'd crossed the never-ending flats of the Midwest, driving toward her new home and the promise of a fresh start.

Nothing was going as planned. Her dreams, once as bright as the pristine Montana sky, had faded like the paint on the large red barn standing sentinel over the Tucker farm. But this was too much. She'd had enough bull in her life, and she was getting out of this car.

Groaning, she looked around in desperation for a way out. An old two-story farm house sat at the end of a dusty driveway. The front door, and her means of escape, a mere twenty feet away.

She pulled her black designer pump from her foot and beat it against the window. Its ineffectiveness against her captor equaled its poor choice as driving footwear, evidenced by the large red blister forming on her right heel.

She studied the beast. His shiny coat seemed to glisten in the afternoon sun. Horns protruded two feet off either side of his huge triangular block of a head, and his neck was thick as a tree trunk. She leaned closer to the window and noticed his horns dotted with red bits that looked like blood, but were probably flecks of the paint that used to be on her rental car door. A large scar extended several inches above and below his left eye. The scar, combined with the way he stamped his foot and shook his enormous head at her, told her this bull meant business.

Turning away from the animal, she tried the ignition once more, hoping the tank had been visited by the *services* fairies and magically filled with gasoline. What little fumes were left in the tank had sputtered out just as she pulled into the driveway and coasted to a stop in front of the house.

She would have to think about that coincidence later, but for now, the car battery still worked, so she depressed the button to roll the window down a few inches. Hot, dry air, smelling of what she assumed was hay, wafted into the car, and the bull, alerted by the sudden movement, slid his tongue up the window, leaving a shiny trail of saliva filled with bits of grass.

Charlie screamed again as his tongue, finding the opening in the glass, snaked into the car, as if searching for the source of the fast food scent. She continued to shriek as she alternately whacked at the huge tongue with her shoe and tried to roll up the window.

Having rid her car of the offensive appendage, she now heard the blessed sound of an engine and turned to see a blue and white pickup pulling into the driveway. She registered a black cowboy hat and dark hair as the truck rumbled past her in a cloud of dust. The window was wide open, the radio blaring guitar-picking country music, and a tan, muscled arm rested against the faded blue paint.

The truck pulled to a stop in front of her car, and she sighed with relief. How low had her life sunk that her hero had just arrived in an ancient pickup sporting a decal silhouette of a naked woman wearing high heels and holding a shotgun, an NRA emblem, and a bumper sticker that read 'Git Er Done'?

The door of the truck opened. As one cowboy boot hit the ground, Charlie had a moment of fear, wondering if she was now in more danger being stranded alone in the middle of nowhere with a three-toothed redneck who fully believed in his right to bear arms.

She reached to depress the door locks, then remembered she had locked the doors earlier when the beast had first charged the car. She was now pretty sure a bull couldn't open a car door with its hoof, but it was a moment of panic, and she wasn't taking any chances.

The rest of her hero emerged from the truck and any thoughts of door-opening cows left her head as she took in the sight of this man. He epitomized the term *hot cowboy*, standing well over six feet tall, wearing faded Wranglers, a sleeveless western shirt, and the aforementioned black cowboy hat.

He was tan and had the solid muscles of someone who spent his time outdoors working hard instead of indoors working out. He rested one of those muscled arms on the open door of his truck as he appeared to survey the red car containing a sweaty blonde being held captive by a twelve hundred pound bull.

Thanks for reading my book!

About the Author

Jennie Marts loves to make readers laugh as she weaves stories filled with love, friendship and intrigue. She writes for Entangled Publishing and reviewers call her books "laugh out loud" funny and full of great characters that are "endearing and relatable."

She is living her own happily ever after in the mountains of Colorado with her husband, two sons, two dogs and a parakeet that loves to tweet to the oldies. She's addicted to Diet Coke, adores Cheetos and believes you can't have too many books, shoes or friends.

Her books include the contemporary western romance Hearts of Montana series, the romantic comedy/ cozy mysteries of The Page Turners series, and her latest hot hockey player's series, the Bannister Brothers Books.

Jennie loves to hear from readers. Follow her on Facebook at Jennie Marts Books , or Twitter at @JennieMarts. Visit her at www.jenniemarts.com .